Ghost
of
Winters Past

by

Gail MacMillan

Ghost of Winters Past

Cover Art by *Tina Lynn Stout*

The Wild Rose Press, Inc.
PO Box 708
Adams Basin, NY 14410-0708
Visit us at www.thewildrosepress.com

Publishing History
First Crimson Rose Edition, 2012
Print ISBN 978-1-61217-315-3
Digital ISBN 978-1-61217-316-0

Published in the United States of America

He got to his feet and looked down at her. The lamps had been turned low. Shadows from the flames on the hearth flitted around the darkened room. A crackle that didn't come from the fireplace snapped through her when she gazed up into those killer blue eyes.

"Travis." His name came as a breathed whisper from her lips. Her arms went up and about his neck. He gazed searchingly into her eyes, then lowered his head to take her lips in a kiss that made her solar plexus do a somersault. Her thoughts tangled. Logic melted into the ether. She soared.

When he released her, every inch of her body felt soft and magically mellow. All her defenses had tumbled. She wanted to spend the night with him, to enjoy every bit of the thrilling mystery that was sensationally virile Travis MacDonald.

"Travis," she breathed, but he began to back away, rubbing his hands on the seat of his pants.

"Sorry." He bit his lower lip. "That shouldn't have happened. I'll go get Doc."

He turned and headed for the door, leaving Michaela still tingling from their encounter, wanting more, so much more, and utterly confused.

"Travis!" His name snapped out in total exasperation. "Travis MacDonald!"

But he was gone, off into the night to get his wolf dog.

Praise for Gail MacMillan

"Written by a superb story teller, *THE CALEDONIAN PRIVATEER* seizes the reader's interest on Page One and doesn't let it go until the very end."

~Irene C. Michel, author & columnist

~*~

"The powerful attraction between Emma Smith, a woman of mystery, and Captain Morgan Reynolds, a handsome rogue of means and determination, sets the stage for the thrilling adventure between the covers of *THE CALEDONIAN PRIVATEER*. Gail MacMillan sweeps the reader into her story with the skill of a master storyteller."

~Stella MacLean, published author

~*~

"This is a wonderful suspense filled romance.... I loved Ms. MacMillan's story of love and piracy and can't wait to read her next one."

~Robin, Romancing the Book Reviews (4 Roses)

Dedication

to Hank DeBruin & Tanya McCready-DeBruin
of Winterdance Dogsled Tours,
and their wonderful canines

Chapter One

"Come on, come on!" Michaela squeezed the throttle as she battled to force more speed from her vintage snowmobile. He had to be gaining on her. Fueled with hatred, he rode a state-of-the-art machine horsepowered to the hilt. She'd seen him leaning against it at the snowmobile garage.

She bent into the windscreen. Swirling snow and encroaching twilight left her only a few feet of visibility, and her headlight bobbed crazily as she bounced over bumps in the old logging road. The light cast a weird play of flash and shadow over the forest ahead of her.

Hairpin turn coming up. She gripped the handlebars. When the turn came into view, she yanked a sharp left.

Snow blasted into her face, the machine careened onto one ski, pitched sideways, and sank into a drift. The engine roared, struggled, then sputtered and died.

"No, no, damn you!" She twisted the key in the ignition. Click, click. Nothing. *Damn, damn, damn.* She pulled her leg out of the snow beneath the tilted side and staggered to her feet. The sled she'd been pulling had remained upright, thank goodness, its cargo of groceries and other necessities for the Lodge held intact by two strategically placed bungee cords.

The sound of an approaching snowmobile brought her back to action. She ripped off her helmet and leather mittens and dropped to her knees. With fingers like frozen sticks, she fumbled open the saddlebag behind the seat. As two black snowmobiles sped past her and whirled back to spray her with snow, her hand grasped the heaviest wrench in the tool kit. Clutching it, she stood and turned to face her pursuers. They braked to a stop, leaving their engines idle, their headlights glaring over her in her predicament.

"Hey, Mikey!" Pulling off his crash helmet and balaclava, the speaker dismounted and waded toward her. "What's your hurry, babe?"

Ralph Frame hadn't changed. She squinted up at him through gusting snow, her fear changing into anger.

"Get out of my way, Ralph." Adrenalin coursing, she drew herself up in front of him. "There's a major storm brewing. I have to get back to the Lodge."

She stared at him, at the black curling hair and dark eyes. Handsome, some would say. Satanically handsome in the shadows from the headlights and the dark, bending trees and swirling snow. Handsome except for that scar...that cursed scar.

"What's wrong, sweetheart?" He moved closer, at six-plus feet towering over her. She smelled whiskey on his breath. "You're looking a little peaked. Something bothering you? Not the..." He slowed his words and ran a black-gloved finger slowly down his cheek. "...the scar?" His tone had deepened with each syllable.

"Your fault." *Face him down, Michaela. You can do it.*

"That's a matter of opinion now, isn't it?" His hand shot out, seized the back of her neck, and squeezed.

"Get your hand off me!" Michaela jerked free. "I wouldn't want to have to file assault charges!"

"Let her go, Ralph!" His companion shifted on his snowmobile. "You don't want that kind of trouble."

"Andy? Andy Murdoch, is that you?" Relief

loosened the knot in her gut. *A witness who might be on my side.* "I haven't seen you since high school."

"Come on, Ralph." The man ignored her. "That's Norm Dunn's niece, Michael Dunn's daughter, for God's sake. Hell, not even Colin will be able to get you out of any trouble you cause her."

"What about you, Andy?" She decided to run a risk. "I hear you've got a wife and children. You shouldn't be running around with this creep."

"Creep, am I?" Ralph Frame's words were a snarl. He shoved her backward into a drift and headed for the supply sled. "I'll show you who's a creep."

He yanked the bungee cords free and thrust them inside his leather jacket.

"Ralph, no!" She struggled to her feet, the softness of the snow hindering her efforts. "I have guests due. I need my supplies."

"Then you'll just have to disappoint them, honey." He lashed out with a booted foot and sent the insulated containers spewing into the drifting snow.

"You miserable...!" She lifted the hand holding the wrench and flew at him.

"Still your weapon of choice, is it, Mikey?" He caught her by the wrist, twisted her arm behind her back, and pulled her close. The stench of liquor wafted over her. Memory flooded back. Fear returned.

"Just remember," he hissed, his mouth hot and moist against her cheek. "Just remember, before you go declaring charges, that I can come up with a few of my own."

"Really?" She struggled. His grip tightened, making her flinch. "Have you forgotten the circumstances?"

"Ralph, let's go. This storm is turning into a blizzard. We shouldn't have come up here. If you hadn't been so damned determined to do a number on Travis MacDonald..."

"Sure, sure." He gave Michaela's wrist a final twist and quirked his mouth into a taunting, self-satisfied smirk. "Since you seem to have lost your supplies for that pile of rotting logs you call a Lodge, maybe you should consider closing down and convincing your aunt and uncle to sell it to me."

"So you can turn it into a gambling den?" She scoffed. "I heard rumors of your plan in Carleton. Small towns are full of gossip. Dream on."

"Yeah, well, we'll see." He shoved her aside and waded back to his snowmobile.

"Wait!" she called. "My machine is broken."

"You have snowshoes, baby." He gestured to the pair strapped to her machine. "And you have legs."

"But there's a blizzard brewing..."

"You should have thought of that before you decided to make a supply run to town." He climbed aboard his snowmobile and replaced his balaclava and helmet. Seconds later, he roared off into the storm.

His companion hesitated, then with a nod at Michaela, followed.

When the sound of their machines had vanished into the roaring wind, Michaela wasted no time. Night had arrived with plummeting temperatures. She returned to the lopsided machine. Maybe she could get it started. Maybe she'd only flooded it. Mentally crossing her fingers, she climbed aboard and turned the key.

A sputter, a splutter, then nothing. She tried again. Then again. Each time the machine's efforts became less until finally it disintegrated into a simple, hopeless click. She dismounted and stared down at the old vehicle. Only one avenue left to her.

Without the headlights from the other machines or her own, she'd been plunged into almost complete darkness. Only the reflection from the snow gave any light. She untied the snowshoes from behind the seat and fastened them to her boots. Then she pulled a miner's headlight from the saddlebags, turned it on, and fastened it over her balaclava.

After a last discouraged glance at the scattered containers, she sucked in a deep breath and headed off up the trail all but obliterated by blowing snow and darkness.

Stay calm. You grew up in this wilderness. You're not more than a mile or two from the Lodge. You've snowshoed ten times that far and never batted an eye. Piece of cake, Michaela, piece of cake.

She hadn't gone far when the realization—and the branches—hit her. Her vision obscured by night and the storm, she'd turned into a thicket, a stand of scrubby, shoulder-high spruce. Pushing aside limbs, feeling the painful scratch of those she didn't manage to avoid across her half-frozen cheeks, she definitely wasn't on the trail...or any trail.

Stopping to get her breath, she remembered the cell phone in her pocket. Totally useless up here in the mountains except on elevated areas, and she wasn't anywhere near one.

The wind howled, black tree shadows gyrated in a *dance macabre* across the snow. The beam from her headlight dimmed, its battery fading. *Don't panic, don't panic. Panic kills in this country. Keep moving, just keep moving.*

And then she heard it. The long, drawn-out, unearthly howl. One howl, then two, then an entire chorus. *Oh, God! A pack of coyotes.* Hungry coyotes. Somewhere beyond the range of her failing headlight they slunk into place, surrounding her. She remembered the young woman who'd been killed by a pair of the animals the previous summer. In winter, food was even harder for them to find.

Again, blending with the wind, the single blood-chilling cry. Closer this time. Then again the chorus...closer. She whirled and glimpsed a pair of glowing yellow eyes just before her light died. In the storm and darkness, Michaela Dunn, attorney at law and temporary manager of Promise Wilderness Lodge, despaired.

I'm going to die. I'm definitely going to die.

A wavering vision began to form in front of her at the edge of the thicket. Glowing with ivory brilliance, its hazy waves undulated before gathering into a male form. A First Nations male form. Clad in fringed buckskins, long straight hair falling over his shoulders, the phantom warrior pinioned her with his stare. Slowly he raised a hand.

Yellow eyes melted back into the night. Their cries dwindled until only the sounds of the storm remained.

Oh, God, I'm hallucinating!

Michaela stared at the specter. His gaze remained riveted on her, his stare seeming to pierce into her mind and body. Moments ticked by. Then, apparently satisfied, he nodded. Turning away, he waved a hand, a gesture she interpreted to mean she was to follow him.

When she didn't, he pivoted back to her, turning from the waist. An impatient jerk of his head brooked no refusal.

Entranced, she plodded after him, the eerie glow that shrouded his silhouette lighting her way. She had no idea how far she'd followed the phantom or how long, but suddenly, and as mysteriously as he'd appeared, he faded back into the night.

"Where are you?" she yelled. "Don't leave me!"

The gale roaring through the treetops was her only answer. She dropped into a crouch. Between the night and the storm and the coyotes, she'd lost her mind. There'd been no Indian warrior to disperse a pack of hungry coyotes. Maybe there'd never even been any coyotes. Maybe...

She jerked alert. Oh, yes, there had been. They were coming again, only this time they were yikking and barking, racing straight toward her. She buried her face in her arms.

Dear God, is this how it ends?

"Hey, where do you think you're going? Doc, get yourself back on the trail, you big mutt!"

A voice. A man's voice. Yelling. Yelling at someone named Doc. Cautiously Michaela raised her head.

Something big and icy and furry slammed into her. Something warm and wet flashed over her face. She screamed.

"Doc, damn it!" The male voice again. "What are you doing?"

A silhouette crusted with snow and topped with an ice-covered fur hat loomed over her. "What have you found? Sweet Jesus!"

Restraining the animal with one hand, he dropped on one knee. "Who are you?" He grabbed the front of her jacket to pull her back into a crouch in front of him.

"Michaela Dunn." Her voice croaked. "My snowmobile broke down. I need to get to Promise Wilderness Lodge. I manage it."

Who is this savage, his face half hidden behind a growth of frozen beard? Not another ghost—please, not another ghost!

"You're Norm and Ida's niece?" The voice out of the frosted outline mirrored amazement.

"Y-, yes." Cold shuddering through every inch of her body affected her speech.

"Follow me." He pulled her to her feet with him, both of them staggering on their snowshoes as they came upright. "I'm on my way to my cabin. It's a lot closer than the Lodge. I have a dog team, but they're pulling a sled full of supplies. You'll have to walk."

"Okay." She could do anything now that she had a definite chance of survival. She didn't know who this man was, but she did know the two things that mattered: he wasn't Ralph Frame, and he was on his way to shelter. She squinted into the storm and saw a bunch of snow-coated animals and a sled piled with containers not unlike those she'd been forced to desert.

"Doc, hike, hike." He turned the dogs back in the direction they'd come and fell in behind the sled. Michaela followed in the path they broke. *So much easier now, so much easier. I can do this, no problem.*

"Come on, get moving!" he yelled back over his shoulder.

Fine. Everyone for himself. Promise Wilderness is no place for weaklings or fainting damsels in distress. This creature seems well aware of the fact. She pulled a mitten across her face to clear her vision and plodded after his vanishing outline.

For what seemed like hours, she followed as dogs and man broke trail. Her breath struggled in and out of lungs she hoped wouldn't freeze. A stitch haunted her left side, her legs ached, her feet became clumsy, half-frozen lumps. Each time he paused to rest the dogs, she risked pulling off her mittens to blow on fingers aching from cold. Finally, when they stopped for the fifth or sixth time—she'd lost count—she saw the outline of a dark cabin a few feet to her right.

"My cabin." He swung back toward her. Tongues lolling, his dogs flopped, panting, into the snow. He released the bungee cords holding his load in place and began to swing containers up onto the verandah. Battling fatigue, she moved to help.

"Never mind." He dismissed her efforts and threw the last container up onto the porch. "Go inside. Turn on the lights. I have to kennel the dogs. Come on, Doc, just a little farther, boy." His tone, even raised as it had to be to overcome the gale, softened as he encouraged the weary dog.

The animal struggled to its paws. His soft growl brought the others up. Dragging the empty sled, they plodded off behind the man and their leader.

Michaela sank down on a step smothered in snow to remove her snowshoes with fingers so cold they barely moved, then shuffled her way up to the verandah.

When she tried the latch, she wasn't surprised the door opened. Most cabin owners in this wilderness area never locked up, especially in winter. Someone might come along in need of food and shelter.

A gush of warmth welcomed her. Heaven could feel no better. She stood savoring the moment, relief engulfing her, making her knees suddenly weak.

Safe at last!

She closed the door and ran her hand along the wall until it encountered a switch. The room flooded with light.

She removed her frozen balaclava and mittens and unzipped her snowmobile jacket. Hanging the clothing on pegs by the door, she scrutinized the place.

Its walls were grey, chinked logs, its floor well-worn pine. A massive fieldstone fireplace dominated the right wall. *Backwoods barracks.*

The furnishings told another story. At the rear, gleaming oak cupboards, matching table and chairs, and stainless steel appliances provided a modern kitchen. The area in which she stood had been outfitted as a living room, with a brown leather couch and chair facing the fireplace. Accompanying lamps and tables appeared rustic, but Michaela guessed they were straight out of a Cabela's Home & Cottage catalogue.

Who was this man she'd followed home? A

comfort-loving Grizzly Adams?

Then it came. The flash. The icy, prickling sensation that made her colder than the blizzard, sicker than the flu. Only this time it was worse. A terrifying sense of *déjà vu* accompanied it.

Something terrifying had happened here, and she'd been part of it. But what, when? Dizziness washed over her. She leaned against the wall.

Keeping her eyes closed, she pulled in a deep, slow breath. *In, out, in, out. Keep going. Keep going. Calm and assertive. Calm and assertive.*

"You okay?" A gush of cold air accompanied the words as he stepped into the cabin followed by the lead dog he'd called Doc.

Her eyes flew open.

"Fine." Confronted by intense sapphire eyes and a full beard bristling with ice crystals, she came out of it. *Good lord, the man is a savage.*

"Surprising." He yanked off his fur hat to uncover thick black hair that curled below his ears. "After a two-mile trek breaking trail through a blizzard."

"After a two-mile trek, alive and not completely frozen is fine, in my opinion."

"*Touché.*" He slapped the hat on a peg by the door and unzipped his parka. "Get out of those frozen boots and clothes." He hung up his jacket and began to remove his snow pants. Under his outer clothing he wore jeans and a black turtleneck.

She pulled off her boots and removed her snowsuit while he disappeared through a doorway to the right, into a room she could see was a bathroom. He returned, rubbing the snow and ice from his face with a towel to uncover dark eyebrows, lashes, and beard. Then, flinging it aside, he headed for the kitchen area.

In her grey sweatsuit, Michaela followed. He took a can of chicken soup from a cupboard and placed it on the counter. "We need hot food."

"Allow me." Her hand shot out to grasp the tin. Their icy fingers met on it, and the moment froze as he looked deep into her eyes. A tingling ripple glanced through her from the point of contact. *What...*

With an intense jolt of willpower, she pulled herself out of it. "Let me help, Mister..."

"MacDonald. Travis MacDonald." He jerked his hand away.

"Travis MacDonald." She barely recognized her own voice repeating his name.

He sniffed. A sneer of distaste quirked one corner of his mouth. Stepping back and turning his face away, he let her have the can.

"You have something against perfume?" *Great! Voice gone squeaky.*

"Against that particular stuff, yes." He turned back to the counter. "Pot in the drawer under the stove."

She opened the can with the electric opener on the counter. She dumped soup into the pot, put it on the stove, adjusted the heat under it, and turned away.

He'd crossed the room to hunker down in front of the fieldstone hearth, where he put a match to the paper, kindling, and logs ready there. Then he stood, watching the dancing flames for a moment, before swinging back to her.

"Sit here." He indicated the couch in front of the fire.

"Okay." She checked the soup before crossing the room to follow his instruction.

"Oh, my God!" She jerked backwards, slamming the back of her knees into the arm of the couch. In front of her lay a bearskin rug. The bear's mouth gaping open in a permanent, silent snarl brought a memory flooding back. Her head swam, her stomach roiled.

"I take it you're not into fur?" His words, cold and passionless, carried disapproval.

"But you are." The words shook.

"Pretty much." When she pulled her stare away from the dead animal to look up at him, she met eyes as cold and hard as the ice on Promise Lake. "I'm a trapper."

She knew hearts couldn't plummet, but at that moment she felt hers perfectly capable. A trapper! Why hadn't he simply identified himself as an ax murderer?

"Really?" From somewhere she regained the ability to reply with a drop of what she hoped was nonchalance. Her father's training at hiding emotions was paying off.

"Yeah, really." He turned back to the kitchen.

Careful to avoid stepping on the fur floor covering, she eased herself onto the leather couch. The dog, the snow on his coat melting to reveal a golden red body beneath, ambled over to sniff her. He wriggled his nose before turning away to stretch out on the rug.

Another anti-perfume creature.

"Doc." Filling a bowl with kibble, he called the dog. With a lazy yawn, the big canine pulled himself to his feet and plodded over to get his supper.

****

"Eat." Five minutes later Travis MacDonald placed a tray with two bowls of steaming soup and a pair of spoons on the coffee table between the fireplace and couch. He picked up one of each and slouched into the chair to the right of the fire.

Glancing over at the bearded, long-haired man frowning into his food, Michaela felt her lips twitch into a sardonic grimace. In romance novels, women got rescued by handsome millionaires. She got Tarzan of the North.

She picked up the remaining bowl and spoon.

The good part is I'm alive and well, and tomorrow I'll be back at the Lodge and never have to see this animal-murdering, perfume-hating lunatic again.

"I'd be grateful if you'd take a shower."

His first half-socially-acceptable words startled her. "Excuse me?"

"I'd be grateful if you took a shower and washed that smell away." He picked up the tray with the empty bowls and headed for the kitchen. "Fresh towels on the shelf in the bathroom."

"Is there a lock on the door?"

"I live alone."

"O-...kay." She replied to his back at the kitchen counter. "The honor system, then."

He grunted a response.

She hesitated, shrugged, and headed into the bathroom. If the hairy brute had been going to attack her, he would have done it by now. A hot shower would be nirvana.

Like the rest of the cabin, the bathroom's walls and floor were well-aged originals. The rest was all recently updated, right down to the washer and dryer behind the door. No bathtub, but a roomy, sparkling-clean shower stall, masculine shampoo and body wash on its shelves. So the creature did practice hygiene.

High-end hygiene. Randy had the same products in the bathroom of his Toronto apartment. And Randy bought the best an up-and-coming attorney could afford. How did this semi-barbarian get expensive shampoo and body wash? More to the point, why? Hermited away in the woods, he had no one to impress, no one to keep from annoying with body odor. Or did he?

Maybe there was a Ms. Semi-Barbarian living nearby. Maybe she even lived here part time, despite

13

his claim to living alone. Michaela swung open the cabinet above the vanity. Male shaving equipment and deodorant, aspirin, and a first-aid kit. Not a Venus razor or tampon in sight.

She glanced at the solitary toothbrush in the holder. More evidence. So he really does live alone. Looking for a fresh one, she opened the drawers. Nothing. Apparently he didn't cater to guests. A navy terry robe hanging on a peg behind the door caught her attention. She took it down, glanced at the label and whistled. She'd bought one just like it for Randall last Christmas. This guy had taste, expensive taste. The enigma regarding Travis MacDonald just kept on expanding.

She stripped off her sweaty clothes and pushed them into the washer. From a shelf above, she took a box of soap flakes, sprinkled some on top, then spun the dial to "Regular." She'd get rid of all evidence of perfume before, as her uncle Norm would say, "it got his dander up" again.

****

"Better?" Carefully avoiding the rug, she brushed past where he was seated in his chair and resumed her place on the couch.

When he looked up at her, she adjusted the navy terry robe more snugly. His gaze roamed from her towel-dried hair to her bare feet. It made her acutely aware of her nakedness beneath.

He sniffed. "Much."

He stood and headed for the bathroom.

She pulled her feet up onto the couch and drew about her a duvet he must have thrown over its back in her absence. Outside, the storm raged on. Wind howled around the cabin, blasting the windows with snow and rattling the panes. She shuddered.

The dog, lying on the rug, muttered and closed his eyes. She adjusted a pillow behind her. The fire was a glow of embers. Warm and comfortable,

Michaela Dunn drifted into sleep.

****

He stood over her, broad chest bare, his only clothing the jeans that hugged his narrow hips. Michaela stared.

Never taking his hypnotic gaze from her eyes, he lowered himself down beside her on the couch.

"Michaela." Her name coming soft and throaty turned body and soul to molten desire. "Michaela."

"Travis." Her whispered word reeked of passion.

Holding her locked in his gaze, he moved toward her. Her lips parted, ready to meet his.

"Are you comfortable?"

Her eyes lurched open. He stood beside the fireplace, a white towel wrapped around his hips, hair and beard damp.

Dreaming. I was dreaming...an idiotic dream.

"You might have gotten dressed." She barked the words.

"I'm headed for bed." He looked down at her, annoyance scowling his features. "And you have my robe."

And, of course, a half-feral creature like you wouldn't have pyjamas...not even bottoms.

"You're okay for the night?" He placed another log on the fire and adjusted the spark screen.

"Yes, I'm fine. Look, I'm sorry about the clothing remark. You woke me and..."

"No need to explain."

Shutting off lights as he went, he strode into the room beside the bathroom. Before he closed the door, Michaela caught a glimpse of a king-sized, quilt-covered bed.

No offer to let me use it. She shifted around to adjust pillows and duvet. *Probably afraid some of my ungodly scent would rub off in it. But, good lord, the man has a body to match my dream fantasy and then some.*

Once in a comfortable position, her back supported against cushions at the end of the couch, she crossed her arms and determined she wouldn't sleep again until she was back in her own bed at the Lodge. *No more crazy dreams for this lady.*

The flames licking around the log he'd added to the fire made shadows dance over the scarred floor and worn walls. The gale shrieked down the chimney.

When will it ever end? I have to get back to the Lodge. Guests tomorrow, and now, thanks to Ralph and his buddy, no supplies. If I ruin Uncle Norm's and Aunt Ida's reputation...

A glance at the window beside the door made her breath catch. Ghostly white against the storm and darkness, he stood, arms crossed on his buckskin-clad chest, his countenance as immobile as stone. For a moment they stared at each other, then his lips relaxed into a faint but satisfied smile. With a slight nod, he melted into the night.

Her breath hiccupped back into rhythm. Pulling the duvet to her throat, she shimmied down beneath it. She'd definitely have no problem staying awake now.

Was this the phantom warrior her uncle had told her about? "The Protector of Promise Wilderness" Norman Dunn had called him. Supposedly he was the spirit of a First Nations brave killed by lumbermen in the mid-1800s when he'd tried to stop their devastation of the forest.

Uncle Norm, you definitely can tell a story. You've got me seeing your ghost.

****

The roar of a snowmobile engine woke her. Sunlight shafted into the room. Morning. And she'd vowed not to sleep. *Damn exhaustion and a warm bed.*

Pulling herself to a sitting position, she saw

Travis MacDonald turn from filling a coffee percolator and face the door. He was dressed in jeans, plaid flannel shirt, and boots. The corners of his eyes squinted. He squared his shoulders. Was he expecting trouble?

The noise stopped at his doorstep.

"Hey, MacDonald, get your sorry ass out here!"

Ralph Frame. Hell and damnation!

Giving her a palms-out signal to stay and another with a finger to his lips for silence, he crossed the room, snatched his parka from its peg, and strode out onto the veranda. He left the door open to let in a gush of frosty air and blinding light as the sunshine ricocheted off dazzling snow.

"What do you want, Frame?"

"We're looking for a woman."

"So what else is new? Murdoch, aren't you married?"

"Right on this morning, aren't you. Too bad you aren't clever enough to stay away from my trap line."

"It's a free country."

"Yeah, well, we'll see what local law enforcement has to say about that. Now about the woman. She had some trouble with her snowmobile last night and didn't make it to her place."

"Then she's probably dead." The words were flat, passionless.

"Not this woman," Ralph Frame sneered. "She knows how to take care of herself, believe me. "

"I don't know anything about her, so you two can pull *your* sorry asses off my property."

"Fine." Engines revved to life. "But," Ralph Frame yelled above the racket. "Remember what I said about my trap line. Remember my brother-in-law is Crown Attorney for this district."

He denied I'm here. Oh, my God! What is he planning to do with me? Keep me prisoner? Quick! Catch Ralph before he leaves...

She was on her feet when she came to her senses.

Ralph Frame left you stranded in a blizzard. This man didn't. And don't forget you and Ralph have a history that doesn't bear publicizing or repeating.

As the machines roared away, he came back inside the cabin and closed the door.

"Nice friends you have." He slung his parka back onto its peg. "They knew you were in trouble last night but waited until this morning to look for you."

"They're not my friends..."

"Right. Grab a cup of coffee." He went to the cupboard and took out a bag of oatmeal. "I'll make porridge. Then we'll hit the trail."

"Why did you lie about my being here?"

"I didn't. Just said I didn't know anything about you. Which is true. And don't bother to try to rectify the fact. I'm not interested."

He poured water into a pot and dumped unmeasured oatmeal into it. His obvious lack of cooking skills made Michaela cringe Even if he didn't plan to do her physical violence, his culinary efforts might be the death of her.

Chapter Two

Travis MacDonald fitted the cliché description "man of mystery" better than anyone she'd ever met. Michaela put the last of the groceries on the Lodge's pantry shelves and thought about how he and his seven-dog team had taken her back to her snowmobile and sled, how he'd righted both and then tinkered at the old machine until it sputtered to life. He'd even cleaned up what was left of her supplies after the coyotes had had a dinner party.

"Thank you," she'd yelled above the roar of the coughing motor. "What do I owe you?"

"This isn't Toronto." His eyes turned icicle-cold. "In this country we help each other." He headed back to his dogs.

So that was it. Michaela mounted her vehicle, turned it toward the town of Carleton, and drove away.

Once she glanced back over her shoulder. In a shaft of dazzling sunlight thrusting through the trees, he stood beside his team. Their golden-red coats freed of ice and snow, they were magnificent animals. She'd never seen dogs like them. Nor met a man like their master. He seemed as much a ghost of winters past as the apparition she'd imagined during the storm. *Darn Uncle Norm and his ghost legends of Promise Wilderness!*

Several times during her trip to town and back she thought she glimpsed a flash of golden red through the trees. A shiver washed over her as she poured sugar into a canister. If she had, what was he doing...protecting or stalking?

Forget Travis MacDonald. You won't be seeing him again. He's some kind of weird recluse-trapper. As for you, Michaela Dunn, you're pushing thirty. Your unfortunate passion for wild crazy guys died out years ago. Ralph Frame put an end to that, once and for all.

The sound of an approaching snowmobile took her attention.

"Hey, Mikey, you in there?" The motor cut.

"Karen!" She headed for the door, a grin curling her lips. She yanked it open. "Welcome, Ranger Dollard!"

"Mikey, thank God!" The rider dismounted to pull off her helmet and balaclava. Shoulder-length blonde hair tumbled free. "When Andy Murdoch reported you might have run into trouble last night in the blizzard, I freaked."

"Not very professional, Ranger." Michaela's grin widened.

"Maybe, but it's not every day someone tells me my best friend is missing in the worst snowstorm of the season."

"Idiot!" Michaela folded the woman into an embrace the moment she stepped onto the verandah. "You and I are a couple of tough cookies. We don't crumble easily. Or freeze."

"Damn it, Mikey!" Ranger Karen Dollard hugged her. "I was afraid...you've been away for years, and I thought maybe..."

Michaela pulled away to look into her friend's face. "I was raised in this country. It'll take more than a little snowstorm to do me in."

"Little snowstorm! Mikey, that was an all-out blizzard."

"Okay, okay. I made it home unscathed, so let's drop the subject. Come inside, and I'll make you a lunch that will justify your coming all the way out here on a well-intentioned if unnecessary rescue mission."

Hmm. Apparently she doesn't know about Ralph's involvement, so enough said.

****

"So when are you going to bring my godchild to visit?" Michaela placed two bowls of chicken fricot on the table in the Lodge's restaurant and sat down opposite her friend.

"Soon. Melissa's been bugging me ever since she heard you arrived last Friday. You're way up on her list of favorite people. Small wonder. Mikey, all those boxes of toys and clothes and books...just because I'm a single parent doesn't mean you have to take on any of my responsibilities."

"Look, I'm having a ball shopping for little-girl stuff. Don't deny me. Have a roll." She held out the bread basket.

"I'm doing just fine, you know." Karen accepted the offer. Avoiding Michaela's gaze, she reached for the butter.

"I'm sure you are."

"Why don't you just say it, Mikey?" She banged her knife down on the table. "Ask me why don't I identify her father and make him live up to his responsibilities."

"I'm letting the question pass because I know it only ticks you off." Michaela ignored the hot defiance in her friend's expression.

"Sorry, Mikey." The ranger gave an annoyed shake of her head. "Sore spot."

"Fine. Changing the subject. When did Andy Murdoch contact you regarding my possibly being in a pickle?"

"About two hours ago. You know I wouldn't waste any time checking out his story."

"What reason did he give for suspecting I might be in trouble?"

"He said your machine wasn't working well

when you left the snowmobile garage in Carleton late yesterday afternoon. He also said you weren't at Promise Lodge when he and Ralph Frame stopped here for coffee this morning on their way back to town from Ralph's chalet." She looked across the table, eyes narrowing. "Where were you, Mikey?"

"Guess I'll have to tell the truth." She grinned sheepishly. "And right on the heels of my big, tough, self-reliant cookie speech."

****

"So you spent the night with the hunky hermit of Promise Wilderness." Karen Dollard's eyes widened as Michaela placed a tray with coffee and two slices of apple pie on their table. "Wow, Mikey, you and your wild guys."

"That was high school stuff." Michaela poured coffee and tried to stifle the flush she felt rising up her neck. "I didn't choose to be found by Feral Freddy."

"Rescued. The verb is rescued."

"Okay, okay." She forked into the pie crust. "So you know Travis MacDonald. What can you tell me about him?"

"Not much, Counselor. He moved into the old Wilson place about five years ago. He and his dogs. Keeps pretty much to himself. Why do you want to know?"

"Just curious."

"Yes, well, I think maybe you should leave your curiosity to burn itself out." The ranger speared a piece of apple and popped it into her mouth. "This guy wants to be left alone, Mikey. If I'm any judge of character, I'd say he has a past, and not a pretty one. Why else would a man in the prime of life choose to hermit himself away in the woods?"

"Don't worry. Travis MacDonald is the least of my interests. I'm here for three, maybe four weeks, to run this Lodge while Uncle Norm and Aunt Ida have a well-deserved vacation. Then it's back to Toronto."

"Is Randall Kirby still your significant other, or has he advanced to fiancé?"

"Hovering somewhere between. Sometimes I think his only interest in me is that if he succeeds in marrying me he's all but guaranteed a position in my parents' law firm."

"Then the man must have more ambition then testosterone." Karen shoved back her chair and stood. "I've got to go. Lots of patrolling to do. I'm the only ranger in the northeastern corner of the county." She headed for the door. "Be careful, Mikey. Ralph Frame owns a chalet halfway up the mountain across the lake. The trail to it passes through your dooryard." She paused and turned back, her expression grim. "He hasn't changed for the better. In fact, he's worse now, cunning and ruthless and absolutely without remorse."

Michaela followed her out onto the veranda and waved as she drove off into the forest. Drawing a deep breath, she paused to savor the beauty of her surroundings. Perfect blue sky, above snow-capped mountains garlanded with sparkling snow beyond the frozen lake, accented a scenario of such beauty she fully understood her great-grandfather's devotion to preserving the area in all its pristine loveliness.

She admired her grandfather—and now her aunt and uncle for continuing to respect his wishes. But what would become of the lodge and the Promise Wilderness when they could no longer maintain it? Norman and Ida Dunn had no children, and Michaela's parents weren't about to abandon their Toronto law practice and lifestyle to run a wilderness retreat. She shuddered at the possibility of Ralph Frame getting his hands on it.

She wished she weren't an only child, that her

parents had had another offspring on whom to pin
their hopes of their progeny becoming one of
Canada's top criminal defense attorneys. She wished
her aunt and uncle didn't see her as being the
family's last chance to continue the protection of
these glorious, feral acres. She wished she were free
to do as she pleased.

*If wishes were horses, beggars would most surely
ride in style.*

With a sigh, she sauntered back into the lodge
and closed the door. The secure, homey feeling of the
old log lodge enfolded her as she leaned back against
the closed panel. The smell of aging log walls, the
strength of the broad planks beneath her feet, the
reverent hush of its shadowy interior, sunlight
streaming in through the windows above banks of
snow, the fire crackling softly on massive fieldstone
hearths at either end of the lounge and restaurant,
even her uncle's old guitar leaning against a wall in
a corner of the lounge... She loved the place. It held
all the good memories of her childhood, years when
she'd spent most of her time with her aunt and uncle
while her father and mother were off "lawyering" as
Norm Dunn would say.

"Michael with Laura beside him could have
saved Jack the Ripper from the gallows if he'd ever
been caught...and if they'd been alive back then,"
her uncle used to joke.

"Norman, what a terrible thing to say!" his
diminutive wife would admonish him. "Michael and
Laura would never defend anyone so notorious."

Back then, Michaela would have agreed with
her aunt. In early January she'd found reason to
differ. Her parents had undertaken to defend a man
accused of murdering his wife and ten-year-old
daughter. Facing the well-groomed business man,
Michaela had felt such a wave of revulsion envelope
her she'd been certain of his guilt. When her father

had called on her to be second chair at the trial, she'd used that reason to refuse.

"You *feel* that he's guilty?" he'd raged. "Are you telling me you have some kind of sixth sense that can detect guilt or innocence? My God, all those days of living alone in the wilderness with your uncle and his wife have warped your brain. Their crazy stories about Indian ghosts and ridiculous promises have finally gotten to you. Well, let me tell you, my girl, you don't need a sixth sense. All you need is a good dose of *common* sense. Until you acquire some, I don't want to see your face in the offices of Dunn and Dunn. Is that clear?"

An hour later she'd telephoned to her aunt and uncle, informing them they could take that long overdue vacation because she'd be happy to manage Promise Lodge for them for as long as they chose to stay away.

Put all that on the back burner. A dozen guests will be arriving within the hour.

****

Michaela placed the last fork at the last place setting and stood back to admire her handiwork. Chili bubbled on the stove, broccoli salad chilled in the refrigerator, rolls waited in covered baskets on each table, and six mincemeat pies cooled on the counter.

Way to go, Michaela. Everything shipshape with a half hour to spare.

The sound of engines gunning toward the Lodge made her turn and head for the door, a welcoming smile on her face.

They're early. Doesn't matter. I'm ready.

The moment she stepped out onto the freshly shoveled veranda her lips sagged. She recognized the snowmobile free-wheeling into her yard at a crazy speed. By the time it whirled to a stop at the foot of her steps, her hands were on her hips, her forehead knotted into a frown.

"Howdy, my little snowbird." Ralph Frame doffed his helmet and balaclava and grinned up at her. "How's chances for a coffee?"

"Not a good time, Ralph. I have guests due." *Damn, I'd love to fly in his smirking face and scream how he left me to die in the blizzard, but I'm alone here. Keep a lid on it, girl. Karen said he's even more ruthless now. And he was bad enough twelve years ago.*

"Well, a minute is all it should take for you to pour me a cup." He dismounted and came up the steps toward her. "This is still an inn, isn't it, open to the public?"

"Yes, it is." Her heart pounding with repressed rage, she assented. "But you'll have to have it at the counter. All my tables are set."

"Fine by me." He followed her inside. "Always did like a stool at the counter. Lets me get closer to the pretty waitresses."

He reached for her, but she dodged behind the counter. With an exaggerated sigh, he unzipped his jacket and took a seat.

"Coffee." She filled a mug and shoved it toward him.

"How about a piece of one of those fine-looking pies?" He jerked a thumb toward her desserts.

"Those are for the scheduled guests, who will be here any minute."

"Ah, too bad. I have a real craving. Hope I don't get weak from hunger and knock over a couple of those tables you have all set up so neat and pretty." Brown eyes narrowed above sardonically smiling lips.

"Okay, okay." She grabbed a small plate and cut into a pie.

"Now that's more like it, Mikey girl. Hey..." He succeeded in catching her hand as she shoved the plate in front of him. "We shouldn't fight. We almost had a good thing going years ago."

"In your dreams!"

"Hey, hey, sweetheart, you're the one who wanted a ride on my super-charged snowmobile, you're the one…" His hand shot higher and grabbed her by the wrist.

The door flew open. A burst of sunlight flooded the room. Travis MacDonald stood silhouetted, a dark shadow in the brilliance, Doc at his side.

"I need to borrow a cup of sugar," he said.

"Like hell you do, MacDonald! Get out! Mikey and I were about to have a romantic reunion."

"Romantic? Doesn't look like it to me." He nodded toward Ralph's hand still gripping Michaela's wrist as she tried to pull away.

"Yeah, well, when you get to know her better, MacDonald, you'll discover Mikey doesn't shy away from a little rough stuff." He freed her, a sneer bringing out the scar on his cheek.

"Would you like a piece of pie, Mr. MacDonald?" Michaela smiled brightly "Mincemeat, fresh and crispy?"

Defuse the situation and be quick about, Michaela Dunn. You don't want your restaurant messed up by a physical altercation between these two.

"Thanks." Travis MacDonald removed his fur hat and parka, hung them on a peg near the door, and crossed the room to take a seat two stools away from Ralph Frame.

"Ah, the hell with it!" Ralph grabbed his helmet from the counter and swung off the stool. "If you're going to be bird-dogging Mikey every step, I may as well shove off…for now. You two must have gotten real close real fast, to bring you running like some kind of toy poodle!"

Travis MacDonald began to extricate himself

from his seat, eyes narrowing.

"Please, ignore him." Michaela caught his arm. "He's always had a foul mouth."

"Watch it, Mikey!" Ralph Frame swung back on her. "This guy can't spend every waking minute guarding you. Not if he wants to keep on raiding my trap line. And when he isn't around..."

Beneath her fingers Michaela felt Travis MacDonald's muscles tighten. "Get out, Ralph. Now."

"Sure, sure, anything you say, my little snowbird. Just remember to watch your back...and your precious Lodge..." He went out, slamming the door behind him.

"Thank goodness." Michaela heaved a sigh. "I was afraid he was going to upset the tables before my first guests arrive. You couldn't have come at a better time. Even if I don't believe you want to borrow a cup of sugar."

"I was checking trap lines, saw his trail turn and head back in this direction. I decided to follow." He looked down at her fingers still on his arm, quirking an eyebrow. She yanked them away.

"As the local knight errant, you deserve better than pie." She went to the stove and began to ladle a bowlful from the pot bubbling on its back burner. "Do you like chili? It's my aunt's recipe, very good with fresh rolls and coffee."

She placed it in front of him along with a basket of rolls and a dish of butter.

"Thanks." He picked up the spoon she handed to him and dug into the thick broth.

"Well?"

"Great. I appreciate good food. I'm not much of a cook."

"Really?" She glanced teasingly at him over her shoulder as she worked at the stove. He was buttering a roll.

"Yeah, really." His lips slowly moved into the first hint of a smile he'd ever given her. "Noticed, did you?"

"I was ravenous and you fed me. I'm not one to look a gift horse in the mouth." She stirred the big pot.

A discreet whine from the floor drew her attention.

"Doc—that's your name, isn't it?" She peered over the counter at the dog drooling a small puddle. "Looks as if you'd like a snack, too. And I've got just the thing."

She went to a refrigerator and took out a roast beef bone. Carrying it around the counter, she presented it to the dog. He lowered his head and whined again.

"What's wrong with him?" She looked up at the man.

"Manners. I'm trying to teach him not to grab...or take food from a stranger." He scooped into the chili without looking at her. "Go on. It's okay. I don't think this lady is going to poison us."

"Thank you." The words came out in a mixture of annoyance and amusement as the dog accepted the food.

****

Ten minutes later Travis MacDonald stood and reached into his pocket. "How much?" He pulled out a wallet.

Italian leather. Randall has one just like it. What is it with this guy?

"No charge. I owe you for a couple of meals, not to mention a pair of rescues."

The sound of approaching snowmobiles stopped further conversation. Shoving the wallet into his pocket, he strode to the door to grab his parka and hat.

He glanced back. "Good food."

Before she could respond, he'd disappeared out the door. She hurried to place his bowl and utensils into the dishwasher and wipe the counter. She couldn't have guests arriving to find leftovers on display. By the time she got to the window, he was vanishing into the forest on snowshoes, Doc plodding behind him.

Why had he fled? Was he afraid someone among her guests might recognize him?

She had no further time to speculate. The confusion of a dozen snowmobiles stopping and parking in her front yard took her attention.

"Welcome!" she called waving and smiling.

****

Mikey waved again as the group roared off on their snowmobiles the following morning. Her guests had expressed their satisfaction in the Lodge, the food, and her services. She walked back inside and examined the register. Group of ten tomorrow, but the remainder of the week looked easy. There'd probably be drop-in guests for meals and a few unannounced overnighters during the following five days, but the bulk of her customers would be weekenders, her aunt and uncle had informed her.

She turned the pages until she came to February 14th. The bookings took her breath away. The lodge would be full for dinner and the night. Valentine's Day! Good lord, she hadn't realized some people would consider The Promise a romantic retreat.

On reflection, she had to agree that it was. Beautiful, peaceful, unspoiled, with those big, log-cabin-cozy rooms. She wondered if she could get a temporary liquor license. She knew there was a strictly enforced law about no alcohol on the trails, and that none could legally be served at any of the establishments along the routes. Still, she'd like to be able to serve champagne once everyone was in off the trails, on that special evening only. Maybe she could put a bottle in each couple's room.

She roamed around the lodge trying to imagine how she'd promote a romantic atmosphere without ruining the rustic appeal of the place. *Hmmm*. She'd have to give it more thought later. Right now, the lunch remains of a dozen hungry guests greeted her. *Mustn't complain. Business is good, and that's what matters.* She picked up a plastic container and began to bus the tables.

Chapter Three

"Hike, hike!" Travis MacDonald ran beside his sled, shouting to his dogs. In spite of the cold, sweat beaded his forehead. Why did he have to be the one to find her, stinking of that rotten perfume? Why did she have to be beautiful? Why did she have to be from Toronto? And a lawyer to boot? She personified everything he despised in a woman, brought back every disgusting memory.

"Haw, haw!" He headed the dogs to the left.

The good part was she didn't seem to like him any better, especially his way of life. He understood that some people had an aversion to trapping, but with her it was a whole lot more. She'd looked as if she were about to vomit when she saw his rug and he told her what he did for a living. Violent reactions like that had to be the result of up-close-and-personal knowledge. But where would a woman from Toronto...?

Back at the cabin, he settled his team in the barn before heading inside, Doc at his heels. He wondered what he could scrounge up for a snack. He *had* to learn to cook. Nothing gourmet, just good, old-fashioned, tasty, stick-to-your-ribs cooking...like the stuff he got at home.

A vision of a body whose curves even a sweatsuit couldn't hide, with a shining tangle of tousled chestnut hair framing a complexion right out of a fashion magazine, even without makeup (he'd noticed when she'd awoken on his couch), darted across his mind.

Forget it! Just forget it. You don't need any more

of the kind of grief that type of woman can inflict on you. Keep in mind your last encounter with a female Toronto lawyer, and how she destroyed your life.

He pulled off his outerwear, built up the fire on the hearth, then headed for the cupboard. Four cans of tuna and an equal number of soup greeted him.

"We'll eat, then make a quick trip to town," he told the dog as he opened two tins of fish. "Got to stock up on food. Checking those traps will have to wait."

****

Travis drove his team to the deserted barn he'd rented to house his SUV, on the edge of the secondary road to Carleton. He backed the white jeep out onto the edge of the road, then led his dogs into the building.

"You guys wait here," he said unharnessing them. "Come on, Doc. Shake a paw. I want to get out to the trap line before dark."

****

"Travis." The owner of the corner convenience store looked up from the newspaper he'd been reading when Travis and Doc entered. "Good to see you. I've got a barrel of bones and scrap meat out back for your dogs. I was wondering when you'd be in to collect it. I don't want it to accumulate. Remember our deal. I save it, you keep it cleaned up."

"I remember, Sam. I meant to come in sooner. Sorry. I won't let it happen again."

"It's okay. Now what can I get you?"

"A lot." Travis took a shopping cart and started down an aisle. "I've been living on canned tuna, soup, and stale bread."

"Hey!" The storekeeper bent over the counter, yelling. "You drop it right now. Travis, he's at it again."

"Doc!" Travis swung back just in time to see the

33

malamute drop a Mars bar. "I warned you. If you continue to shoplift, you'll have to stay in the jeep. Sorry, Sam. Put it on my bill."

"Ah, let him have it." The storekeeper grinned at the dog who stood, head drooping, tail between his legs. "He's a good guy except for his kleptomania." He walked around the counter to confront the repentant-looking dog. "Here." He picked up the purloined bar and pulled off the paper. "Enjoy. On the house."

Doc cast a glance in Travis's direction.

"Oh, okay, go on, take it. But don't do it again. If it was a T-bone steak, Sam would be calling the cops. Damn, that's all I'd need."

"Had trouble with the law, Travis?" Sam Mathers cast a suspicious glance in his direction.

"Let's just say I prefer not to have the guys in red coats hassling me."

****

Back at his cabin, he put the dogs in the barn and stowed his groceries. He glanced at his watch. Three o'clock already. It would be dark in a couple of hours. With a regretful look at the coffeemaker, he knew there was no time for a quick cup.

"Stay here and look after things," he ordered Doc, who glanced up from his food dish as his companion headed for the door. "I don't trust Ralph Frame not to try to vandalize the place."

****

Moving through the hushed bush, he watched a brilliant sunset spilling over the mountains. It cast a surreal reddish hue over their crests. A pair of deer paused in the glow. He stopped to savor the moment. Like a painting, a wilderness masterpiece. Man, he loved this country. He pulled in a deep breath, then forced himself forward. There were traps up ahead and he had to get them.

He was bent over a beaver trap when the first

blow hit. It sent him sprawling headfirst into the snow. The second connected with his midsection as he struggled to his knees.

The abuse that followed was swift and brutal. Within minutes, Travis MacDonald lay unconscious and bleeding in the snow.

****

Blood reds and deep purples flooded the late afternoon sky above the mountains across the lake as Michaela finished preparations for the guests due the following afternoon. Her Aunt Ida had taught her to cook for a crowd. Now pots of beef stew, stacks of freshly baked rolls, and several pans of apple crisp filled the kitchen area with aromas guaranteed to whet even the feeblest appetite.

Time to take a break. She poured herself a cup of coffee and sat down at one of the restaurant tables. Her feet hurt, but a sense of satisfaction outweighed the discomfort.

That apple crisp does smell sinfully delicious.

The scent of the food brought Travis MacDonald's cooking to mind. An idea flashed across her mind. She stood and headed for the counter. She hadn't known how to repay her debt to him, but now she could, at least partially. She pulled a cooler from under the counter and began to ladle beef and vegetables into a container.

Twenty minutes later she drove off into the receding light of the January day on her uncle's old snowmobile, the cooler full of food strapped behind her. Although the hermit probably wouldn't be overjoyed to see her, he couldn't help but welcome a decent meal.

She enjoyed the drive through the darkening forest. Her months of staying at the Lodge with her aunt and uncle had given her confidence. In winter, with bears in hibernation, the area offered few dangers...aside from meeting up with Ralph Frame or starting out with a storm brewing. She cringed at the memory of her recent foolishness regarding the second danger.

A rising moon provided sufficient light to allow her to follow the trail. Within fifteen minutes she'd arrived at the cabin. When her headlight flashed over the pelts hanging on the outside wall, she swallowed hard.

Ignore them. Just ignore them.

She turned off the engine, to be greeted by the barking of dogs from the barn. Removing her headgear, she dismounted and stared up at the cabin. No smoke rose from its chimney. The windows were dark. Surely he would have a fire going and lights turned on by this time of evening, if he was at home. Where could he be? It wasn't as if the area had a flourishing night life.

A shiver of apprehension crept up her spine. She remembered Ralph Frame's threats. Her hand slid into the saddlebag holding an emergency tool kit and found a wrench. Clutching it, she went slowly up the steps.

"Travis?" His name echoed out into the silent shadows, black and impenetrable, in the moonlight. Not a single breeze stirred. A coyote howled, an owl hooted. Michaela moved close to the door. "Travis MacDonald, are you inside?"

A fury of barking erupted.

"Doc?"

Silence.

"Doc, it's Michaela. Remember me?"

Again, silence.

Hoping her introduction would appease the dog, she tried the door. It gave inward.

"Doc, I'm coming in." She eased into the black interior. "It's okay, boy. I'm looking for Travis."

A low growl to her right established the dog's location. Sliding her fingers along the wall, she found the light switch. Lamps flashed on, and she saw the malamute near the couch, hackles on end, crouched, ready to spring.

"Doc, it's okay." She stood still, heart pounding. "Where's Travis? Why are you alone?"

Slowly the big dog's fur returned to normal position, his stance relaxed. He looked up at her and whined.

"Come here." Michaela held out her hand. "I need your help. You have to find Travis."

As if he understood, he sprang toward the door.

"No, no." She slammed it shut. "You're not running off to find him on your own. I'll get my snowshoes and put a lead on you. *Then* you can take me to Travis."

****

It wasn't difficult to find the trail by which Travis apparently left his camp yard on a regular basis. In the illumination of the headlight she'd strapped to her forehead, she could see snowshoe tracks forming a hardened path into the bush. Even if they hadn't, Doc, lunging at his leash, would have dragged her in the right direction.

Her arms felt pulled from their sockets as she fought to hang onto the lead she'd fashioned from rope found in Travis's cabin. A wind coming out of the northeast reached down into her lungs, warning of its deadly potential. She stumbled as she battled to keep up with the dog's frantic pace.

No wonder this guy and his buddies have little trouble pulling a sled with a man the size of Travis on the runners. Lucky I learned to run on snowshoes as a kid, or I'd be face down in the snow! Maybe I could have done this on my own. Travis left a legible path.

That idea vanished when they broke into a wide meadow where all evidence of the man's passing had been obliterated by snaking drifts. Doc paused, sniffed the air, then threw back his head and howled.

"Don't tell me you've lost the trail!" She panted. "Come on, Doc. Find Travis!"

The dog put his nose to the ground. He circled and then, with a lunge that all but pulled Michaela off her feet, set off at a gallop.

"Whoa! Or whatever means slow down!" Stumbling and lurching, she clung to Doc's leash. The beam of her headlight danced crazily around the open area. When they entered the trees again, the big dog slowed to walk. Sniffing, he circled until he picked up the trail. When he did, Michaela felt she could once again have followed it on her own. The snowshoe tracks, protected from the wind, were easy to follow through the bush.

Ten minutes later, Doc stopped. She staggered to a halt behind him and saw an opening ahead. Not a large one but recognizable as a frozen pond. In its centre, a beaver lodge rose in a snow-crusted pile. Doc's nose quivered as he tested the air before he lunged off again, Michaela lurching headlong behind him.

"Whoa!" she cried.

The dog stopped the moment they burst into the clearing, threw back his head, and howled a long, mournful cry that made her hair tingle. Swinging her light, she saw the reason.

A body, blanketed with blowing snow, head turned to one side, lay belly down beside the winter-stilled stream.

"Oh, God!" She dropped the leash and scrambled toward the figure. Doc beat her to the spot. By the time she arrived, he was licking his master's unconscious face.

"Get back, Doc!" She knelt. It took all her strength, but she managed to roll the man onto his back. "Travis!" She took his head into her lap.

"Travis MacDonald! Can you hear me? It's Michaela Dunn...and Doc."

Her heart flip-flopped with fear. Was he dead? His right eye was swollen and discolored, his left cheek bruised an ugly purple. She pulled off her mittens and was trying to find a pulse in his carotid artery when he moved and moaned. His good eye slowly opened a slit. He muttered something she couldn't understand...

"Travis, what happened?" She slid back his mittens and began to massage his wrists.

"Disagreement over...traps." His lips, blue from cold, barely moved.

"Someone attacked you? Who?"

"Not important..."

His eye began to close.

"You stay with him, Doc." She scrambled to her feet. "Keep him safe. I'll go back for my snowmobile and your sled. It's the only way we can get him out of here."

For insurance that the dog would stay with his master, she tied his leash to a nearby tree. Re-entering the forest, she glanced back. A lump rose in her throat. The malamute had lain down against Travis, his head on the man's shoulder.

"Good dog," she whispered.

****

"Argh!"

Travis MacDonald groaned as she urged him toward the dog sled she'd attached to the snowmobile. His weight against her shoulder threatened to collapse her. She gritted her teeth.

"Come on, Travis. Just a little bit more. Try. We're almost there."

"Cold," he mumbled. "Dead cold."

"I know, I know. We'll have you back at your cabin in no time, and I'll get a fire going. Now try to help yourself just a little more."

He heaved a shuddering breath. With her help, he drew himself up.

"Good. Just a bit more."

When he finally dropped into the sled, her body went weak. She pulled a survival blanket from the snowmobile's saddle bags, tucked it firmly around his body, and turned to mount the machine on knees threatening to desert her.

"Michaela?" The rasping voice, barely audible above the howling wind, stopped her.

"Yes?"

"Thanks."

"Just returning the favor, my man." She struggled to keep the tone light as fear grappled to take over her emotions. "Sit tight. I'll have you back in your cabin safe and warm in no time."

She climbed aboard and started the engine.

"Doc, hike!" she yelled to the dog.

He bounded off, leading the way through the drifting snow.

Twenty minutes later, once again stumbling under his weight, his arm across her shoulders, she helped him up the steps to his cabin. At the top, he lurched backward. Clinging to the front of his parka, she planted her feet and managed to right him.

"Come on, come on, damn you!" Nearing exhaustion, Michaela was all out of gentle platitudes. "Help yourself!"

"A real sweetheart, aren't you?" He ground out the words between clinched teeth.

"Exactly the kind of sweetheart you need right now, Travis MacDonald." She leaned him against the cabin wall while she pushed open the door. "Now," she resumed her position under his right arm. "Walk!"

****

He lay ensconced in his bed, beneath the duvet, a half hour later. A fire crackled on the hearth in the room outside the bedroom door.

"Beef stew." Michaela sat beside him and held out a steaming cup. "I was bringing it to you, along with some other homemade goodies, when I discovered you missing. This is the broth. I don't think you're up to vegetables and meat just yet."

She put her hand behind his head, into the mat of dark curls, and raised him to take some of the liquid.

"Good." He paused after the first swallow.

"Drink it all." She held the cup to his lips as he tried to lie down again. "You need to recover your strength."

"Won't help me recover my dignity." He looked up at her with his good eye. "Having a woman undress you when you can't stop her doesn't do much for a man's ego."

"Oh, I'm sure the undressing part wasn't a first." She pressed the cup of broth against his mouth again. He choked down another gulp. When he'd finished, sputtering, she wiped his beard with a hand towel and lowered him back onto his pillow.

"No, it wasn't, but having my underwear pulled off when I'm too weak to resist is. I'm okay now. You can go."

"No, you aren't, and no, I won't." She stood. "I'm staying the night. Where is your generator? I want to make sure it's fueled."

"Shed out back." With a sigh, he closed his good eye. "Leave it alone. You'll only foul it up."

"Hardly. I run Promise Lodge, remember? I know how to refuel a generator."

"Okay, okay, do your worst. I'll fix it tomorrow." His head lolled to one side. Doc heaved a sigh and climbed onto the foot of his bed.

"Good boy." Michaela patted his head. "You're the only who could possibly want to be near someone so grouchy." She turned toward the door.

"Wait a minute."

"Yes?" She swung to face him.

"Do I have all my teeth?"

"Definitely." She smirked. "Male vanity rears its head. A sure sign of recovery." She paused. "It was Ralph Frame and Andy Murdoch who did this to you, wasn't it?"

"Not important. You'd better hit the trail. Your guests, remember." Again, the last tinged with sarcasm.

"None before tomorrow night. I'm staying until tomorrow morning. Oh, and by the way, I'm not wearing a drop of perfume. No need to worry about offense to your olfactory system."

The expletive that erupted from the bed made her mouth quirk up at one corner.

****

Michaela was returning from the generator shed, flashlight in hand, when she heard the roar of approaching snowmobiles. Not wanting to be seen until she knew who the newcomers were, she switched off her beam and huddled into the shadow of the cabin beside the verandah. Her snowmobile parked out of sight against the rear wall of the cabin wouldn't warn anyone of her presence.

As two machines roared into Travis's fire break and skidded to a halt, the malamutes in the shed broke into full voice.

The new arrivals cut their engines but remained astride to look up at the lights glowing from Travis's windows.

"Seems he made it home." Michaela recognized Andy Murdoch's voice. "Hell, that's a relief."

"Relief?" Ralph Frame guffawed. "You didn't seriously think he'd die out there after the little hiding we gave him? Man, if he couldn't take it, he shouldn't be in this country, never mind tampering with our trap lines."

"Yeah, well, I don't want a murder charge haunting me. I've got a wife and kids."

"You got the guts of a chicken, Murdoch. You don't care about that homely little mouse you married. If she left you tomorrow, you'd be well rid of her."

"Don't talk crazy, Ralph. You know our house and my job at the mill depend on my keeping Jenny happy. If her father found out some of the stuff we've been doing..."

"Okay, okay. So the mill manager bought his daughter a husband with a bungalow and a foreman's job. As for this MacDonald, he must be sleeping it off or he'd have heard our machines. Listen to those dogs! Man, their howls are enough to make your blood run cold. I swear they're more wolf than dog."

He switched on his machine. Seconds later, both visitors roared out of the yard.

Michaela walked slowly around to the front of the cabin. She'd been right. Ralph Frame and Andy Murdoch were responsible for Travis's condition. A trappers' war. Well, maybe he deserved what he got. She looked at the pelts on the cabin wall and shuddered.

She stepped inside to find her patient, the duvet wrapped around his bottom half leaning on the bedroom door frame.

"I heard snowmobiles. Frame and Murdoch?"

"Yes. They're gone now. Back to bed."

She slipped an arm around his waist. Hard as steel.

"Okay, okay." He struggled free. "Leave me alone."

"Fine. Fall on your face." She released him and went to sit on the couch. "See you in the morning."

Again an expletive as he turned and hobbled back to bed.

****

Michaela awoke in pre-dawn darkness to a discreet rattling sound. Pulling herself up on an elbow on the couch where she'd spent the night, she saw a shadowy figure fumbling with the coffeemaker.

"What are you doing?" She rubbed her eyes. "What time is it?"

"Making coffee. It's six a.m." In jeans, plaid shirt, and grey woolen socks, he turned to her in the shadowy cabin and snapped on the light above the stove.

"Go back to bed. I'll do it." She struggled to her feet and flinched at the crick in her back. "That is one lousy place to sleep."

"I told you to go home." He turned back to filling the machine with water. "I'm perfectly..." The pot dropped from his hand and spattered the rest of the water over the floor. "Damn, now see what you made me do."

"What I made you do!" Michaela was at his side, stooping to pick up the unbroken container. "I'd say weakness is a whole lot more to blame. Go, sit on the couch. I'll finish up here."

Stubborn blue eyes met a pair of determined green. Zapped by a bolt of something that snatched her breath, she stared up at him. She heard him suck in his breath. The next instant she was in his arms, being kissed, skyrockets exploding in her mind and body.

She swirled away with him, lost in new sensations, lost in a wonderful world of wilderness winter and the man who personified it. If he was a ghost and he kissed like this, she'd welcome the paranormal anytime.

Lost in the passion of the moment, she pulled him to her. He grunted.

"Damn ribs!" He flinched away, the words a

sharp gasp. Taking a step backward, he rubbed his chest. "Sorry about that. Knee-jerk reaction. Won't happen again."

Ice water splashed in her face could not have shocked Michaela more. No man had ever pulled away from Michaela Dunn. *She'd* always been the one to put a stop to romantic moments that didn't please her.

"Okay, fine."

He rubbed his hands on his thighs and turned away. "Yeah, okay."

"I'll make breakfast." Michaela tried to bring her racing heart and catapulting senses back under control.

He headed toward the cold hearth. "I'll start a fire."

"No!" She caught him by an arm. "I'll do it. Just as soon as I make the coffee."

"Are you going to do everything for me until you think I'm well enough to again take care of every detail of my existence?" He loomed over her. "I thought you said you had guests coming today."

"I do, but I wouldn't leave anyone wounded in the wilderness." She glared up at him. "I'm not about to leave...at least, not until I've fed you a decent breakfast."

"Argh!" He limped to the couch and eased himself down onto it. "Okay, do what you feel you have to. Then get the hell out of here."

"Jesus cured ten lepers and only one thanked him." Michaela remarked sententiously as she finished measuring coffee and pushed the Brew button.

"Yeah, well, you're not Jesus and I'm no leper, so you can put that analogy to rest."

Cranky or what? Definitely a sign of recovery.

Chapter Four

An hour later, she climbed aboard her snowmobile and headed back down the trail toward the Lodge. She'd made his breakfast, fed and watered his dogs, and lighted his fire...on the hearth. Telling herself she'd done all she could, given his belligerent attitude, she drove off into a beautiful wilderness morning.

Snow sparkled like diamond crystals on the ground and from the branches of trees. The bitter wind that had haunted the area in the night had fallen away. Now a crisp, cold calm held the Promise in its grip and made everything appear fresh and unsullied.

Beautiful and at times harsh, this pristine wilderness was nevertheless fragile. Clear cutting that destroyed every tree in its path, whether worthy of use or simply considered in the way, would utterly destroy this area. Without forests on the mountains to hold soil in place, silt would wash down into Promise Lake, ruining the spawning areas of fish that each year made their way up the streams and rivers to deposit their eggs. Wildlife would have no refuge from harsh winter winds, no food to sustain them through the cold months.

Dismounting in front of the venerable old inn a few minutes later, she gazed up at it and felt a wonderful, warm feeling wrap itself around her heart. The word "home" resonated through her thoughts. She tried to brush it aside, but when she crossed the threshold it echoed persistently.

****

Michaela paused in adding tomatoes to a batch of chili. Someone was coming. She turned down the burner under the pot, smoothed her apron and patted her hair.

"Auntie Mikey!" A small creature in a pink snowmobile suit, face hidden in a matching balaclava, arms extended, toddled through the doorway.

"Melissa Dollard, what a wonderful surprise!" Michaela scooped up the cold bundle that was her friend's daughter. "I hope you have room for a couple of chocolate chip cookies. I have a fresh batch in the oven."

"Yumm!" the toddler cried as Michaela stood her on a chair and began to divest her of her outerwear.

"I see you're right at home, Miss Melissa." Karen entered, one large and one small helmet under her arm. "You remembered to thank Auntie Mikey for all the goody packages she sends, I hope."

"Thank you, Auntie Mikey." Now free of her snowmobile suit, the child reached up to hug Michaela. "I 'specially love the big fluffy dog. He looks like Doc."

"Doc?" Michaela looked questioningly at Karen.

"She knows Travis and his team." The ranger avoided Michaela's gaze as she lifted the child to the floor.

"Travis and Doc come to visit sometimes." Melissa explained, heading toward the kitchen area. "Are the cookies ready, Auntie Mikey?"

"They should be done just about now." Casting a puzzled glance over her shoulder at Karen, Michaela headed toward the stove. "Get Mom to hoist you up onto a stool at the counter. You can have cookies and milk while we have a coffee." She pulled a covered bowl from under the counter. "I mixed this just for you. It's homemade play dough. You can practice making cookies."

"Cool!" Melissa held up her arms to her mother. "Boast, Mommy, boast!"

They were finishing their coffee when the door opened and Travis stepped inside.

"Interrupting a girls' time, am I?" It had been four days since Michaela left him at his cabin. Evidence of his facial injuries was fading.

" Uncle Travis!" Melissa jumped to the floor, staggered to regain her balance, then ran to throw her arms around his knees.

"Good lord, Travis!" Karen Dollard stared at him. "Mikey told me you had an incident on the trap line, but I had no idea...Ralph Frame and Andy Murdoch, no doubt?"

"Nothing I care to talk about. Hello, Kitten." He scooped the child up in his arms, grimaced as her small feet hit his ribs, then grinned and planted a kiss on her cheek. Michaela had never seen such delight in his expression. "I didn't know you were here."

"You hurt your face, Uncle Travis." The child touched his discolored cheek. "Did you fall down? Does it hurt?"

"Only when I laugh." He tickled her ribs, and she giggled. "So don't tell me any funny stories."

"Is Doc outside? What about the other dogs?"

"Yes, they're all here."

"Take me for a ride...pleeeeze!" She threw her arms around his neck and squeezed.

"Sure. That is..." He glanced at Karen. "If your mom says it's okay."

"Of course. Now that you're here, I won't have any peace until you take her."

Karen started to get up. "I'll get her dressed."

"Sit, enjoy your coffee." Travis placed Melissa standing on a chair and took the small pink suit from the peg by the door. "Melissa and I are old hands at getting into this rig, aren't we, girl?"

"Sure are, Uncle Travis." She steadied herself with one hand on his shoulder as he bent to put her feet through the bottoms. "You sit, Mom."

"Okay, okay." With a resigned grin, Karen reseated herself on the stool and watched as Travis dressed the child.

"See you later, Mom, Auntie Mikey!" Melissa called back over his shoulder as he carried her outside.

"Have fun." Karen swung back to her coffee. "What?" She met Michaela's questioning gaze. "Oh, for heaven's sake, Mikey, you don't think Travis MacDonald is her father?"

"The time frame fits. He came here four or five years ago, Melissa is three—going on eleven, from the way she talks. And, in spite of what you've said about his past, you trust him with your most precious possession."

"Okay, okay, I'll tell you the sorry truth. Travis MacDonald helped me out when I ran into trouble with a bunch of drunken snowmobilers last winter. They figured they didn't have to listen to a woman, law enforcement officer or not. Travis and his dogs arrived just in time...Travis and Doc, that is. I think those guys were more afraid of that big malamute than they were of either Travis or me. Anyhow, they'd disabled my snowmobile. Travis drove me home with the dogs. When Melissa saw his team, she fell in love, and nothing would do but for Travis to promise to come back in the morning and give her a ride. He's been doing it ever since. Too bad..."

"Too bad what?"

"Too bad he had some kind of experience that soured him on women. You must admit he's a waste, hermiting himself away."

"Apparently not too completely to pay visits to you and Melissa." Michaela eyed her suspiciously.

"Okay, okay, suspect what you will. We've both

been good at keeping secrets, haven't we, Michaela Dunn? Now can we move on to other topics? Like where you got that killer sweater? And don't even get me started on those jeans."

Chapter Five

"Got any more of that great stew, Mikey?" a customer called from the back of the lodge dining room. The place was packed, with only a table for two still unoccupied in a far corner.

"Comin' right up, Kelsey." She took a fresh bowl from the shelf and ladled out a generous serving. Her plaid shirt was damp, her hair twisted into a knot on top of her head and wilting in the heat of the stove, but she loved every minute.

Straightening from placing the bowl in front of the customer, she saw the door open. A couple entered, looked around, then headed for the unoccupied table. When they pulled off their protective headgear, Michaela recognized them with a start of surprise.

"Jenny!" She hurried to greet the woman. "Hi! Welcome!" And then, "Hello, Andy." Her last two words lacked the alacrity of the first three.

"Hello, Mikey." The woman looked up. Michaela saw the dark circles under her eyes, the gauntness of the pale face. Jenny Murdoch had never been pretty, but at least, when Michaela had previously known her as a teenager, she'd had the advantage of youth.

"I haven't seen you since you were married, Jenny."

"Yes, well, Andy and I don't go out much together." She glanced at her husband before her gaze flitted back to Michaela.

"What can I do for you?" Michaela made an effort to defuse the tension she sensed brewing between the couple. "I've got a full house, but I can offer you dinner."

"Look, Mikey, we really need a room." Andy Murdoch looked at Michaela and winked. His face was flushed and he reeked of liquor.

Drinking again. And driving a snowmobile. Poor Jenny. I'll have to get them off the trails.

"It's our anniversary." Jenny looked shyly up at Mikey. "Mom offered to keep the girls...we have two daughters...so Andy...that is, we decided to come up here to the Lodge."

"Yeah." He leered. "But it wasn't Jen's first choice. She wanted to go to Halifax to a dinner theatre. Dinner theatre, for God's sake! How lame would that be!"

"The only vacancy is the honeymoon suite." Michaela swallowed the chunk of annoyance threatening to color her reply as she forced a smile. "It's more expensive than the other rooms. However, since it is your anniversary, I'll let you have it for the price of a regular room. It has its own fireplace and a Jacuzzi."

"Now that sounds like a place where a man could have a real good time...with the right woman." He let his gaze roam up and down Michaela.

"I'll get it ready for you." Battling the put-down simmering behind her polite words, she turned away. He'd been drinking. She had a moral responsibility to get him off the trails.

****

With the only illumination a fire crackling on the hearth across the room, the king-sized bed plumped with quilts and pillows looked romantically inviting in the softly dancing shadows. In the adjoining bath, thick white towels and robes waited beside the Jacuzzi. Michaela opened the curtains on the garden doors to give a full view of the silver moon hovering over the frozen lake and snow-iced mountains.

She paused to admire her handiwork. *Pretty darned romantic.* Suddenly Travis MacDonald was all over her imagination.

Damn, what am I doing! She gave her fantasies a kick in the behind, turned, and went back down the corridor to her guests.

****

By 10:00 p.m. her guests had retired to their rooms, ready for a good night's sleep in preparation for a full day in the wilderness tomorrow, beginning early in the morning. Michaela made a final check of the dining room with its tables set for breakfast. *Everything shipshape.* She snapped off the lights. In the glow of the fires burning low on the hearths, she headed for the door to lock up.

Oh, no! She wilted as she heard the roar of approaching engines. *Not more guests at this hour.*

The machines stopped in the dooryard. Seconds later the door banged open. Ralph Frame and two male companions burst in.

"'Evening, sexy." He grabbed Michaela around the waist and drew her so close the stench of rum on his breath made her grimace. "Where's my buddy Andy? We're on our way to my place for a little poker game. He promised to meet us here."

"Meet you here?" Michaela wrenched away from him. "No way. He's with his wife. They're celebrating their anniversary."

"Well, now, isn't that just too sweet!" Ralph slapped his leather mitts down on a table. He was mean drunk. Michaela had seen it before. "Damn it, he's spent the last five years with that Minnie Mouse! Be a good girl. Go tell him his buddies are here."

"Ralphie, that you, boy?" Andy Murdoch appeared from the bedroom hallway, bare-chested, waving a bottle in his hand and swaying on his feet.

"Where did you get that?" Michaela pointed to

the flask.

"Brought it with me, innkeeper. I know this is one hell of a dry spot."

"We're waiting, Andy." Ralph snapped. "Get dressed. I've got lots of booze over at the chalet."

"Andy..." Michaela tried to protest, but Ralph narrowed his eyes at her.

"Leave it, Mikey." His tone brooked no further protestations.

"Give me two seconds. I'll be right with you." Andy Murdoch headed back toward his room, bumped into a doorjamb, cursed, then lurched out of sight.

"Ralph, he's in no condition to be out on the trails." Michaela rounded on the man. "Neither are you or your friends. We're filled for the night, but your friends can sleep on the couches in the lounge, and I'll let you have my room. I'll sleep in my aunt and uncle's apartment."

"Ah, come on now, Mikey." Ralph leered at her. "Sleeping in your room without you wouldn't be any fun at all. Come on, guys. Let's wait outside. There's still a few swallows of Jack Daniels left in my bottle, and lots more when we get to the chalet. Who needs this desert with its prissy landlady."

Laughing, his companions followed him outside.

****

"He wasn't always so insensitive." Jenny Murdoch, one of the lodge's terry robes wrapped about her, huddled in a corner of the loveseat in the honeymoon suite and clutched a teacup in her slender hands.

"No, I'm sure." Michaela reached for a plate on the tray she'd brought to the suite. "I'm sure he's not now. Peer pressure doesn't end with adolescence, you know." *Whoever said white lies were easier than the truth must have been an idiot.* "Have a cookie. These oatmeal-raisin are genuine comfort food."

"I'm sorry, Mikey." She shook her head and turned away. "I haven't much of an appetite. Oh, I hope Andy has enough sense to stop before he gets us any deeper in debt to Ralph Frame."

"Andy owes Ralph money? How did that happen?"

"Gambling." Jenny Murdoch stood and went to the window to stare out into the bitterly cold night, clutching her steaming mug. "High stakes poker games like the one they'll no doubt be having tonight." A shudder shook her slender body. "Oh, Mikey." She turned toward her, desperation shriveling her features. "Andy owes Ralph over eighty thousand dollars already! Ralph says Andy can get a mortgage on our house, but if we did and my father found out, he'd be furious. He gave us that house and Andy's promotion at the mill as wedding presents. I know he'd fire Andy, and then where would we be? Andy keeps thinking his luck will turn, that he'll be able to win it all back, but that's impossible. Ralph Frame is a cheat! I wish he was dead!"

****

Michaela was placing chicken into a pot to simmer for a fricot when she heard snowmobiles approaching. She glanced at the clock above the stove. Ten a.m. All of her guests except Jenny, who appeared to be sleeping late, had breakfasted earlier and hit the trails. Were some of them returning?

Wondering if there'd been a mishap, she crossed to the door. When she opened it, a twinge of apprehension snagged in her stomach. The two machines stopped at the verandah steps bore RCMP logos, and their riders wore law enforcement badges on their shoulders.

"Good morning." One of the officers spoke as they dismounted, removed their helmets, and approached. "Michaela Dunn?"

"Yes. Good morning, officers. What can I do for you? Coffee? Breakfast?"

"Thank you, no." The first officer came up the steps and stopped squarely in front of her. "I'm Corporal Palmer, and this is Constable Roy. May we come in?"

"Certainly." Michaela moved aside. She'd met a lot of law enforcement officers during her years as a criminal attorney. She could read trouble in their stance as easily as advertising on a twelve-foot-high billboard.

Pulling off their headgear, removing mitts, and loosening the top fastenings on their jackets, they followed Michaela into the dining area.

Preparing for a serious talk. Good lord, what is wrong?

"Let me get you some coffee." She struggled to keep their meeting pleasant and non-confrontational. "I just made a fresh pot."

"No, thank you, Miss Dunn. We want to get straight to the point. Did you have a guest here last night named Andy Murdoch?'

"Yes, Andy was here for dinner." *Don't lie and don't over-explain. The facts, just the facts, as basic as possible until I see where all this is going.*

"But he didn't stay the night?"

"No."

"Do you know what he did after dinner, where he went?"

"First, he went to a room with his wife. Later he left with friends." Michaela could stand the suspense no longer. "What is this all about? Has something happened to Andy Murdoch?"

"He was involved in a snowmobile accident around midnight."

Michaela's breath lurched inward. "Was he injured...?" She couldn't speak the other possibility.

"Not seriously." The officer relieved her fears.

"Just a few bruised ribs and minor cuts and abrasions, but he did destroy his machine. When his blood alcohol level was taken at the hospital shortly afterwards, it was well over the legal limit. We've been informed that Mr. Murdoch had been drinking before he left the Lodge and that he purchased alcohol from you. May we see your liquor license?"

"I'm sure you already know I don't have one." A hollow, sickly feeling invaded her stomach. *Now* she knew where this was going. She also knew who the informant had been, who had said Andy purchased liquor from her. "You know it's illegal to sell alcohol at snowmobile stops."

"Then how did Andy Murdoch manage to be intoxicated shortly after leaving here?"

"He brought alcohol with him." Sweat began to trickle down her body. "He and his wife had dinner with the rest of the guests, and then they went to our honeymoon suite to celebrate their wedding anniversary. When he came out of their room a couple of hours later, he appeared to have been drinking."

"Is there liquor in the premises?" Corporal Palmer looked squarely into her eyes. "Any at all?"

"Yes, in my aunt and uncle's private apartment. It's kept in a locked bar for their exclusive use. I didn't sell any."

"Miss Dunn, I hope you understand how serious this is. Someone could have been killed." Corporal Palmer wasn't about to let her off the hook. "With the increasing number of injuries and deaths that occur on our snowmobile trails each winter, we're cracking down."

"I understand. But, as I've said, I didn't supply alcohol to Andy Murdoch or anyone else."

"We found several empty liquor bottles on the trail leading up here." Constable Roy pulled a flask from inside his jacket and held it up for her consideration.

"On the trail leading up here. I can't control what some people do out in the bush. Since they were on the trail leading *up* here, doesn't that tell you they didn't get them here?"

"*Touché*, Miss Dunn." The corner of Corporal Palmer's mouth quivered into a sardonic grin. "I see you've lost none of the skills that made your family famous in the criminal justice system."

"I know law enforcement people often frown on what my family does for a living." She struggled to keep her cool. "But it's their job."

"Mikey?" Jenny Murdoch stood in the doorway of the corridor leading to the bedrooms. She clutched the terry robe to her throat, eyes huge and frightened, her face the color of chalk. "What's happened to Andy?"

"Officers, this is Jenny Murdoch, Andy's wife." Michaela introduced the woman.

"There's been an accident, Mrs. Murdoch." Corporal Palmer's voice was professionally considerate. "Your husband has been injured but not seriously. I'll take you to him." He turned to Michaela.

"As for you, Miss Dunn..." He pulled a paper from an inside pocket of his jacket. "You're being shut down, pending a full investigation." He handed her the notice. "Crown Attorney Best issued this closure order before we left town."

"But you can't do this! I have guests arriving! My aunt and uncle need the business! Don't you understand? This is peak season for Promise Lodge!"

"I am sorry." Corporal Palmer remained coolly professional. "Mrs. Murdoch, if you'll get dressed for the trail, we'll accompany you to the hospital."

****

A half hour later Michaela drove past the lane that turned into Ralph Frame's chalet halfway up the mountain that rose on the far side of Promise Lake. She had to fight the urge to roar up to his elegant hideaway and tell him what she thought of him and his underhanded ways. But she couldn't. She had guests to prevent coming, and the mountain summit above Ralph's chalet was the only place she knew she could get cell reception. She gunned her motor and drove on.

At the top, she stopped, dismounted, and took out her phone. Within twenty minutes she'd either contacted all the people on her reservation list or left messages for them. She checked for incoming messages and was startled at the number seeking reservations. She answered each with a refusal, shoved the cell back into her pocket, and zipped it shut. There was no way she could accept any of them until she got this mess straightened out. Anger surged through her as she headed back down the mountain. This time she didn't resist the urge to turn in at Ralph Frame's open gate.

The owner himself came out onto the veranda of his Swiss-style chalet perched on a ledge overlooking the lake. He was wearing his snowmobile suit, helmet under his arm.

"Well, this is a surprise. Come for a visit, Mikey? Grizzly Adams of Promise Lake lost his appeal? But then, your men always did have the shelf life of a banana."

"You miserable heap of bear droppings!" she yelled. She didn't dismount or turn off her engine, aware she might have to make a quick getaway. "I wish you'd get caught in one of your own traps! I wish you were dead!"

"Now that's not a very nice thing to say to an old friend." He smiled at her. "You made a big mistake, selling Andy that whiskey. I'd have thought a smart big-city attorney like you would have better sense. And wishing all kinds of bad luck on me in front of witnesses..." He shoved open the door. "Girls, come on out and let Ms. Dunn know what you overheard."

Two blondes wearing skin-tight jeans and turtlenecks trotted, shivering, out onto the verandah.

No trouble to guess their profession. Or what they'll do for money. Damn my big mouth and temper.

"Heard yah!" The tallest one taunted Michaela. "Can we go back in by the fire now, Ralphie?"

"Sure, sure, girls. Just don't forget her exact words, okay?"

Arms wrapped around their bodies, they shivered their way back inside.

"Argh!" Stonewalled, Michaela revved her motor and gunned out of the yard.

Glancing back, she saw he'd mounted his machine. She gritted her teeth and tried to urge more speed out of her uncle's old snowmobile.

Seconds later he passed her in a cloud of flying snow, momentarily blinding her. Several yards up the trail he swung his vehicle sideways. Swerving to avoid him, Michaela lost control. As her machine careened to the left, she flew into a snowdrift several feet away.

"You okay, babe?" Ralph was beside her, pulling her to her feet. "Man, you really got to learn how to drive one of these things."

"Bastard!" She wrenched free and glared at him. "Miserable bastard!"

"Back in fighting trim. That was quick. Sorry I can't say the same for your machine."

He jerked his head in the direction of the upset snowmobile. Its engine sputtered a few times before it fell silent. "Looks like you might have killed it instead of me."

"Damn you, Ralph Frame!" Michaela shoved him out of her way and strode back to the silent vehicle.

"If you made me ruin Uncle Norm's snowmobile…"

"Cool down, kid. It's a piece of junk. Norm should have bought a new one years ago. Remember, I own the only RV dealership for sixty miles. I might have given him a deal, under certain conditions."

"My uncle isn't a rich man!" she snapped as she tried to shove the snowmobile upright. "He has to deal with balance sheets and red and black ink. But if you're thinking he might have agreed to sell Promise Lodge in return for a deal on one of your crappy snowmobiles, you don't know Norman Dunn at all!"

"Chill out, Mikey." He caught her by an arm and swung her to face him. "How about coming back to the chalet for a drink? I'll send the girls packing. I have some choice chardonnay." He winked at her. "Your company might just make me reconsider my memory that Andy bought booze from you. I might even tell the Mounties I know he brought it with him."

"You are a despicable…" Her invective ended at the sound of dogs yelping.

Travis MacDonald and his team appeared, coming up the mountain trail. The musher drew to a halt beside them.

"An accident?" He gestured at Michaela's snowmobile.

"Hardly." She struggled to hide the relief his appearance had given her. "Long story. Will you give me a ride back to the Lodge?"

Travis looked from one to the other. "Sure. Hop aboard. What about your machine?"

"I'll have to find someone to tow it back to the Lodge," she said.

"Hope you haven't been hustling my trap lines, MacDonald." Ralph Frame stepped closer. "Hope you learned your lesson last time."

Travis MacDonald rounded on him with a

swiftness that startled Mikey and made her catch her breath. Blue eyes flashing, he faced his tormentor.

"What if I haven't, Frame? It's two against one now." The musher indicated Doc rumbling a warning at his side. "Your kind of odds, right?"

"Okay, okay. Take your rotten wolf and get off my property. I swear, you're like some kind of damn ghost from a winter a hundred years ago, appearing out of nowhere when you're least wanted."

Travis gave him another blood-chilling stare, then turned his team.

"Hike, hike!" he yelled, and the dogs were off down the mountain.

****

"Thanks. You arrived at just the right moment." Mikey got out of the sled in front of the Lodge and looked up at Travis MacDonald. "You *are* like the wilderness ghost."

"Huh!" He fastened the dogs to the verandah. "Do you have a backup machine to use until your other one is repaired?" He straightened and looked at her.

"Aunt Ida's is even older. It's in the barn, but I think it would take a bit of tinkering to get it back in running order. I'll have to find someone to tow Uncle Norm's down the mountain and out to Carleton for repairs."

"You can't stay here without transport." He began to separate the dogs. "I'll show you how to harness the dogs, and then I'll leave these guys, and Doc, and the sled with you until tomorrow. I'll return in the morning and take the full team back to get your machine."

"How will you get home with no sled? It's getting dark. You can't snowshoe that far at night."

"Have you got any cross country skis?"

"Sure, a bunch in the barn. Sometimes guests

want to explore the country that way, but they won't make traveling much faster than snowshoeing, in this deep snow."

"They will when I harness my dogs to pull me. I've done it before. These guys know the drill and the way home."

"I've heard of it. It's called skijoring, isn't it? A sport that originated in Scandinavia—Norway, I think. The skier attaches a line from the dogs' harness to a hook on a belt around his waist..."

She stopped as he pulled the item from a saddlebag on the back of his sled.

"You really are prepared." She indicated the snowshoes strapped to the sled's side, and the belt in his hands.

"Can't leave a whole lot to chance in winter in this country," he muttered gruffly, strapping on the belt. "That's one reason why I use dogs. They're a whole lot more dependable than snowmobiles, never mind that they're quieter, don't have to be gassed up, and create only biodegradable residue."

"Yes, well, I don't have a team of malamutes, so..."

"You do now." He pointed to the four dogs tied to the porch with Doc sitting beside them. "Here, let me show you how to harness them. Remember the commands? Gee is right, haw is left, hike is go, and whoa is stop. You won't have any trouble with them. Doc will keep them in line, don't worry."

"You're trusting me with your dogs and sled?"

"You're Norm and Ida's niece, so why wouldn't I? Keep Doc in the Lodge with you tonight." He turned to face her, blue eyes intense. "The others will be fine in the barn. Ralph Frame hasn't come down the mountain yet, and he has to pass through your dooryard to get to the road to Carleton. He's not a happy man right now, but you'll be safe with Doc in residence. Frame has a healthy fear of my boy. I'll get those skis and head out."

He started toward the barn. She hesitated, then called out, "Thanks. I owe you one...again."

He waved a dismissive hand without turning back.

"Travis?"

He rounded to look at her.

"What?"

"Are your dogs a specific breed? I've never seen any quite like them."

"They're called Moon Glow malamutes. I bought them from the kennel that developed the strain. Now can I go?"

"Forgive me for being interested."

"Argh!" He started off again.

"Travis!" An afterthought occurred to her. "You can stay the night. Room Number One is available...as are all the others...maybe permanently."

"What? What are you talking about?" She had his full attention as he turned back to face her.

"It's a long story." Suddenly she needed someone to listen.

He drew himself up and looked back at her. "I've got time."

"Okay. Settle the dogs in the barn and come inside."

****

"Bastard!" he shoved back his chair and stood to pace the length of the restaurant. "He's well named...Frame. That's what he did. Framed you. He likely suggested to Andy Murdoch that he should bring his wife here for their anniversary. He knew he'd bring liquor. Probably made him a gift of it...twelve-year-old scotch or the like. He probably scattered those bottles along the trail himself for the RCMP to find." He stopped in front of her. "You need a good lawyer. Can you afford one?"

64

"Nothing subtle about you, is there?" She looked up at him and tried to sound annoyed. She failed. The bruises were fading, and he was able to trap her once again with those amazing blue eyes. "But, yes, I can. I'm going to defend myself."

"Defend yourself? Hey, now, just a minute. Even a hillbilly like me knows only a fool tries to be his own attorney. You need a professional."

"I *am* a professional." She stood and faced him. "In Toronto I'm a member of my parents' law firm, Dunn and Dunn."

"Mom and Pop operation, is it?" Skepticism colored the words.

"Hardly." She felt annoyance pushing out despair, putting her back in fighting trim. "If you'd ever been accused of a serious crime in that city, you'd have come across their names. They're one of the top, if not *the* top, criminal defense lawyers in Toronto."

"What about you? Gotten any mass murderers off the hook lately?"

"Damn you!" She whirled and strode behind the counter where she banged a frying pan onto the stove. The memory of the man she'd refused to defend flooded back. "I'm sorry I confided in you! I'm sorry you came along when Ralphie was giving me a hard time! I'm sorry..."

She broke off. Suddenly he was behind her, swinging her into his arms, covering her mouth with his, crushing her against him, turning her knees to jelly, making her head swirl, her heart leap to the back of her throat. Neon lights flashed across her consciousness. *Wow, wow, wow!*

When he finally let her come back to earth, she collapsed against the counter.

"What in hell was that?" Her words came out as a croaking whisper.

"Another knee jerk reaction?" He backed off a

couple of steps, looking down at her with blue eyes that made her want to leap right back into his arms...and so much more. "Dangerous move, that. It could"—he let a corner of his mouth quirk up—"get way out of control."

"Yes, yes, it could." Michaela headed for the refrigerator. *Don't let me stagger. Please, please, don't let me stagger.* The kiss had shaken her equilibrium to its roots.

"So we'll put things on hold." He walked back to the table and sat down. "Is that what you want?"

"Sounds like a plan." She jerked open the refrigerator door. "Now, how about an early supper. How does steak and baked potatoes sound?"

"Darn good." He stood again. "I'll light the fire in the lounge."

"While it's cooking, I'm going to check the register and make sure I've cancelled reservations far enough in advance."

****

Her finger sliding down the names on the page froze to a halt.

Pencilled in the margin in her aunt's small, neat handwriting was a notation she'd missed.

Shane Gray and party of ten! She couldn't believe it. The Premier of the province and his entourage were due in two days. A sick feeling welled in her gut. It could ruin the Lodge's reputation when they learned it had been closed because of a liquor violation.

Then a thought struck her. Hadn't Ralph said his sister was married to Colin Best, the Crown Attorney? Amanda, that was her name. Michaela remembered her from high school. Gossip in Carleton declared that said Crown Attorney had political ambitions. Hardly a man to allow the Premier to be inconvenienced when it was within his power to prevent it.

66

She looked up, a smile stretching her lips wide.

"I think I may just have thought up a solution to my dilemma," she said, looking over at Travis, seated in the lounge reading a newspaper. "And it won't take all that much lawyering at all. I'll need a lift to town in the morning."

"A lift?" He looked up.

"You and your dogs. I'm willing to pay cab fare."

"O-kaaaay..." The word came out slowly.

"If you don't want to, just say so," she snapped. "I'll get there somehow."

"I'm willing." He folded the paper and placed it on the table. "But you may be risking your reputation by arriving in Carleton with a man the locals have branded a fugitive."

"*Are* you a fugitive?"

"Depends on your definition of the word. Still want me to drive you?"

"I'll risk it. But what about *your* reputation?" She slanted him a sideways glance as she removed the steaks from the grill.

"I don't get you."

"Your reputation as a hermit, a loner, a man of mystery." She narrowed her eyes over the last three words and lowered her voice to a whisper.

"Yeah, well." He pushed back on his chair and let a shadow of a grin curl his lips. "I guess I'll just have to risk it, too."

****

"A fine meal." Travis MacDonald shoved back his chair and rubbed his belly appreciatively. "More than sufficient payment for a trip to town and back."

"Really?" She stood and began to gather up their dishes. "In Toronto it wouldn't earn an elevator ride."

"In Toronto, a million dollars barely buys decent shelter." He got up and began to help her.

"And you'd know all about Toronto?"

"Yeah, well, I can read, and I do have a radio." He headed for the counter with his cup, plate, and cutlery.

"More evidence of the global village syndrome."

"Right." He swung to face her. "Need help with the clean-up? If not, I'll bank the fires and head off to bed."

"No, I'm fine. Go ahead. I'll be doing the same shortly. A confrontation with Ralph Frame always tires me."

An hour later Michaela sat in her bed across the hall from room number one and tried to concentrate on her book. She'd found it in her aunt's bookcase. It had looked interesting: nice, light, bedtime reading. Now she wasn't so sure. The romance between the handsome, virile hero and the heroine trapped by an avalanche in a mountain cabin only served to conjure up images of the man in the room across the corridor.

She'd never experienced sensations like those produced by the kisses she'd shared with Travis MacDonald. The book slid to her lap. Certainly he was a fascinating creature, mysterious and earthy, with a fantastic body and gorgeous blue eyes. But his effect on her had been more than physical. She'd felt as if she floated off the floor, then swirled away into a world of ecstasy beyond anything she'd ever encountered.

Maybe he *was* some kind of ghost, some kind of mythical creature who had the power to mesmerize women with a single kiss.

Disgusted with her fantastic ramblings, she picked up her book and turned the page, only to discover her feelings described by the author. She plunked the romance onto the nightstand and snapped out the light.

Grow up, Michaela Dunn, and stop believing in fairy tales. Just because the guy has rescued you more than once, don't go thinking he's your knight in shining armor with some kind of a magical kiss.

****

The roar of a snowmobile engine roused her into pitch blackness. Glancing at the luminous dial on her bedside clock, she saw it was midnight.

As the machine's headlight flashed through her window, she heard the door of Travis MacDonald's room open.

"Travis, what is it?" She bolted upright.

"Stay in bed," his voice, gruff from sleep, advised. "I'll see who it is."

"But..."

"Stay. You're not open for business, remember? So unless whoever it is happens to be cold or starving, I'll send them on their way."

"You're right." With a discouraged sigh she sank back against her pillows.

"Hey, Mikey!" Ralph Frame's drunken voice came to her. "Come on out and party! I've got a bunch of guys up at the chalet who'd like to meet an honest-to-god big-city female lawyer!"

Incensed, Michaela sprang out of bed and grabbed her terry robe. She thrust her feet into fuzzy slippers and headed for the restaurant.

Travis had turned on lights, including the verandah one. In jeans, boots, and unbuttoned plaid shirt, he was about to open the door, Doc by his side.

"Travis, no!" She ran across the room and grasped his arm. "Ralph is drunk! I can tell by his voice. When he is, he can be violent. Turn off the lights and maybe he'll go away."

"Somehow I doubt that." Booted footsteps on the verandah gave truth to his words.

"Hey, Mikey!" The door was yanked open and Ralph Frame, swaying on his feet, stood in front of them. Travis caught Doc by the collar as the malamute emitted a warning snarl.

"Well, well!" He stumbled into the room. "Grizzly Adams again. Getting right addicted to the hermit's charms, are you, Mikey? Why don't you come on up to the chalet with me, and I'll show you a little civilized entertainment."

"Get out of here, Ralph." Michaela drew herself up and faced him. "Haven't you done enough damage already?"

"Come on, sweetie. You used to be almost a good sport." He ran a finger down the scar on his face. When she flinched, he grinned. "That was one hot night, remember?"

"I said get off my property, Ralph."

"And what if I refuse? What if..." He made a grab for her arm, but Doc was quicker. He lunged, catching the man just above the wrist.

"Damn! Hell! Get him off, MacDonald!" Ralph Frame wrestled with the snarling dog.

"Doc, leave it!" Travis grabbed the animal by the collar and pulled him away. "And you leave us." He faced the man before him, who was bent over nursing his arm. "Otherwise, I might just lose my grip on my dog."

"Okay, okay!" He turned away clutching his wrist. " But if he's broke the skin, I'll see to it he's destroyed! That animal is just plain vicious!"

He lurched out of the Lodge and onto his snowmobile. After a few fumbling attempts to start it, he succeeded and roared out of the yard.

"We shouldn't have let him go." Michaela stared after him.

"What?" Travis slammed the door. "The man was drunk and belligerent! You couldn't seriously have been considering asking him to stay the night."

"It was the last thing I wanted to do, but he is intoxicated."

"Yes, well, it is midnight, time most snowmobilers are off the trails. Anyhow..." Travis glanced out the window beside the door. "He's headed across the lake, and his is the only place over there. He's not likely to meet anyone."

"I guess." She paused a moment. "Travis, I'm glad you were here. I'm relieved I didn't have to confront Ralph alone."

"I didn't do anything. Doc chased him off." His lips quirked. "Ralph Frame is more afraid of my malamutes than he is of me. That's why he chose to…"

He broke off and headed toward the bedroom corridor.

"That's why he and probably Andy Murdoch chose to attack you when you were checking trap lines. They know you don't take Doc or any of the dogs with you then."

"Did I say that? You're jumping to conclusions, counselor."

Chapter Six

"Climb aboard." Dressed for the trail, his breath forming fog in the frosty air, Travis MacDonald waited for her at the bottom of the Lodge steps, his dogs harnessed and ready. The sun, sending slender golden shafts through silent, glistening trees, promised a clear day.

Muffled in her snowmobile suit and boots, Michaela Dunn came down from the verandah to settle into the sled.

"Ready?" he asked.

"Ready."

"Hike, hike! Go, Doc!"

With a lurch that threw back her head, they were off at a gallop. Travis let the dogs run, blowing off excess energy before he brought them to the more sedate pace they'd assume for the drive to Carleton.

Gliding through a winter landscape of Christmas card beauty, he felt his entire being come alive. The serenity of the surroundings embraced him. He delighted in every freewheeling moment of his existence in its embrace, its invisible power to heal.

When he'd first arrived in the Promise Wilderness the process had been slow, but gradually he'd begun to feel better. The stress and misery he'd left behind in the city had drained away, like the contents of a spiritual abscess, the relief from its swelling palpable with each passing week.

Now she'd come along, reeking of fancy perfume, yet she fitted into this wild country as perfectly as her hips filled out the eye-magnet denim of her jeans.

He gave himself a mental shake. *Burned once, shame on you; burned twice shame on me.* His mother's words of advice echoed across his mind. She was a smart lady, his mother.

"Travis, look!" Pointing ahead, Michaela broke into his thoughts.

"Whoa," he called softly to his team and looked.

On the edge of a clearing they'd entered stood a pair of deer. Michaela's mittened hand covered his on the sled rail.

His heart lurched. *Hell and damnation! The woman is casting some kind of stupid spell over me!*

He jerked free and yelled to his team. "Hike!"

They broke into a trot. The deer whirled. White tails raised, the pair leaped gracefully into the trees.

"Why did you do that?" She swiveled to look up him, her cheeks pink from the cold, emerald eyes indignantly bright.

"It's still a long way to Carleton. It's only a couple of deer."

"Really, Travis!" Annoyance and exasperation tainted her response.

Good. Fed up with me again. His response had gotten the desired reaction.

****

"It isn't necessary for you to stay with me," Michaela muttered out of the side of her mouth. They sat in Colin Best's outer office in the century-old courthouse an hour later. "But since, according to you, you decided before we left the Lodge to companion me all the way, you might at least have shaved."

She glanced around the glass-and-chrome office, its sleekness proclaiming expensive renovational superiority over the rest of the dingy old building. Travis followed her visual appraisal. Even the Crown Attorney's prim, efficient-looking, forty-something secretary exuded polish and sophistication. She cast a disapproving glance over at the pair before rolling her hazel eyes skyward.

"I told you," he hissed back. "I'm the brawn, you're the brains. The tougher I look the better. We don't want Ralph Frame or his brother-in-law to think they can bully us on either level. Talking of appearances, where's your lawyering getup? I thought you'd bring a bag stuffed with a tailor-made suit and six-inch stilettos. Those cords and that turtleneck make you look more like…"

"Like a wilderness lodge keeper? At the moment, that's exactly what I am. We don't know there'll be any need for serious legal maneuvering…yet."

"Yeah, right," he guffawed.

The intercom on the secretary's desk buzzed. The woman picked up the receiver and turned her back to the pair to speak into it beneath their hearing.

"Wonder what nice things she's telling him about us?" Travis slouched in his chair. "Wish I had a cigar or a wad of gum that would make her order me to 'take that out of your mouth!' Too bad the bruises on my face are nearly gone."

"Quiet! She'll hear you." Michaela jabbed her elbow into his ribs.

"Ugh!"

"Sorry. Forgot about your ribs."

"Mr. Best will see you now." The woman didn't bother to rise, merely pointed to the closed door behind her.

"The respect level is pretty near rock bottom in here, wouldn't you say?" Travis muttered as they passed her desk. Michaela's booted heel found his toe.

Together they entered the ultra-modern office with so much sunlight flowing in through its floor-to-ceiling windows that it caused them both to blink.

Silhouetted against the glare, the Crown Attorney got up from his desk and came forward to greet them.

"Miss Dunn, this is an honor. I'm familiar with some of the more celebrated cases in which your family's firm has been involved. Come in, come in." His words hiccuped slightly over the last sentence as he looked up at Travis.

Colin Best, of medium height, blond, a poster boy for the art of male grooming, extended a manicured hand and flashed a toothpaste-ad smile. He was dressed casually in tan pants and a rust-colored sweater with the collar of a pale yellow shirt showing at its neckline.

"Excuse the outfit," he said. "I allow myself the luxury of dressing down when I'm not expected in court."

"Mr. Best." Michaela accepted his welcome and offered a smile Travis noticed didn't extend to her eyes. They remained emerald cold. "Thank you for agreeing to see us without an appointment. This is my...neighbor, Travis MacDonald."

"Ah, our famous hermit, Promise Lake's mystery man." He extended his hand again. "Good to meet you at last."

Travis's mouth curled at one corner. A reply didn't have time to reach his tongue before Michaela's boot once again found his toe.

"May I get you something...tea, coffee?" The Crown Attorney indicated a bar across the room. "Possibly something a little stronger?"

"Thank you, no." Michaela sat in one of the two chairs he indicated in front of his desk. She crossed her legs and sat up pertly. *A woman using her feminine appeal for all it's worth.* It was working...at least on one too-long-celibate trapper. Even in cords and a turtleneck Michaela Dunn was one sexy woman. Willing himself not to think about it, he took up a bodyguard stance behind her, arms crossed on his chest.

"We're anxious to get the closure on my Lodge removed," she was saying. "I have to re-open today."

"Of course. However, I'm sure you're aware this is a serious charge, considering your location and the recent RCMP initiative of zero tolerance of alcohol on snowmobile trails. It's my duty to support the officers wholeheartedly."

"I appreciate that fact, Mr. Best." Michaela's words were controlled and professional.

Travis couldn't help admiring her from his place behind her chair.

Quite a lady.

"However," she continued taking a sheaf of receipts from her briefcase. "As you can see from these receipts, there's no record of liquor being sold at the Lodge that night…or ever."

"All well and good, Ms. Dunn." He leaned back in his chair and steepled his fingers. "But on this occasion, according to Andrew Murdoch, you included a bottle of whiskey with the room. This, in essence, means you sold it to him."

Major problem. Travis crossed his fingers inside his folded arms. *Come on, Michaela. Pull out a rabbit.*

"I did not include liquor with the room." *Man, she's one cool cookie under fire.* "Mr. Murdoch must have brought it in with his luggage. Ask his wife. She'll tell you I didn't sell them whiskey or anything else of an alcoholic nature."

"The officers already have. She's not certain where he got the bottle. She didn't see it in their luggage. When she came out of the bathroom he was pouring them each a drink. He said he'd found it on the nightstand."

Travis saw Michaela's shoulders heave as she drew a deep breath. *Had she expected the wife to support her? Well, that idea had just taken a hike.*

"I didn't sell it to him. I'll swear to it. And I didn't place it in his room. Furthermore, those liquor bottles the officers said they found along the trail were between the Lodge and Carleton. That excludes the possibility that they were purchased at my inn."

"Come on, Miss Dunn, think. People leaving your establishment could have thrown them away as well."

"If they did, they didn't get them at Promise Lodge."

"My brother-in-law believes differently. From gossip on the trail..."

"I assume he can produce someone aside from his best friend who will swear to having purchased liquor from me?"

"Certainly not. People won't admit they've been drinking and driving a snowmobile."

"I thought as much." Her tone tinged with sarcasm.

Easy, Michaela, easy. Don't lose your cool now. Travis wet his lips.

"Ralph said you'd be belligerent. He said you and he had had a relationship in high school. He said you'd been very much the woman scorned when he'd refused your overtures. He also said you'd tried to interest him again and..."

"What? The man must be insane. I'm engaged to a Toronto lawyer named Randall Kirby."

Travis felt as if a fist, a very large fist, a fist much larger than Ralph Frame's, had suddenly been rammed into his gut. *Engaged! Hell and double hell!*

"Engaged? Well, that does tend to cast a bit of a shadow over the situation." Colin Best struggled out of his surprise and adjusted his bottom on his chair. "However, that's not the reason for our meeting."

"No, it definitely isn't," Michaela resumed her cool. "I need to get the Lodge re-opened immediately.

Premier Shane Gray and his entourage are due shortly. I'm sure this province's top elected official wouldn't welcome the news that his much-needed winter vacation plans have to be altered. He is, as you know, an ardent snowmobiler."

"The Premier is coming to the Lodge?" Colin Best sat bolt upright, his eyes widening, manicured hands clutching the edge of his desk. "I had no idea. Are there any social events planned, get-togethers, parties?"

"Not that I'm aware. To the best of my knowledge, the Premier simply wants to rest and enjoy the outdoors. But..." She continued slowly. Behind her back Travis could imagine green eyes narrowing, lips tightening in a cold, calculating smile. "I might be able to arrange a chance encounter... That is, if I'm permitted to re-open in time. Perhaps a serendipitous after-dinner drop-in?"

"That would be wonderful, wonderful!" Colin Best was on his feet, rounding his desk, rubbing his hands together. "I could put forward some of my plans for next year's election...subtly, of course. You may have heard I've been proposed to be his party's representative for this district in the next election. If Mr. Gray sanctioned the nomination, I'd be a shoo-in."

"Of course, your meeting with him won't be possible unless you lift the ban on my lodge." Michaela lowered her head. *Brilliant strategy. Studying her hands in pretended indifference while she waits for his reply. One terrific little actress. Yeah, terrific actress...never once giving out a hint she's engaged.*

"Yes, well, I think I can deal with that little problem." He stood and stepped around the desk to stand beaming down on Michaela. "I'll have Mildred type up a document dismissing the case against you. Ralph's testimony wouldn't have been sufficient evidence to take the matter to court. You can re-open immediately. Lots of preparations to make for the great man's visit, right?"

"Right." Michaela arose. "Thank you, Mr. Best. I'm glad we were able to come to an understanding." Travis noted her emphasis on the last word. *Subtle but definite.*

"Oh, no, *thank you*, Miss Dunn." He followed them to the door with such alacrity that Travis imagined him dancing like Doc when the dog wanted a treat. "You will let me know when to 'serendipitously' arrive at Promise Lodge, won't you?"

"Of course." She paused and spoke again without looking back. "You'll inform your brother-in-law of your decision?"

"Of course."

"You can also," she rounded on him with such suddenness that it startled even Travis, "instruct him to stay away from Promise Lodge. Furthermore, he's to stop harassing Mr. MacDonald."

Leaving the Crown Attorney gaping, she pulled open the door and strode out. Travis paused for a moment. *What a woman!* He nodded curtly to the man before he followed Michaela from the room.

****

"So you're engaged." He walked beside her, his strides lengthening to keep up with her rapid pace as they headed up Carleton's main street.

"Yes, well, sort of. What's it to you?" Her response snapped at him.

Bad timing. Back off, man.

"Nothing, nothing at all. Anyhow, you were brilliant in there."

"Thank you." Her tone relented. "I admit I had some shaky moments. If that pompous ass didn't want to get into politics so badly, I would have been up a very long creek without even a breadstick for a paddle. I hated to make a deal with that man."

"Okay, your strategy worked. Now can we slow down? People are staring."

"Maybe it's not the speed. Maybe it's because I'm with the mysterious hermit of Promise Lake." She glanced up at him, and he saw her annoyance recede. A glint of humor coming into her eyes, she slowed her steps. "Thanks for backing me up in there."

"I couldn't do much. Someone kept stepping on my toe."

"Your support nevertheless is appreciated. Let me treat you to lunch. Do you prefer MacDonald's or the hotel restaurant?"

"The former, hands down. I can't imagine marching into a hotel restaurant dressed like I am and with fading bruises and my reputation."

****

With the sun of the short winter day sliding toward the mountaintops, they drove back to the Lodge. The dogs, tails curled over their backs, trotted easily along the snowmobile trail. Pulling the man, woman, and sled appeared to take only the slightest effort. A clear late afternoon sky promising a moon-lighted, frost-crackling night normally filled Travis with a pleasant feeling of contentment. This time it didn't.

Michaela was engaged to some guy in Toronto; no doubt some jerk who dressed like a model for GQ and smelled ever so faintly but ever so sexily of some kind of men's scent with a triple-digit price tag. As if something as simple as a scent could rule passions and emotions!

He caught himself up short. *Damn right it could. Her perfume turns me off like a faucet. So maybe there is something to that male body spray crap. Maybe I should...*

"Travis?" She looked up at him, green eyes wide

and bright, cheeks glowing pink from the cold.

"Yeah?" The word came out harder than he'd intended.

"Want to stay for supper at the Lodge? I took one of Aunt Ida's famous lasagnas out to thaw before we left, and some homemade rolls. I can whip up a salad as a side. There's also a couple of pieces of cheesecake in the fridge."

"Better get back to the cabin," he replied gruffly, even though her description of the meal made his mouth water. All that waited for him at his place was a tin of chunky soup and a dead-cold hearth. "I have to check the trap lines tonight."

"Of course." A deep freeze fell over her tone. "I *almost* forgot you're a trapper. It won't happen again." She swung back to face forward, neck and shoulders stiff.

"I am what I am." He retaliated with equal coldness. "Hike, hike!" He jumped off the sled to run behind it. "Hike, hike!"

The dogs, eager to get home, yelped and leaped into their harness.

Chapter Seven

"Listen, I'm telling you." Travis MacDonald gave the malamute his severest look. "Don't shoplift again. You could end up in an SPCA kennel a long way from the freewheeling lifestyle you're enjoying now."

Tongue lolling out of one side of his mouth, Doc looked up at the man.

"Come on, take me seriously. I don't want any more trouble with the law."

The dog jumped to his feet and leaped up to place his paws on Travis's chest. "Grinning, are you?" He relented and rubbed the dog's ears affectionately. "Okay, so maybe I am getting a bit paranoid. Now hop down. You're way too heavy on a chest recovering from Ralph Frame and company."

The dog resumed his place on the rug. Travis looked out a window. In the thickening twilight, wind howled around the corners of his cabin. Rubbing his ribs, he flinched. He still hurt. He wondered if *she'd* care if she'd known the true extent of his pain during the first couple of days after the incident. She'd probably have insisted on his staying at the Lodge. Even now he might be sitting in front of her hearth, his belly stuffed with lasagna and cheesecake, feeling secure in her safety.

Damn! And he'd thought all he wanted was to be rid of her...her with her chestnut curls and big green eyes and body that wouldn't quit. He fought to edit his thoughts. Her that stank of perfume, her that was a Toronto attorney, her that was engaged to another man.

But what about those two kisses? Maybe they had been a knee-jerk reaction, but they were definitely something that had been on his mind from the moment she'd peeled herself out of the snowmobile suit in his cabin on the night of the blizzard. That and a whole lot more. All it had taken was a couple of opportunities when she didn't reek of that three-hundred-dollars-an-ounce memory to knock down all his defenses.

Come on, man! She's got animal-rights activist written all over her. You can't go ruining your reputation by getting involved with her.

He'd watched her expression when she saw his hat and mukluks. He remembered her horrified expression when she'd encountered his bearskin rug.

Repulsed, turned off to the core. Well, good. All that was good. Perfect, in fact. Just what should have happened. He felt the flesh around his eye and flinched.

Doc, lying by the fire, looked up at him, and whined.

"Yeah, yeah, I get it. If you'd have been with me it wouldn't have happened. And don't try and tell me I should be grateful to you and Michaela Dunn for finding me before I froze. I know all about her kind, Doc, and, believe me, you don't want to get involved with any of them." A blast of snow hit the windows, rattling the panes.

"Going to be a wild one," he muttered. In spite of his recent declaration, his thoughts went back to Michaela. She wouldn't be able to reinstate reservations until the following morning. The possibility of drop-in guests was unlikely. She'd be alone in that big old Lodge. Was Ralph Frame at his chalet across the lake plotting God only knew what?

He paced the floor, rubbing his hands on the back of his jeans. His ribs hurt when he made any quick moves, but he was feeling a lot better. The day's exercise and fresh air had revived him. He made a decision.

"We're heading out, Doc." He reached for his outdoor gear hanging on a peg by the door.

****

"It's Travis MacDonald." Doc by his side, he stood on the Lodge porch and pounded on the door.

"Travis?" She opened the door to peer out into the driving snow.

Hair damp and tousled, wrapped in a pink chenille robe that looked as soft and inviting as the curve of her neck and hint of cleavage at its top, she must have been fresh out of the shower. Smelling incredible, she assaulted his senses in a full, hard, frontal attack.

Sweet Jesus, where is that miserable perfume when I need it!

"What are you doing out on a night like this? And in your condition? Come in. Doc, you, too."

She stepped aside to allow him and the dog to enter. As she shut the door, he pulled off his snow-crusted hat and mittens and brushed frozen precipitation from his bearded face.

"Just passing." The words sounded stupid even as he said them, but he hadn't planned anything better.

"Really?" She stood back from him, hands on her hips, green eyes narrowing. "Strange night to be out for a drive."

"Yeah, well, the dogs were putting up a fuss." Turning his hat in his hands, he shuffled his boots. "They like a challenge. Their kind of weather."

"Okay." Her mouth quirked up at one corner. "Put the other six in the barn and come in by the fire. I was just making a hot drink. Join me?"

"All right." He jerked his head in agreement. "Doc, you stay here."

****

"Man, what's in this?" Travis lurched back from the cup. Cold to the bone, he'd taken a gulp from the steaming mug she handed him.

"Brandy, et cetera. Uncle Norm's personal recipe for the ultimate chill-chasing hot toddy." Her eyes twinkling wickedly, she looked at him over the rim of her cup. "You're supposed to drink it slowly. What did you think it was…hot chocolate?"

"I wasn't expecting something with the kick of a Missouri mule."

"Not much of a drinking man, I take it."

"Beer's my usual. Not into the hard stuff. But…" He took a sip, this time cautiously. "This is good…if you take it easy."

"Okay, now that we've got that behind us, how about the truth of this visit." She leaned back and gave him a penetrating stare. "You weren't really taking the dogs for a fun run, were you?"

"No." He drew a deep breath, winced as it hurt his ribs. "I wanted to make sure you were okay. You helped me out. I don't like to be beholden to anyone."

The last sentence came out hard and harsh.

"Sorry to hear that. In this country, neighbors often help neighbors." She cast him a sly, sideways glance as she paraphrased his words to her.

"Okay, fine."

"Now I'm heading off to bed." She stood and looked down at him, her drink cradled in her hands. "You and Doc can take room number one."

She turned and headed down the corridor.

Man, this stuff is strong. After a near abstinence over the past few months, it was hitting him hard. He could feel it to the tips of his toes. Staying the night definitely wasn't the thing to do. The wind had lessened. He'd have no trouble making it back to his place.

He crossed the room and pulled on his parka. Twenty minutes later he had his dogs harnessed to the sled.

Across the lake, through the trees, halfway up the mountain, he saw the lights of Ralph Frame's chalet. With brandy warming his mind and body, he made a decision. He'd pay the guy a quick visit. Advise him it wasn't a good idea for him to hassle Michaela Dunn.

"Hike, hike!"

Above him the Northern Lights danced crazily.

Watching them, he remembered the stories he'd heard from his great-uncle about these winter phenomena. According to the old man, Pierre Gassendi, a French scientist, had named the occurrence Aurora, for the Roman god of the north wind. Caused by high-speed particles from the sun striking the ocean of gasses above the earth, resultant shimmering lights gyrated across the night sky.

He remembered the legends his mother's uncle had told as he gazed at the wreathing shafts of multicolored lights leaping high into the dark sky, then doubling back on themselves only to shoot upwards once again.

In the Far North, Uncle George had said, people claimed they'd heard the Northern Lights speak in the whistling voices of migratory birds. Auroras, they claimed, were sent to buoy up people's spirits during the long, dark days of winter. Other cultures offered more sinister explanations, believing the lights to be the souls of the dead who died from violence, with the red aurora representing their blood.

This final tale sent a chill racing through his veins. The Northern Lights had turned crimson.

Chapter Eight

Michaela gazed out the lounge windows and watched the Northern Lights practise their exotic moves high above Promise Wilderness. She'd heard the door close and gotten up to find Travis gone. Feeling restless and uneasy, she made a cup of hot chocolate and curled up in a chair in front of the garden doors of the lounge area, fascinated by Nature's display of silent fireworks. Sometimes green, sometimes multicolored, they shot up into the night sky before bending back on themselves like lightning contortionists. Their glow cast an eerie illumination over the winter landscape of lake and mountain.

She shivered and drew her terry robe more tightly to her throat. Legends of the mystical powers of these winter specters sent a mental chill coursing through her. The hot chocolate in her hand cried out for a splash of brandy.

She was about to head for her uncle's apartment when she saw something moving out on the lake. Dogs. Travis and his dogs. In the ghostly glow, like phantoms of the wilderness, they were crossing the frozen expanse.

Oh, God, no! They couldn't be headed for Ralph Frame's chalet!

Had Travis found something wrong in his trap lines again and was heading up to confront his enemy? No, no, no. He was too sensible to do anything that crazy. He'd probably decided to take a look at her snowmobile and see how much work it would be to pull it back to the lodge.

That theory didn't make sense. He should be resting his dogs in anticipation of pulling her snowmobile across the lake in the morning. Furthermore, how could he hope to do a decent examination with only the Northern Lights to illuminate the machine?

Pouring a splash of Norman Dunn's best brandy into her mug, she hoped Travis MacDonald wasn't about to do anything foolish...not where a reptile like Ralph Frame was concerned.

When she glanced out the window again, she flinched. The greens of the wreathing lights had turned red. She remembered the legends about this change and sudden death.

The man and his dogs vanished into the trees on the far side of the lake.

Oh, God, Travis, why did you have to pick tonight to cross the lake toward Ralph Frame's cabin!

****

Michaela awoke with a start to what sounded like a veritable army of snowmobiles roaring past the Lodge. She glanced at her bedside clock. 8:00 a.m. She'd overslept, no doubt thanks to the brandy. She scrambled to her feet and padded into the lounge in time to see a string of snowmobiles heading across Promise Lake at high speed.

What could Ralph Frame possibly be up to that would warrant such an influx this early in the morning? A thin stream of smoke rose from the trees at the location of his chalet. A breakfast poker game?

With a shrug, she turned away from the window and headed for the shower. She didn't care what Ralph Frame was up to, just so long as he left her and the Lodge alone.

Her thoughts turned to more immediate concerns. If Travis didn't return soon, she'd have to snowshoe across the lake and up the mountain to reinstate the reservations she'd cancelled, if she wanted business to resume. She hoped she didn't get caught up in the group that had just crossed the lake. She didn't want anything to slow her down today.

Reflecting on Travis' midnight jaunt across the lake, she wondered what he'd been thinking. Maybe she shouldn't have fueled him with that powerful toddy. Hopefully he'd arrive soon and explain it to her. Even if his purpose in crossing the lake last night had been to try to get her snowmobile going and he'd failed, he and his team could take her up the mountain to the cell phone reception point a lot faster than she could snowshoe. She wished he'd waited for morning to make the attempt.

The memory of those crimson northern lights sent a shiver of apprehension over her in spite of the warm, gushing water.

****

She was finishing her breakfast when she heard his "whoa" from the dooryard. A moment later, he strode into the restaurant, Doc by his side. She was again struck by how much a part of the wilderness he and the malamutes appeared to be. She felt a tingle of excitement start in her solar plexus and slide sensuously up over her body.

"Got any of that grub left?" He gestured to her plate. "I could do with a meal before I head across the lake to fix your machine."

"Sit." Pushing back her chair, she stood. "I'll whip you up an omelet." Struggling to contain her inner heat, she headed for the stove.

"Sounds good."

"Travis, where were you going last night when I saw you crossing the lake?"

"Just took the dogs out for a run." He removed his jacket.

"Really? I find it difficult to believe they needed

89

exercise after the trip to Carleton yesterday and then down here from your cabin."

"Are you expecting guests?" The sound of approaching machines saved him a reply.

"Not today." She crossed the room and rubbed frost from the window. "Oh, no, it's Corporal Palmer and Constable Roy! What has Ralph accused me of now?"

"Good morning, Ms. Dunn." The officers entered, pulling off their headgear.

"Good morning, officers. What can I do for you?"

"Actually it's not you we've come to see." Corporal Palmer looked at Travis. "It's your friend."

"Me?" Travis turned to face the officers.

"Yes, sir. Angus Jones, justice of the peace, has issued a warrant for your arrest in connection with the burning of the chalet across the lake and the murder of Ralph Frame."

"Murder!" Mikey caught the edge of the counter. A tsunami of nausea washed over her. "When?"

"Some time during the night. The smoldering remains of the chalet across the lake and a body we have reason to believe is that of the owner, Ralph Frame, were discovered early this morning. There was a bullet hole in its chest."

"Dear God!" Michaela slumped into a chair.

"I'm sorry, Ms. Dunn. I understand the deceased was a friend of yours." Corporal Palmer spoke as Constable Roy blocked the door, feet astride.

"An acquaintance. You couldn't expect me to rank him as a friend after he had my Lodge shut down."

"No, I suppose not." He turned back to Travis. "You're to come with us now, Mr. MacDonald."

Constable Roy made a move to cuff Travis's hands. He wasn't quick enough. With a roar Doc leaped and caught the officer by his sleeve.

"Doc, no!" Travis swung toward the startled

officer. "Off!"

Muttering, the dog released the constable's arm and backed away.

"Down!" Travis ordered. With a growl, the malamute slowly stretched out on the floor, never taking his predator gaze from the Mountie's blanched countenance.

Michaela held her breath. One wrong move and Doc would spring into action again.

Crouching beside the dog, she grasped his collar. She doubted she could stop him if he seriously decided to free himself, but she would at least be in a position to give it her best effort.

"Cuff him, Constable." Corporal Palmer ordered his pale-faced junior officer. "MacDonald has the animal under control. He won't risk its attacking a law enforcement officer and facing a put-down order."

"This is crazy!" Travis was incredulous.

"You can't be serious! Angus Jones issued the warrant?" Michaela jumped to her feet, the dog rising with her hand on his collar. "I remember him. He was elderly when I was a teenager. He must be eighty or older now. On what evidence did he issue a warrant?"

"On evidence photographed by the person who first arrived at the crime scene this morning...pawprints everywhere, fresh pawprints, since that light snowfall late yesterday afternoon. Mr. MacDonald is the only musher within a hundred miles. Furthermore, it's a well known fact that Ralph Frame and Mr. MacDonald were rivals for prime trapping areas. We've been informed that Mr. Frame and Mr. MacDonald had several altercations recently, both verbal and physical. A witness declares he overheard him threaten to kill Mr. Frame as a result. "

"Andy Murdoch!" The name hissed from

Michaela's lips, steam from her boiling outrage.

"We're not at liberty to name names at this point, Ms. Dunn. We have to get Mr. MacDonald back to the detachment for questioning."

"I can't believe you're resting the entire case on the hearsay of one prejudiced witness!"

"There's more." The officer drew a deep breath before continuing. "A cursory examination of the crime scene has revealed that the victim was, as I've said, shot. The bullet passed through his body. A forensic team from the city is sifting through the ashes at this moment. We know Mr. MacDonald owns a deer rifle. On a search of his cabin earlier this morning, we discovered it had been fired recently."

"You searched my home?" Travis spat out the words.

"With a completely legal warrant." Corporal Palmer was quick to defend the action.

"I assume you've confiscated the rifle?" Michaela felt a cold chill around her heart.

"Miss Dunn, I'm not at liberty to discuss the case with you. Come along, Mr. MacDonald."

"Take care of my dogs." Travis put on his jacket and hat and held out his wrists for the handcuffs.

"You know I will. Hang in there. I'll have you out of this mess in no time."

"Yeah, right." Sarcasm tainted the two words as Constable Roy clamped him into handcuffs.

Travis allowed the officer to urge him out the door. Clinging to a rearing Doc, Michaela followed. As they put their prisoner onto the back of one of their machines, Doc lunged, roaring with every ounce of wolf blood he'd inherited from his ancestors. Michaela stumbled and fell to her knees but managed to retain her grip on his collar.

"Doc, no!"

"Doc, stay." Travis turned to the dog. "Listen to

Michaela."

With a whine, the dog reluctantly settled to stand tense, glowering at the Mounties from Michaela's side as their machines roared out of the dooryard.

Michaela was left alone with a team of huskies and a pounding heart.

I have to talk to Dad. The epiphany hit her like a snowball in the face. *Much as I hate to admit it, I need his help.*

Chapter Nine

Michaela roused the huskies from their snuggled positions in the snowdrift near the door and led Doc to the head of the line. She had to get up the mountain to make cell phone contact with her father. The dogs were the fastest and most efficient means. Snowshoeing could take all day, and she didn't have the time to waste.

"Help me, Doc." She picked up the harness to put him in place at front. "What goes where?"

The malamute whined and backed into position. Swinging his head, he seemed to point to the dog who would be pulling directly behind him.

"Okay, I get it. Look at how he's harnessed. Got it. Just hold still."

Shortly she had Doc strapped in place. *Three weeks ago, standing in my parents' offices in TO, I could never in my wildest dreams have seen myself in this position.*

"Doc, you're in charge. I'll have to trust you. Be a good boy."

She got to her feet, turned the team toward the frozen lake, walked to the back of the sled, and climbed on the runners. Gripping its rails like grim death, she drew a deep breath and yelled, "Hike, hike!" in the best imitation of Travis she could manage.

Her head jolted back as the team took off at a gallop down the broken trail. For a few moments she thought she'd be thrown, but shortly she got into the rhythm of the ride. *Wow! What a rush! No problem to see why Travis loves it.* "Hike, hike!"

The dogs put on a burst of speed. A wind had arisen, gusting snow across the barren lake surface, limiting her vision and hearing. They'd reached the far side and were rounding a bend in the trail when she saw the snowmobile coming toward them.

"Haw, haw!" she yelled.

She could have remained silent. Doc had realized the danger and drawn her and his team well to the left, out of harm's way, before her cry.

"Whoa!"

Again a needless command. Doc brought his followers to a safe stop clear of the trail. The snowmobile skidded to a halt several feet away.

"Karen?" she said as the rider dismounted and pulled off a helmet.

"Mikey, what on earth are you doing? Where's Travis? "

Michaela quickly recapped the morning's events.

"Are they crazy?" Karen Dollard stared at her friend when she'd finished explaining. "Travis MacDonald is no killer!"

"That's a matter of perspective. He does kill animals, but I suspect murder is out of his league. Anyway, given Ralph's character, I'm sure there's more than one person who might like to see him dead."

"So you're headed up the mountain to call your dad and get his advice?" Karen looked over her shoulder. "Maybe not a good idea to take these dogs so near the crime scene. There are forensic guys all over the place. They might think it's a good idea to get a few hairs from these dogs to prove they were near Ralph's cabin."

"You're right. But I do have to phone Dad."

"There's good reception at Travis's cabin. It's at just enough of an elevation to make it possible. I'd advise you to go there instead."

"Thanks, Karen. I will. "

She turned the team awkwardly with "Gees" and "Haws" and caught the ranger suppressing a grin.

"What?" she asked, once she had them facing down the mountain.

"A musher you ain't...yet."

"What do you mean 'yet'?"

"Somehow I have a feeling you and Travis MacDonald are heading into a relationship. If you are, he'll make a musher of you. He loves those dogs."

"Relationship with a trapper? Come on, Karen. You know my feelings about those brutes."

"Okay, okay. But when you get to his cabin, take a close look at those pelts hanging on the outside wall. Check his outbuildings for traps. Maybe then you'll understand why he has a deer rifle. Now I have to be back on patrol. Good luck with getting Travis sprung."

She climbed onto her snowmobile and, with a wave, headed off up the trail.

"Hike, hike!" Michaela made a jump for the runners as the dogs started off at a gallop, missed, stumbled, and staggered after sled and dogs. She managed to scramble aboard as they reached the lake.

Make a musher out of me, right! If I survive this run, I'll consider it the pinnacle of my dog-sledding career.

By the time they'd reached Travis's cabin, the dogs had slowed to a trot. Nevertheless, they failed to stop when Michaela yelled "whoa!" but continued on until they reached the barn that was their kennel.

"Tired and hungry, thank God!" she breathed as she got off the runners and went to unharness Doc. Before long six dogs lay stretched out in the straw in the barn. She'd let them rest before feeding. With

Doc beside her, she went up to the cabin.

She paused on the veranda and stared at the pelts, her innards roiling. "Examine them," Karen had said. Her long-time friend was above pulling any cruel trick. Gingerly she reached out and turned one over in her hand. A fleck of white caught her eye. She took it between shaky fingers and read "Made in China."

"Fake!" The word burst like air from a pricked balloon. She turned them over one by one. All fake.

But why? Why would Travis MacDonald go to all this bother and expense to make people believe he was a trapper? Was it simply to give him a supposed source of income that would keep people from knowing how he really made a living? And if so, why? Was he the fugitive some locals had branded him? Was he living off the proceeds of crime? Was that why he chose to hide his features beneath a growth of hair and beard?

Was that why he could afford the luxuries in his cabin? If she defended him and a criminal past emerged, where would it leave her and her flagging career in Toronto?

Doc whined. She looked down at the golden-red malamute staring up at her.

"I have to make a decision, Doc," she said placing her hand on his head. "I have to decide if I trust your master."

Doc butted her hand, then threw back his head and howled his haunting wilderness cry.

"Okay, okay, I'll give it a go. My legal career is pretty much in the dumpster anyway."

She opened the door and went inside. The place was neat, clean, cold, and silent. The sky had clouded over, casting the rooms into a shadowy ambience. She shivered.

"We'll start a fire, then I'll go back to the barn and feed your buddies," she told the dog.

A half hour later, with the dogs fed and watered, she wandered into his bedroom. Neat and tidy. Bed made...she opened the closet door...clothes hung up. She turned to the dresser, hesitated, then opened the top drawer. Good God! Silk underwear! Who was this guy! She had to know more before she attempted to defend him, before she was sure she could defend him. Feeling as if she was violating his privacy in the extreme, she slide her hand under the folded garments.

Ah-ha! The Italian leather wallet he'd pulled out at the Lodge when he'd offered to pay for a meal. She opened it gingerly. Inside was money, several hundred dollars at least, and a driver's license and birth certificate. The latter two had been issued to Travis MacDonald. They gave his place of birth as Yellowknife, Northwest Territories.

So he was who he said was, at least in name. And that was it. No credit cards, no photos, nothing. Searching the remainder of the cabin revealed no further information. She'd have to go with what she had.

She picked up her cell and dialed her father's office.

"Michael Dunn's office." Janet Harris, her father's efficient secretary, answered.

"Janet, it's Michaela. May I speak to my father?"

"Michaela, child! Are you all right? I was terrified you'd be eaten by a bear down in the wilds of New Brunswick!"

"I'm fine, Janet. Don't worry about bears. They're all in hibernation. Will you put me through to my father?"

A pause. "He's been in court all morning, sweetie. I'm not sure..."

"That he'll welcome the diversion of a call from his prodigal daughter? Trust me, Janet. I'll deal with the man."

"I guess it will be all right. He did win his case. And Michaela?"

"Yes?"

"Do take care. I'm sure that, even if the bears are all asleep, there must be other terrible creatures in the forest...wolves and lord only knows what else."

"I'll be careful, Janet. Thanks for your concern."

The phone beeped.

"Michael Dunn here."

"Dad, it's Michaela."

"Ah, come to your senses, have you? Well, you're too late. I've completed the case for that man you damned as guilty. Got all charges dismissed. The press had a field day. I'm only sorry my daughter wasn't at my side to share in the glory."

"I suppose I should congratulate you—"

"But you're still convinced he did the deed? Good God, Michaela, do you still believe you've got some kind of sixth sense that allows you to know who's naughty and who's nice?"

"I've met this man." She ignored his sarcasm. It definitely wasn't the time to get into an argument with him. "We've become...friends. He's been arrested for a murder I'm confident he didn't commit. I want your insight on how I can go about getting him cleared of the charge."

Silence. Michaela held her breath.

After a seeming eternity, he spoke. "I hope you haven't become involved with this fellow. Do you realize what the media would do with a thing like that? Do you know what it could do to the firm's reputation? God knows what Randall would do if he thought you'd gotten mixed up with a murder suspect."

"No personal involvement. He claims to be a trapper. That should give you a picture of our relationship."

"Well, then, why in heaven's name are you proposing to help him? Ever since your uncle allowed you to witness that bear caught in a leg-hold trap..."

"Okay, okay, Dad." Michaela felt her insides beginning to swirl unpleasantly at the image his words conjured. "Uncle Norm didn't *allow* me to witness anything. We came upon it by accident. My decision to defend Travis MacDonald has nothing to do with what he is or was. It's simply because I believe he's innocent." She paused. "And he saved my life."

"Saved your life? Good God, Michaela, what trouble have you gotten yourself into now?"

"I got turned around in a blizzard near the Lodge. Travis found me and took me to his cabin for the night. If he hadn't, I would probably have frozen to death."

"Michaela, how...?"

"Dad, I'll tell you all about it some day when I have time. At the moment, that's all you need to know."

"Give me a minute. Let me think."

Silence. Michaela imagined she could see the wheels of her father's astute legal brain revving. Then he cleared his throat.

Here it comes.

"I'll throw all the resources of this firm behind you, provided you make certain the media is aware of its part in the proceedings once you get him acquitted. Afterwards, you're to get yourself back here and resume your position in this business and as Randall's intended."

"Yes to the first condition even though you know how I hate publicity-mongering." She paused and drew in a deep breath. "As to the second, I'll think about it."

"Sorry. Not good enough. Call me when you're ready to be reasonable."

"No, wait! Don't hang up!" She paused to pull in a deep breath. "Okay I agree." The last sentence was a sigh of resignation.

"That's better." The smug note of satisfaction in his voice made her fingers clench the phone like grim death. "Now give me the details."

Damn! Did he always have to win?

When she'd finished, she heard him draw a deep breath. Good. He was about to give it his best shot.

"Okay, here's how we're going to play it." She heard a rustling that sounded like papers, and she knew he was making notes. "I have an idea how the legal system works down there. Remember your mother and I started our legal careers in Carleton. First I'll get in touch with Judge Drew Anderson. He's probably gone ice fishing at this time of year. That's how Colin Best got that old fool Angus Jones to issue an arrest warrant on so little evidence. Probably handed over a little cash in the process. I'll have Drew investigate. Then I'll get in touch with some friends I have in forensics up here and see what they can find out from their colleagues in your area about that bullet. If it didn't come from MacDonald's rifle..."

"Thanks, Dad."

"No need, Daughter. Just live up to your promise."

"Bye, Dad. Say hello to Mom for me. Love you both."

She punched End and drew a deep breath. Everything her father had advised made sense. His offer to contact his friend, local judge Drew Anderson, and experts in forensics on Travis's behalf was exactly the type of assistance she'd been hoping to obtain.

Reflecting on the conditions to which she'd agreed, she grimaced. Well, what else could she have done? She owed her life to Travis MacDonald. If she managed to clear him of this murder charge, they'd be even. She could walk away from him free and clear.

But did she want to? He wasn't a trapper. Aside from that fact, what else did she have against him? He did have those amazing blue eyes and a body Chippendales would hire in a heartbeat, never mind that he came across as a man of mystery, a feral intrigue in a sexy package.

Grow up, Michaela Dunn. You're not eighteen and looking for a cheap thrill with the hermit of Promise Wilderness. Anyhow, you've just pledged your soul back to Dunn & Dunn Attorneys at Law in Toronto, never mind Randall Kirby...

She glanced toward the window. Dark. She'd have to stay the night. The Lodge would be all right. There were no scheduled guests. If anyone did come along, they'd have to make themselves at home. The auxiliary heating system had been set to kick in at the appropriate drop in temperature.

So what now? Food. Definitely food. And then sleep. Tomorrow will be a full day. With Doc at her heels, she began to explore the cabin's kitchen area.

Good lord, was this how the man lived? Cupboards full of cans, a freezer stuffed with frozen dinners... Michaela pulled out a boxed meal, brushed frost from its top, and grimaced.

Hamburg steak, mushrooms, onions, gravy. Remove plastic from potatoes before microwaving. Probably the plastic is the tastiest portion.

She removed the plate from its box and sniffed the rigid mass. *Oh, well, when in Rome.* She shoved it into the microwave, punched in the appropriate time, and stepped back, hands on hips, to wait.

Maybe he has wine. Anything to make the sludge being hummed to hot more palatable.

The idea sent her searching the cupboards. Behind a cabinet door in a far corner she discovered several bottles of an excellent vintage. More pieces of the puzzle. She selected a bottle of red, thinking it was a shame to waste such fine drink to accompany the mess she was about to call supper.

What the heck. In the morning, with luck, she'd have the man exonerated of a murder charge. The least he could do was provide her with a bottle that might make her evening bearable.

A half hour later Michaela threw the empty paper plate into the garbage can and headed into the bathroom, her third glass of wine in hand. "Time for a long, relaxing shower, Doc," she called out to the dog stretched out on the bearskin rug she'd discovered was also fake. "Guard the door."

The sound of an approaching snowmobile halted her. It stopped in front of the cabin. Michaela placed her glass on the kitchen countertop and went to the window beside the door. The rider dismounted and came up the steps. A woman. The gait and shape gave that much identification. But who? Curious she moved to answer her knock.

"Mikey!" The visitor pulled off her helmet and balaclava and shook long, blonde hair free. "Surprised as I was to see lights in Travis's cabin tonight, I never suspected I'd find you here."

"The feeling is mutual, Amanda." Michaela struggled to keep from gaping at the woman who was Ralph Frame's sister and Colin Best's wife. "My condolences on your loss." She recovered sufficiently to acknowledge the woman's bereavement. "What in the world brings you up here tonight? I'd have thought..."

"That I'd be busy playing the grieving sister?" She pushed past Michaela and flung her headgear onto the couch. "I'm hardly the type." She paused and looked around the room, a smug smile moving her lips. "And there are a few loose ends I have to tie up...like things I left here."

"Are you telling me you were involved with Travis MacDonald?" Michaela felt the words hiccup incredulously from her lips.

"Telling you loud and clear, Miss Big City." She rounded on Michaela. "Don't think you're his one and only. Ralph told me how he took on the job of being your knight in shining armor. That really annoyed me. I thought I was special to the brute. After all, how many women would bother to come all the way up here to sleep with a big hairy creature like Travis MacDonald."

"You apparently did." A sick feeling roiled in her stomach as Michaela faced the woman.

"Yes, well, he does have those terrific blue eyes and a body that just won't quit. And in bed... But then I take it you know all about the above."

"So what brings you now?" Michaela fought down the reflex to deny Amanda's words. Much more effective to leave her guessing. "You apparently know Travis has been arrested on suspicion of murdering your brother?"

" That's why I'm here. I have to gather up a few things I left behind. With the mess he's currently in, he's all yours." She strode across the room, but as she started to enter the bedroom, Doc, hackles up, blocked her way.

"Get this brute out of my way!" She turned on Michaela. "I have to get my stuff. Can't you just imagine how much more vigorously my husband would prosecute Travis if he knew about us?"

"You're not afraid I'll tell him?"

"What, and give Travis yet another motive for killing my brother? Ralph was threatening to tell my husband about our affair if I didn't get Colin to wangle acquittal for Ralph on all the charges laid against him over the years. Now get that wolf out of my way."

"Doc, come here." Michaela took the dog by the

collar, and Amanda proceeded into the bedroom.

She returned in seconds, stuffing a flimsy black nightie into a pocket of her snowsuit.

"That's it...I hope." She snatched up her headgear and headed for the door. "If anyone finds anything else that might incriminate me, be a dear and pretend it's yours."

She went out into the darkness, slamming the door behind her.

"Damn, damn, damn!" As Amanda Best's snowmobile sputtered to life and roared off down the trail, Michaela strode to the door and banged her fists on it. So Travis had been having an affair with that hard-faced piece of trash.

She gave herself a good, swift mental kick in the butt. So what. It wasn't as if there'd been anything between her and the hermit—She grimaced at the inaccuracy of the term—of Promise Wilderness. A couple of mind-blowing kisses did not a happily-ever-after make.

But they were a couple of mind-blowing kisses that made you feel like a teenager getting her first, that made you feel like you'd never really been kissed before.

With a deep sigh, she turned away from the door. None of what Amanda Best had said changed the fact that Travis MacDonald had saved her life. She'd defend him with every ounce of her skill. But that would be it. Once she'd freed him, she never wanted to see him again.

Twenty minutes later she emerged from the bathroom wrapped in a large white towel and paused, looking into the bedroom. She couldn't sleep in there, not after Amanda Best had bragged about her relationship with him.

The duvet she'd used on her previous nights at the cabin lay tossed over a chair beside the fireplace. She snatched it up. Although the couch wasn't comfortable for sleeping, it was the only alternative.

What would it be like to share that king-sized bed with him? She pulled the duvet over her shoulder and snuggled beneath its warmth. Would he prove as earthy and virile as he looked? A warm thrill washed over her. Would she ever get the opportunity to find out? She gave herself a sharp mental shake. Given what she now knew about his previous relationship with Amanda Best, how could she even think of the possibility?

****

Michaela woke early the following morning. She hadn't had a good night. For most of it, she'd lain wakeful and restless, hoping her father would be able to work his magic and come up with one of the spectacular defenses for which he was famous. She worried whether maybe his years-ago friendship with Drew Anderson had dissipated or that exonerating information wouldn't be forthcoming from his forensic contacts.

When she'd finally managed to drift off, she was tortured by dreams—or were they nightmares?—of her and Travis together, about to make love, when Amanda Best crashed into the cabin, swinging her long blonde hair and laughing. Travis had wrenched away from Michaela to take the woman into a passionate embrace.

The next instant he was pulled away by Corporal Palmer and Constable Roy, handcuffed, and dragged from the cabin while Doc, confined somewhere in the background, roared his protest.

She awoke in a cold sweat, clutching her pillow in white-knuckled fists. *Damn, damn, damn! What's wrong with me?* She fussed around, trying to get herself comfortable, but she succeeded only in tangling the duvet into a pile. Plunking herself down into the mess, she'd finally drifted off into more unpleasant fantasies about Travis, including a possible criminal past and involvement with other women.

As soon as she thought her father would be at his desk, she called, heart thudding. *Please, please...!*

"Dad?"

****

While she ate a quick breakfast of coffee (terrible blend), toast, and porridge, she concentrated on the day ahead. She probably wouldn't get to see either the judge or Travis until 10:00 a.m. She'd stop at Sam Mather's convenience store and pick up something packaged to eat that would see her through until lunch. She'd have to use his washroom to change into her "lawyering" getup.

"You can come with me once we get to town," she told Doc, who sat eyeing her toast with unblinking interest. "I know you can't wait to see Travis again."

****

Sam Mathers wasn't on duty behind the counter when Michaela and Doc entered. Instead, a stern-looking middle-aged woman eyed them both coldly.

"Good morning," Michaela smiled. "I need some groceries, but before I shop I would like to use your washroom to change clothes. As you can see"—She indicated the heavy jacket and pants she was wearing—"I've just come in off the trails. I have an appointment in Carleton that requires something a little dressier. I have it here in my packsack. It will only take a minute."

The woman looked over her granny glasses, her stare cold and appraising.

"Sam has been a friend of mine for years. My name is Michaela Dunn."

"Norm and Ida's niece, the one that's running the Lodge?" She put her hands palms down on the counter and eyed Michaela from head to toe.

"That's me." Michaela gave the woman what she

hoped was her most appealing smile and held out her hand. "And you are?"

"Mattie Hendricks." She hesitated before she took Michaela's hand in her cold, dry one.

"Margaret Hendricks' mom? I went to school with Margie."

"Yes, you did. You had a bit of a reputation back then."

Michaela felt a hot blush rising up her neck.

"Yes, well, that was a long time ago. Now, what about my using the washroom?"

"All right, I guess. What about the dog? You can't take him in there with you."

"No, he'll be fine out here. Doc, stay." Michaela hefted her backpack and headed for the washroom down a corridor at the rear. "Thanks, Mrs. Hendricks. Say hello to Margie for me."

The woman grunted.

Chapter Ten

"Where's Doc?" Michaela, dressed in a smart grey suit, white blouse, and black knee-high boots, stepped back into the retail section of the store and looked around for the dog. She'd taken time to restyle her hair into a neat pile at the back of her head. Over her arm she carried a long, camel-colored coat.

"Had him nabbed for shoplifting." The woman's eyes and words sparkled with malice. "Caught him stealing chocolate bars. The Mounties took him away."

"What!" Michaela, packsack in hand, was running toward the door. "Where did they take him?"

"To the lockup at the RCMP detachment. Said they didn't have time to go all the way to the SPCA shelter on the far end of town with a murder investigation under way."

As she jumped into Travis's SUV, Michaela wondered what had prompted the woman's vindictive actions. She shoved the key into the ignition, then froze as she remembered. Her daughter Margie had had a thing for Ralph Frame, but Ralph had been concentrating on Michaela. He'd shown absolutely no interest in the chubby, aggressive Hendricks girl. Margie had blamed Michaela for her inability to attract Ralph. Apparently so did her mother.

Turning the jeep out onto the snow-packed road, Michaela sighed. Even from the grave Ralph Frame was reaching out to foil her. Now she had two clients to spring.

****

Travis leaned back against the cement blocks of his cell. How in hell had he ended up here? When he'd moved to Promise Lake, he wanted only peace and quiet, time to forget and heal, and an opportunity to protect that pristine wilderness. Now here he sat, charged with murder, listening to the drunk in the next cell vomit.

He wondered how Michaela was making out with his team. Big city lawyers didn't generally come equipped with a working knowledge of malamutes. He hoped Doc would look after her. He hoped she wouldn't take the dog into any situation where he could shoplift. He shook his head ruefully. He was probably the only musher in history to have a kleptomaniac sled dog.

The sounds of a scuffle erupted from beyond the steel door to the office area of the RCMP detachment. Another prisoner, a belligerent one this time, it appeared, was about to join him. He hoped whoever it was hadn't been drinking.

When the door banged open, Travis lurched upright. At the end of a pole, strangling in a choke collar, Doc fought against the two officers endeavoring to get him into the detention area.

"Doc, no! Easy! Whoa!" Travis's commands brought the dog to an instant halt. He stared in the direction of the voice. His tail began to wag. Throwing back his head, the malamute gave a long howl.

"Makes my skin crawl." Constable Roy suppressed a shudder. "Are you sure he's a dog, sir?"

"Reasonably sure." Corporal Palmer opened the door of the cell opposite Travis's. "Put him in here, Constable. We'll see what's to be done with him later. Right now we have a murder investigation to complete."

Doc, recovering from his initial joy at seeing his master, lunged toward Travis, all but throwing the officer against the bars.

"Doc, no! Behave. Do as you're told." Travis's words quieted the leaping dog. After a baleful glance at his master, he allowed himself to be thrust into the cell across the common area. As the door clanged shut behind him, he howled again.

"I like dogs," Constable Roy muttered, wiping sweat from his forehead. "But that one has to be mostly wolf."

"He is a beautiful animal." Corporal Palmer paused to admire the caged malamute. "I'm sure your lawyer friend will be able to clear him of all charges once she makes restitution to Sam's Convenience."

"Shoplifting, was he? Sam couldn't have been on duty." Travis gripped the bars and stared across at his dog. "He knows I always pay for whatever Doc filches."

"As a matter of fact, he wasn't. It was Mrs. Hendricks."

"Ah-ha, Mattie Hendricks. I might have known. Had a few run-ins with her myself. What did he take this time?"

"Apparently your friend Miss Dunn was in the washroom for some time. He had ample opportunity to purloin whatever he wanted. In all, it consisted of two Mr. Big bars, a package of Smarties, and a few strings of licorice."

"If he ate all that junk, I have to warn you, he's going to be sick."

"Too late, I'm afraid." Corporal Palmer's normally professionally calm expression twisted with distaste. "That happened in the back of the patrol car. Constable, you'll have to take it to Auto Clean and get it flushed."

"Yes, sir." The young officer hesitated.

"Now, Constable."

"Yes, sir. I was hoping to let it air a bit before I had to drive again, that's all."

He turned and left the cell block.

"Kids." Corporal Palmer's mouth quirked up at one corner.

****

The door to the cell corridor opened and Corporal Palmer came in followed by a woman Travis didn't immediately recognize. Her knee-high ebony boots shone below a camel-colored calf-length coat hanging open over a grey suit and snow-white blouse. She wore her hair pulled back into a bun and looked so coldly professional she brought a shudder of remembrance washing over him. In her left hand she carried a laptop case.

"Michaela?" He came slowly to his feet.

"I'd like a moment alone with my client." She turned to the officer. "You'll come for us when the judge is ready, I presume?"

"Of course, Miss Dunn." He inclined his head and left, closing the heavy steel door behind him.

"Doc, how are you doing, boy?" Instead of going to Travis, she headed for the malamute's cell and knelt to extend a welcoming hand. "We'll have you out of here in no time, don't worry. That nasty woman had no business calling the cops on you for a few chocolate bars. And as for saying you snarled at her, well, we know that's a fabrication."

"Hey, what about me? I've got a lot more hanging over my head than filching a few treats."

"You certainly do." She stood, swung to face him, putting her hand on her hip. "A fine mess you're in, Mr. MacDonald. Looks as if you could use a little help...even if it is from a Toronto lawyer who once reeked of your least favorite scent."

"Once?" He walked to the bars and took them into clenched fists.

"I've shelved it...at least for the present. I never did like it all that much."

"But Randall Kirby did?"

"He did. Now let's move away from the personal stuff and get down to hard facts. I've been talking to my father and..."

"Ah, another big-city, high-power..."

"Listen, do you want to be cleared of these charges or just keep on rattling your cage?"

"Cleared, definitely cleared." He let his hands fall to his side. Drawing a deep breath he looked out at her. "Okay. Let's get started. I won't be a charity case. I can pay."

"You already did when you found me in that blizzard. If I succeed, we're even. Agreed?"

"I never considered you owed me."

"Well, I did. And I don't like it. So listen up. Here's our strategy."

****

An hour later they stood before Judge Drew Anderson in his chambers, with Colin Best beside them.

"Take a seat, all of you." The handsome, white-haired judge waved a hand at them as he sat behind his massive oak desk. "Can't bear looking up."

As soon as they were seated, he leaned back in his chair, grey eyes examining each in turn.

"Okay, let me have it. First you, Mr. Best."

"Your honor, Travis MacDonald, seated on my left, stands accused of murdering Ralph Frame. On what he considered sufficient evidence, Justice of the Peace Angus Jones issued a warrant for his arrest. If you'll allow me, I'll summarize that evidence."

"Go ahead, Mr. Best. But make it brief. I have a busy day ahead."

"Yes, sir, of course, sir." Colin Best looked smug as he glanced at Michaela. "Firstly, Mr. MacDonald is the only musher in our area. Tracks of multiple dogs were found near the site of Mr. Frame's burned-out cabin. It's well known in the community that there was no love lost between the accused and Mr. Frame. Mr. MacDonald continually interfered with Mr. Frame's trap lines. For confirmation of this fact, I can bring in Ranger Karen Dollard, who investigated these allegations on several occasions. In fact, I have a witness who will testify to having heard Mr. MacDonald threaten to kill Mr. Frame. A couple of weeks ago, this animosity between the two men broke into a physical altercation. Mr. MacDonald apparently got the worst of it. I submit, your honor, that Mr. MacDonald killed Mr. Frame in an act of retribution for this beating."

"That's it?" The judge's forehead creased into a frown. "Angus Jones decided those scraps of circumstantial evidence were sufficient cause to issue an arrest warrant for murder? Mr. Best, what were you thinking? I strongly advise against such rash action." He turned to Michaela and his tone lightened. "Now let's hear from you, counselor. Although it's hardly necessary, given what I've just heard."

"I agree, Your Honor." Michaela smiled at the man. "I would like to add that forensic evidence found at the scene further exonerates my client. A bullet that apparently killed Mr. Frame found in the remains of the cabin has been identified as having been fired from a .38 calibre hand gun, not a deer rifle, which is the only weapon RCMP investigators found during a search of Mr. MacDonald's premises."

Travis almost let his mouth gape open. She'd gotten forensic information that could have taken another lawyer days, maybe weeks, to obtain.

"Furthermore..." She drew a breath and continued. "A wildlife biologist called to the scene could not definitely declare the paw prints in the vicinity of the cabin had been made by malamutes, the type of dogs Mr. MacDonald owns. Heat from the fire had melted most of them. He admitted they could just as easily have been made by large coyotes. There are a number of them in the area."

For the first time since his arrest, Travis began to relax. He had one kick-ass attorney.

"On the basis of what I've just heard, I hereby dismiss the charges against Travis MacDonald." Judge Drew Anderson stood, and the others followed his example. "Mr. Best, next time you see fit to urge the issuing of a warrant in my absence, please make certain you have a great deal more conclusive evidence. If you'd gone to trial with nothing better than what I've heard here today, this young lady would have made you look like a fool. Good morning, lady and gentlemen."

He strode past the group toward the door. As he passed Michaela, he favored her with a wink.

He leaned close to her ear. "Say hello to your father for me."

"Thank you, Your Honor. I will."

Ah-ha! Michael C. Dunn, QC. I should have guessed. My beautiful barrister's state-of-the-art backup.

Travis MacDonald's legal counsel smiled sweetly at Colin Best. He scowled and stepped aside so she and Travis could follow the judge out of the office.

"Miss Dunn, how about a statement?" A television reporter forced her way to the forefront of the group of press on the steps of the courthouse as they emerged.

Travis stared. Where had this crowd come from? Who had alerted them, and why so many? Surely the arrest of a murder suspect in a small town in northern New Brunswick wasn't of sufficient interest to draw a crowd of paparazzi.

A light bulb flashed in his brain. Of course! Publicity for Dunn & Dunn, Attorneys at Law.

Michaela's appeal for help had come with a price tag—that the press be given a full account of her success.

Watching her expertly fielding questions and smiling into the cameras, he came to a few more conclusions: Judge Drew Anderson's timely return to Carleton and that fast forensics report? Yeah, only someone with power to burn could have effected those results. Someone like Michael Dunn.

"No pictures." He shoved aside a camera thrust into his face and headed for the parking lot.

"Thanks," he said when Michaela joined him at his SUV. "Colin Best may have had weak evidence, but I know I wouldn't have gotten a hearing as quickly as I did if you hadn't intervened."

Doc was waiting for them in the driver's seat, his nose to the glass. He let out a long, agonized whine.

"Okay, okay." Michaela unlocked the door and let the dog leap out to greet his master.

"Whoa, easy, boy!" Travis warded off the malamute's exuberant greeting. "I missed you, too, even if we were confined in the same jail." He turned to Michaela. "Thanks for springing him."

"Not much of a feat." She shrugged, repressing a smile as she watched dog and man, both happy to be free again. "I paid for the junk food and that was it. Actually, Sam Mathers was distressed by Mattie Hendricks' actions. He insisted on giving me a bag of bars for Doc to make up for his inconvenience."

"Yeah, well, I think we'll reserve those for a while. He may have escaped punishment for theft, but I'm not sure Constable Roy has forgiven him for barfing his booty all over the back seat of the patrol car."

"You'll probably be receiving a sizeable bill for clean-up."

"No problem. Guilty as charged in that case,

right, Doc?"

The dog, still dancing around them like a pup, yelped happily.

"Okay, okay, get into the Jeep." Travis held the door open. "Man," he drew a deep breath. "Sure is great to breathe fresh air. That poor guy in the next cell had a definite stench."

"Worse than my perfume?" She turned to shoot him a mocking glance.

"Okay, okay, sorry about that. Are you going to drive, or will I?"

"I'll drive, but when we get to the garage, you can harness the dogs."

"Finding it a chore?" Grinning, he jogged around to the passenger door.

"I need time to change out of this getup before we head back in the sled. You can drop me off at the Lodge. My snowmobile is still lying on its side up on the mountain, if you remember."

She shoved the key into the ignition, and the long camel-hair coat fell open to reveal a shapely leg encased in a black stocking and calf-hugging boot. He stared.

"Interested?" She slanted him a glance, her hand pausing on the gear shift.

"I may be a hermit, but I haven't lost my appreciation for a nice leg."

"Apparently not." She wrenched the truck into drive with more than necessary force, and it jerked forward.

"Hey, easy on my transmission! What do you mean, 'apparently not'? You and I haven't exactly been a hot item."

"No, but you and Colin Best's wife are." She swung the truck out onto the road, and he lurched with the force.

"Again, easy on my truck. I have no idea what you're talking about. Me and the Crown Prosecutor's wife? Come on. "

"Oh, so I guess her see-through black nightie just materialized in your bedroom?" She gunned the vehicle to the top of the speed limit as she headed out of Carleton.

"See-through black nightie?"

"She arrived up at your cabin last night to retrieve it and God only knows what else. I didn't accompany her into your bedroom while she collected her leftovers."

"This is crazy! Karen Dollard is the only woman who's been in my cabin since I moved into it...aside from you."

"Ah-ha, the plot thickens! Are you telling me that you and Karen..."

"Karen and I are friends." He glanced over at her. "Not jealous, are you?"

"Hell, no!" She swung the truck into the drive in front of his garage. "Get out and harness the dogs while I change."

Fifteen minutes later Michaela seated herself in the sled behind seven eager-to-be-off huskies.

"Ready?" Travis stood beside the sled and looked down at her.

"Ready."

"Hike, hike!"

Doc howled, happy to be back in his element, and leaped against his harness. The other dogs broke into a gallop behind their leader.

Travis understood. It felt good to be out of that prison and into the freedom of the wilderness. He jumped onto the runners and glanced down at Michaela, snuggled into the sled in front of him, a robe wrapped about her. The day was cold, gray, and windy, but he enjoyed every minute, every breath of sharp, clear air. The woman in front of him had made it possible. Maybe he'd have to adjust his opinion of Toronto lawyers, especially ones who'd recently abandoned the fancy perfume another man had enjoyed.

What kind of a man is this Randall Kirby? Probably tall and very well groomed, totally ready for the cover of GQ. Probably the kind of guy who goes to spas and gets manicures. Probably a wimp who couldn't handle seven malamutes if his life depended on it.

Hell, why should he care? He wasn't about to get seriously involved with the woman in his sled. He'd had enough of city women whose morals weren't any better than those of an alley cat. Maybe he was old-fashioned. Jessica had damned him as such. So what if he was. His old-fashioned ideas had saved him from what he now knew would have been a personal and professional life of frustration, one he couldn't have borne for long.

What about Michaela Dunn? Was Randall Kirby her one and only, or were there a whole bunch of ex-lovers back in Toronto? A hot boil flooded up through his body. The idea of Michaela with any other man...

Fool! Fool! Fool!

****

"Thank you." Michaela climbed out of the sled in front of Promise Lodge. "Come in. I'll make us a meal before you start back to your cabin."

"Not impressed by my grub supply?" He let a grin quirk a corner of his lips.

"Not to be unkind, but yes. Put the dogs in the barn and come inside. I think I can find some leftovers they'll appreciate."

"I won't refuse. The take-outs from the greasy spoon across the road from the jail weren't exactly satisfying, especially with the guy in the next cell vomiting and a murder charge hanging over me. Now another favor."

She paused on her way to the steps and glanced back over her shoulder at him. "Ask."

"Will you let me take a shower before we eat? I slept in my clothes in a cell next to a drunk vomiting up whatever he'd ingested over the last day or so. I feel filthy."

"Sure. I'll show you to my uncle and aunt's apartment. You can use his razor and soaps. Travis?" She stopped him as he started for the bedroom corridor.

"Yes?" He turned back.

"That deer rifle. You use it to put out of their misery the animals too severely injured to be released, don't you?"

"Yeah, well." He rubbed his hands together and blinked as he met her distressed expression. "Sometimes it's the only thing I can do for them."

"I understand." The words were soft and choked. "Thank you."

He jerked a nod of acknowledgement before he headed down the hallway.

"I'd suggest you borrow some of Uncle's Norm's clothes but your waist line and his are too many sizes apart."

"No problem. I can live in these a little while longer."

****

Shortly, showered and feeling much better even though he'd had to redress in his unwashed clothes, he joined her at a table in the restaurant.

"I grilled pork chops and baked a couple of potatoes in the microwave," she said. "I have applesauce to go with it. Not exactly gourmet cuisine, but it will stick to your ribs for the journey back to your cabin."

"Looks great." He sat down as she placed a well-filled plate in front of him.

"Coffee?" She held a pot poised over his cup.

"Please. I'll need a shot of caffeine to keep me awake until I get home. I'm bushed. Can't wait to fall into my bed and sleep a good twelve hours."

"Your bed." She replaced the coffee pot on the warmer and sat down across from him. "The one you *didn't* share with Amanda Best."

"That's the one. Or Karen Dollard. Or anyone else. My bed is a virgin." He slanted her a sly, teasing look.

A flush rising up her cheeks, she straightened her shoulders and turned her attention to cutting her pork chop.

Good. Not too sophisticated or blasé to blush over a sexual innuendo.

"How is your pork chop? More applesauce?" She picked up the bowl and held it out to him.

Changing the subject to get away from it, too. Better follow her lead or this conversation could get away out of hand.

"Everything's fine. Michaela, what say we take a stab at solving this murder?" The words were out before he had time to consider them. Or really know where they'd come from. "It's the only way I'll be out from under suspicion once and for all."

"We'll see. Hadn't you better hit the trail soon? It's getting late."

****

"'Morning." Karen Dollard poked her head around the door of the restaurant. "Any chance of breakfast for a starving ranger?"

"Karen! Come on in. I'm just having my own. I'll be happy to have company. Pancakes and sausages okay?" Michaela got up from the table where she'd been eating and headed back to the stove.

"Perfect." The ranger placed her headgear on a table near the door and began to unfasten her jacket. "You're alone?"

"So far. I'm expecting guests for dinner and the night. Why?"

"Just thought..." She looked around

speculatively. "That I might find Travis MacDonald pullin' on his britches at Promise Lodge this fine winter's morning."

"What?" Michaela paused, spatula in hand, and swung to face her friend. "Why on earth would you think Travis MacDonald had spent the night here...with me?"

"Well, he did save your life, and now you've saved his, and you know he's not a real trapper..."

"It would take a lot more than those facts to make me fall into bed with the hermit of Promise Wilderness. Especially since..." Her voice trailed off. She shouldn't have said that.

"Especially since? Since what? Come on, Mikey. Tell me."

"Actually..." Michaela returned her attention to filling a plate with sausages and pancakes. "Amanda Best paid me a visit at Travis's cabin the night he was incarcerated. She said she'd come to collect a few things she'd left in Travis's bedroom. She walked out waving a nightie that was mostly not there."

"What? Travis and Amanda? Get real, Mikey. You know what a nasty piece of work she can be. I've known Travis for over four years and, believe me, he ain't that lonely yet. And never will be. She's not his kind of woman. That's a definite."

"Are you sure?" Michaela set the plate in front of her friend and poured coffee into her cup.

"Trust me. I know what Travis MacDonald likes in a woman, and she's not it."

"Really?" Michaela slid back onto her chair, narrowing her eyes as she looked across at her friend.

"Oh, come on, Mikey. You can't seriously suspect I'm his type. No matter what the secrets of Travis's past, I'm darned sure they include some pretty sophisticated living. I definitely don't measure up to that kind of lifestyle."

"Sophisticated? How do you figure that?"

"Just some of the stuff he says and does. Didn't you tell me he hates your expensive brand of perfume? Do you think he made that discovery here in Promise Wilderness?"

"No." Michaela dragged the word out slowly. "Still, it's hard to believe a man who lives as he does ever wore a suit and tie, hailed a cab, or attended a cocktail party."

"Really? I bet cleaned up he'd give you one big surprise."

"And you'd know?" Michaela shot her friend a quizzical look.

"When he first arrived here, he had only the beginnings of that tangle of hair and beard. He's quite a looker under that growth." Michaela saw Karen watching her over the rim of her coffee cup as she raised it to take a sip.

"Did he give you aspirations?"

"I can't deny I cast an eye over him. He arrived here the week after Andy jilted me for Jenny. I was looking for some way to make Andy regret his decision."

"So you thought the handsome newcomer might just be the answer?" Michaela felt a surge of something she wouldn't acknowledge as jealousy flush over her.

"Maybe I did. Old news, now. Anyhow, enough about Travis MacDonald. Let me tell you about Melissa's latest adventures."

They spent the rest of the meal enjoying the exploits of Karen's daughter. Finally the ranger stood. "Thanks for the breakfast, buddy. How much do I owe you?"

"It's on the house, of course." Michaela got to her feet, still nagged by the uncomfortable feeling that had caught her at Karen's admission of her attraction to Travis. "You just continue keeping the

Promise safe and secure. That's the best payment you can offer."

"I'll do my best." The ranger fastened her jacket and picked up her headgear.

Michaela stood in the doorway and waved as her friend drove off. Then she went slowly back into the Lodge. As she closed the door behind her, she was doing the math that included Travis's arrival in the Promise Wilderness, Karen's broken engagement, and Melissa's birth.

An hour later Travis knocked briefly before stepping into the Lodge restaurant. "Everything okay here? Thought I'd stop by and check, on my way to get your snowmobile."

"Great, thanks. I'm grateful for your offering to try to fix that old machine. It could be a challenge. Have you any experience with motors?"

"Farm equipment. I think I can manage."

He turned to leave.

"Farm equipment?" Michaela stopped him. "Were you a farmer before you came here?"

"I grew up on a farm."

"And afterwards?"

"Afterwards doesn't matter. I'll come back for you when I get your snowmobile going. You'll need to drive it across the lake."

Michael went to the window and watched him drive away, the dogs dashing exuberantly along the trail packed hard by the increased traffic across the lake to the crime scene. Her thoughts went back to Karen, Melissa, and Travis.

****

She drove her restored snowmobile carefully across the lake, exhilarated that Travis had been able to get the old machine running. Without her own mode of transportation she'd felt disabled, not in control of dealing with the demands of the Lodge. Those dogs and their harnessing were still a challenge.

Halfway across, she saw two snowmobiles pull up in front of the Lodge. Even at that distance she recognized their distinctive style and logo. RCMP. Corporal Palmer and Constable Roy. What did they want this time? Surely they weren't looking for Travis again.

She stopped and dismounted a few feet from where the two officers waited.

"Good morning, gentlemen." She slipped back into her defense attorney mode. "What can I do for you?"

Travis, who had been close behind her with the dogs, halted his team.

"We'd like you to accompany us to the detachment in Carleton," Corporal Palmer said. "There are a number of questions we believe you can answer."

"Questions? About what?" She removed her headgear and shook her hair free.

"About where you were and what you witnessed on the night of Ralph Frame's death. Apparently you blamed him for the recent closure of your Lodge."

"Opportunity and motive?" She disguised her dismay as she looked at the officers. "I assure you I didn't kill Ralph Frame."

"Then it won't take long for you to reassure the Crown Attorney. Please come along with us. Do you prefer to take your own machine or ride with one of us?"

"I saw lights in the Lodge the night Ralph Frame died." Travis came to stand beside her. "Ms. Dunn was at home."

"So you're supplying her with an alibi?" Corporal Palmer's eyes narrowed as he turned on Travis. "You're barely out of the woods yourself, Mr. MacDonald. I'd avoid involving myself any further in this investigation, if I were you. Come along, Ms.

Dunn."

He took her by the arm. Doc, standing beside Travis, snarled.

"Easy, boy." Travis quieted him.

"I have guests arriving at 4:00 p.m. for supper and the night—the Premier and his friends, for God's sake! I can't leave the Lodge!"

"Go along with the officers." Travis touched her on the shoulder. "Settle this thing once and for all. I'll see to your guests."

"But you can't cook!"

"No, but I can defrost. Judging from what I've seen you pull out of that massive freezer, I'm sure I can find something."

Awash with apprehension, Michaela mounted her snowmobile and headed down the trail between the two officers.

What will he do? He can't possibly manage meals and guests. My aunt and uncle's business will be ruined!

****

"So, Ms. Dunn, it appears you had a score to settle with the murder victim." Colin Best sat behind his desk and steepled his fingers.

"I was annoyed with him, yes. Who wouldn't be, when he was instrumental in having my business shut down, albeit it temporarily." She looked across at the Crown Attorney, narrowing her eyes. "But certainly not sufficiently to kill him."

"Maybe not because of that single incident, but you held a running grudge against Mr. Frame from your high school days here in Carleton, didn't you?"

"That was years ago. We were kids. He made a pass. I hit him."

"I think it was a great deal more than that. My wife told me her brother said you were responsible for that scar on his face, that you disfigured him with a wrench."

She hesitated. Her stomach roiled. *No way out of this but the truth.*

"He drove me into the woods on his snowmobile after he'd promised to drive me home from a Christmas dance. When he headed into the woods instead of turning toward my aunt and uncle's house, I yelled for him to stop, to take me back to town." She paused, cold sweat trickling between her breasts as memory flooded back.

"Go on." Colin Best wasn't about to give her a break.

"He was going so fast I knew if I tried to jump I'd probably break a leg."

She paused and sucked in a deep breath.

"Come on, Ms. Dunn. We don't have all day." Colin Best's satisfied expression rankled her.

She fought the urge to bury her face in her hands. "He drove into the woods until he came to what I later learned was called the old Wilson cabin. He dragged me inside and attacked me. He forced me back against the cupboards. There was a hand pump there. I raked my hand around, looking for something to use to defend myself…and found a pipe wrench that must have been used to work on the pump."

She paused, closed her eyes, and sucked in a long breath before continuing. "I lashed out. My blow connected with the side of his face, and blood gushed over both of us. He…roared obscenities."

"And?"

"I ran, actually got his snowmobile started and headed back down the trail he'd followed to bring me there. About a quarter mile away, I realized I couldn't leave him there, injured, perhaps seriously. So I went back.

"He'd gotten outside the cabin by the time I arrived and was trying to stanch the bleeding with his balaclava. At first he refused to let me help him and only continued to yell at me. Finally he must have realized he needed my help. He let me put snow on the wound and wrap my scarf around his face. Then I drove him back to Carleton. At the snowmobile garage, I called an ambulance, waited until it came into view, and then ran."

"Why didn't Mr. Frame prefer charges?" Constable Roy asked.

"Think, Constable." Corporal Palmer's tone reflected annoyance. "The man had been wounded attacking a young woman. It was in his best interest to keep quiet. Until recently, apparently," he continued, looking at the Crown Attorney. "When one of Mr. Frame's acquaintances decided revelation of the incident would cast suspicion on Miss Dunn."

"What are you suggesting, Corporal?" Colin Best rounded on the officer, eyes flashing angrily.

"I'm simply mentioning the fact that this incident hasn't surfaced for over ten years. Now, suddenly…"

"Yes, well, Corporal, there's more." A smug smile crossed the Crown Attorney's face. "You threatened to kill my brother-in-law during that little scuffle, didn't you, Ms. Dunn?"

"If everyone who yelled a threat when they're terrified carried it out, we'd be wading in bodies." Michaela managed to keep her cool and face the man, even as she recalled screaming the threat at the man pinning her against the cupboard and tearing at her clothes.

"Perhaps, but nevertheless…"

"Look, I've answered your questions to the best of my knowledge. Now I have to get back to the Lodge. The Premier is due at 4:00 p.m."

"The Premier?" All smugness vanished from Colin Best's expression. "Tonight, at Promise Lodge?"

"Yes, and the only one there to greet him and his

group will be Travis MacDonald—who, as far as I know, has zero experience in the hospitality business and less, if possible, in food service."

"Well, then, we'll terminate this interview." The Crown Attorney stood. "Gentlemen, you can leave us," he told the two Mounties.

"So the Premier is arriving at 4:00 p.m." Colin Best swung to face her as soon as the two men had left the room, his expression burning with eagerness. "Have you arranged for my meeting with him as you promised?"

"I didn't promise, just suggested it might be a possibility. Mr. Gray and his wife are counting on having a relaxing few days with close friends. They made that quite clear in their reservation information. I don't think they want uninvited guests."

"But surely, if someone were to arrive unexpectedly, you wouldn't turn them away, now would you, Ms. Dunn? Especially if that someone was willing to take your recent statement as gospel and leave you in peace to run your Lodge?"

"That sounds suspiciously like a bribe, Mr. Best."

"Definitely not. I never for a moment believed you had anything to do with my brother-in-law's death. Bringing you in was just a formality. Had to be done to clear the air, you understand. And on a previous occasion, you will remember, you more or less said you'd arrange for me to come by."

What a sycophant!

"Perhaps you could drop in...briefly...for dessert around 7:30." She got up and turned to leave.

"That would suit very well." He followed her to the door.

"I'll be contacting my father later this evening, Mr. Best." She swung on him abruptly. "I'll be requesting he fly down from Toronto to be present at our next intervicw."

"Oh, I doubt that will be necessary." The man's face paled under his tanning-bed color. "We've covered most of what I needed to know today. Anyway, I'm sure a high-profile attorney like Michael Dunn is much too busy to come away down here for a case that won't involve anyone he's connected with."

"I'll leave that for him to decide." Michaela met his gaze squarely. "If he thinks there's even the vaguest possibility I may need his assistance, he'll be on the next flight to New Brunswick."

She yanked open the door and strode out.

Chapter Eleven

Corporal Palmer drove Michaela back to the snowmobile garage. With twilight bringing shifting shadows into the bush, she climbed aboard her machine and headed for the Lodge as fast as she dared press the old machine. Visions of Travis spilling spaghetti sauce into the Premier's lap danced through her head.

In the yard she found a parked collection of snowmobiles. Light and laughter flooded out into the crisp cold of the winter night. Two men in snowmobile suits stood on either side of the door. *Security people.* She dismounted and went up the steps, pulling her wallet from inside her jacket.

"Michaela Dunn, current proprietor of Promise Lodge." She flipped it open and handed it to the man on the right.

"Looks okay." He examined her ID in the illumination of the porch light. "You're expected." He opened the door.

Light, warmth, ripples of laughter, good-natured conversation, and the music of a guitar and someone singing a country western tune greeted her. She stepped inside and looked around. The place was next to overflowing, each table with a full complement of diners. At the middle table the Premier and his wife sat chatting and laughing with their companions, coffee and slices of pie in front of them. On one of the stools at the counter sat Travis MacDonald strumming her uncle's old guitar and singing. Michaela paused to listen.

Pretty darn good. Maybe that explains his

mysterious past. He's a runaway country music star.

She hung her headgear on a peg by the door, unfastened her jacket, and revised the thought. Definitely not a professional musician. If he were, he'd be gyrating around the room, not sitting quietly in front of his audience.

"Travis, how about another slice of that great pie?" The Premier tapped an empty plate when the song ended. "Best I've had in ages. And maybe a bit more coffee?"

"Yes, sir." Travis laid aside the guitar and reached toward the counter. Picking up a plate holding more pie, he took the coffeepot in the other hand. "Ice cream with that, Mr. Premier?"

"Definitely. Can't remember when I've had such a great meal or such a good time. Do you know 'Blue Eyes Cryin' in the Rain?' It's Linda's favorite." He took his wife's hand on the table and smiled at her.

"I'll give it try, but I'm no Willie Nelson."

Travis returned to the counter, picked up the guitar, and resumed his seat on one of the stools. As he strummed the first few bars of the old country classic, Michaela felt a sigh ease through her lips. Once again, Travis MacDonald had saved the day. In fact, it looked as if he'd *made* the day, judging from the mood of the guests.

"Good evening, Mr. Premier." Michaela crossed the room to greet the guest of honor. "I'm Michaela Dunn. I'm managing Promise Lodge while my aunt and uncle are on vacation."

"A pleasure to meet you, Ms. Dunn." Shane Gray stood to accept her extended hand. "I mean it. Your family has done a remarkable job in protecting and maintaining this place as a wilderness retreat. And all without a penny of government assistance, I might add. A sterling example of what dedication and hard work can accomplish. Please pass my compliments along to your relatives."

"Thank you, sir. I will."

"Great host you've got in Travis MacDonald." The Premier resumed his seat. "He certainly knows how to make a group feel welcome. Not only does he serve up a delicious supper, he's one fine musician."

"I'll be sure to tell him you're happy with his service."

She was about to continue behind the counter to take over serving duties when she heard another snowmobile approaching. Seconds later loud voices from outside announced the arrival of someone the security guards didn't plan to admit.

"Excuse me, Mr. Premier." Michaela headed across the room. "Enjoy the music and dessert. I'll take care of this."

Outside she found Colin Best angrily forcing ID under the noses of the two guards.

"You fools! I'm the local Crown Attorney! I'll have your badges for this outrage! I'm an invited guest! Tell them, Michaela."

He swung on her. She suppressed a smirk at his calling her Michaela, not the distancing "Ms. Dunn" he'd used in his office.

"Mr. Best is my guest, gentlemen." She drew a deep breath. "I'll vouch for him. He is exactly who he says he is."

"Very well." The guard handed back the ID folder. "But he isn't on the guest list or identified as a person to be welcomed this evening."

"A late invitation." Michaela opened the door. "Come in, Mr. Best."

Once inside she whirled on him. "Okay, you're here. I'll take you to the Premier's table and introduce you. You can have dessert and coffee with him *if* he invites you. I don't have a bed for you, so you'll have to head back to town tonight."

"That's all I require." Nose in the air, he followed Michaela to the Premier's table as Travis

MacDonald finished his song to cheers, whistles, and applause.

Leaving Colin Best cloying in a manner that would have befitted Mr. Collins of Austen's *Pride and Prejudice*, she continued to the counter. Seated on a stool in front of it, she faced the man putting plates into the dishwasher, a quizzical smirk twisting her lips.

"What?" He turned from the waist to look at her.

"You're just one giant human puzzle, Travis MacDonald," she said leaning on an elbow on the clean surface. "I never thought you could pull it off, let alone make a huge success of the evening."

"I've had experience hosting shindigs." He straightened, punched in the wash cycle, picked up the guitar, and headed out in front of the counter. "Any requests, folks?" he asked.

A cacophony of titles burst out.

****

A half hour later all the guests had left for their rooms. Plans for the morning included an early start on the trails. Most stopped by the counter behind which Michaela and Travis were working to thank them for a wonderful evening. Only the Premier and Colin Best remained seated in the middle of the room, deep in conversation.

Finally Shane Gray stood.

"I'm sorry I can't throw my party's support behind your candidacy, Mr. Best," he said. In the near-empty room, Michaela and Travis couldn't help overhearing. "But after your brother-in-law vigorously and publicly proposed a gambling establishment here in the Promise Wilderness, supporting you would make it appear our government is in favor of such an enterprise. Did you know he recently informed the media that you, as his sister's husband, were one hundred percent behind the scheme?"

"Yes, but that was without my knowledge or consent…"

"We're against gambling, as you must be well aware." The Premier ignored his protests and continued. "We're also against any further violation of such pristine wilderness areas as the Promise Lake region. If not for Mr. Frame's proposals, which voters would assume we support through an endorsement of your campaign, we might have been able to support your candidacy. You have my condolences on his passing. Good night, Mr. Best."

The Premier turned to Michaela and Travis. "Good night, folks. Thanks for a great evening."

"But Mr. Premier—Shane—my brother-in-law is no longer a factor in my future plans. Surely any negative shadows his unfortunate plans might have cast in my direction are gone. Surely…"

"Mr. Best, Ralph Frame was long and loud in announcing his plans to anyone who would listen. His murder has only served to underscore the inherent dangers in promoting such an endeavor."

"Yes, but that's not going to happen *now*. When I become the elected official for this area, I'll support wilderness protection. I'll speak out against gambling, I'll…"

"Voters have long memories on election day. The upcoming polls promise a close race. I can't take the risk of having someone with questionable associations on my team."

He strode off down the corridor toward the suite where his wife waited.

For a moment the Crown Attorney stood staring after him. Then he rounded on the couple behind the counter.

"Well, what are you two staring at?" he snarled. "I'd think you'd both be accustomed to my brother-in-law's ability to ruin lives!"

He grabbed up his snowmobile gear and strode

out, slamming the door after him.

"Well." Michaela looked up at Travis. "Seems even from the grave Ralph Frame can reach out to foil people's plans. You know, when I met you, I thought you were a ghost of winters past. Now I think Ralph is that ghost, coming back to haunt us all with his nefarious deeds."

"Yeah, well, could be. The part about Ralph, that is. I've never considered myself a spectral anachronism."

"Wow! Aren't the big words flying tonight! Karen was right. You do have a degree of sophistication that belies your hermit-recluse persona."

"Ah, so you and Ranger Dollard were discussing me. Casting lots to see who would become the woman of my dreams, no doubt?"

"She only said you had more than a dab of big city in your make-up. Don't get carried away."

"Okay. Subject dropped. Regarding the evening, aside from the Crown Attorney's putdown all went well." Travis wiped the last table, threw the cloth on the counter, and went to bank the fire in the lounge. "Guests all fed and watered and safely in their rooms."

"I don't think I remembered to thank you." Michaela sank down on the couch in front of the hearth and watched him add logs and replace the spark screen.

"No need. I haven't played guitar in years. Must have sounded pretty rusty."

"Not to my ears. Come. Sit. Tell me about your hosting and musical past."

"No way." He sat down in the chair to her left and stretched long legs out toward the fire. "It's not something you need to know or that I want to share."

"Okay, then at least explain your phony trapper

routine. When I was considering defending you, Karen told me to examine those pelts on your cabin wall. Phony as a three-dollar bill, just like the bear rug on your floor. I'll bet the same goes for that fur hat you wear. Why?"

"No reason I shouldn't tell you, now that Ralph is dead." He rubbed the back of his neck. "I had to find an excuse to be out along Ralph's trap lines, so I ordered a bunch of fake fur stuff off the Internet and pretended to be his competitor. I also had to have some visible means of income, or I'd soon become a person of interest to the boys in red serge. Actually I spent my time destroying Ralph's traps, freeing any animals I found in them that weren't seriously injured, and..."

"And putting out of their suffering those who were," she finished softly, as he lowered his head and looked at his hands.

"Yeah, that's about it. Rotten practice, trapping."

"Agreed. I thank you for your concern and your undercover work. But if you aren't a trapper, how do you make a living? You've got eight mouths to feed."

"Made some money before I decided to hermit myself away in the Promise Wilderness, invested it soundly. Keeps me in bacon and beans."

"And very little more." She remembered his cupboards.

"Yeah, well, I could buy more stuff, but I can't cook, so what would be the use?"

"You cooked very well tonight."

"Pulling containers of your aunt's super stew out of the freezer and defrosting it isn't exactly cooking."

"But the pies weren't cooked."

"Not a big deal there, either. Rolls were a bit more tricky. They may not have been thoroughly thawed when I put them on the table." He grinned. "Nobody complained. They must have softened with room heat."

"Well, anyhow, you saved the day. Now I have to go to bed. I have to be up at 5:00 a.m. to start breakfast for this crew." She stood and looked down at him. "You'll be staying the night? I presume the dogs are settled in the barn. You'll have to sleep in my aunt and uncle's apartment. Everything else is full."

"No problem. But would you mind if I brought Doc up here? He's not accustomed to sleeping with his crew. It will put his nose out of joint. I left him in charge in the barn when the guests began to arrive...not everyone enjoys a 100-pound malamute begging for tidbits."

"Sure, go get the boy."

"Thanks, but before I do, tell me. How did you make out today with the local law enforcement guys?"

"Actually that's the reason Colin Best got in here tonight. I made a deal, agreed to have him meet the Premier. After that, he couldn't absolve me of suspicion quickly enough."

"Once again, the Premier to the rescue...even though he has no idea of what a hero he's become around here." A sardonic grin curled the corners of his lips.

He got to his feet and looked down at her. The lamps had been turned low. Shadows from the flames on the hearth flitted around the darkened room. A crackle that didn't come from the fireplace snapped through her when she gazed up into those killer blue eyes.

"Travis." His name came as a breathed whisper from her lips. Her arms went up and about his neck. He gazed searchingly into her eyes, then lowered his head to take her lips in a kiss that made her solar plexus do a somersault. Her thoughts tangled. Logic melted into the ether. She soared.

When he released her, every inch of her body felt soft and magically mellow. All her defenses had tumbled. She wanted to spend the night with him, to enjoy every bit of the thrilling mystery that was sensationally virile Travis MacDonald.

"Travis," she breathed, but he began to back away, rubbing his hands on the seat of his pants.

"Sorry." He bit his lower lip. "That shouldn't have happened. I'll go get Doc."

He turned and headed for the door, leaving Michaela still tingling from their encounter, wanting more, so much more, and utterly confused.

"Travis!" His name snapped out in total exasperation. "Travis MacDonald!"

But he was gone, off into the night to get his wolf dog.

Chapter Twelve

Damn it, where was his common sense! Travis shucked his clothes and headed into the bathroom of Norm and Ida Dunn's cozy apartment. Michaela Dunn was everything he didn't want to get involved with ever again. And he wouldn't. No, sir, he wouldn't. She could wrap those soft arms around his neck any time she chose, kiss him with a passion that made every male fibre in his body roar, but he wouldn't let himself become mixed up with her.

He turned on the water, adjusted it to warm, then changed his mind. Swinging the tap to cold, he stepped into the stream and yelped. Nothing like icy water to bring a man back to sanity.

As he lay in the king-sized bed twenty minutes later, he knew there wasn't enough cold water in all of the Promise to stop him thinking about Michaela Dunn. Hell, he'd just caught himself fantasizing about them running Promise Lodge together, making a success with its pristine location and amazing menus. He'd visualized himself offering dog sled excursions to guests as together he and Michaela slowly lessened snowmobile traffic in favor of canine transport. He grinned into the shadows from the fire dying on the hearth on the other side of the room. He might even sing and play a bit.

Damn it! He rolled away from those seductive shadows. Staring at the empty pillow next to him, he realized all his ideas were moot without her sharing them.

****

He woke early the next morning, washed,

brushed his teeth with one of the new toothbrushes he'd found on a shelf above the basin, pulled on his clothes, and headed for the restaurant. He wasn't surprised to see Michaela, dressed in sweater, jeans, and apron, busy at the stove.

"What can I do to help?" He stopped in front of the counter.

"Really, Travis, it isn't necessary." She turned, shoving her hands into the apron pockets. "I can manage."

"I know you can. Still, I have time to spare, now that I don't have Ralph's traps to dismantle. Don't try to tell me another pair of hands wouldn't be welcome."

"No, I definitely won't. Okay, you can set the tables. I gather, from last night's success, you managed that acceptably well." She slanted him a teasing glance.

"No one complained." He joined her behind the counter and began to pile forks, knives, spoons, and napkins onto a tray.

"Travis, about last night..." She paused beside him. "I shouldn't have..."

"No need to explain. I've had thank-you kisses before. I should probably apologize for my over-reaction." He paused in putting napkins onto the tray. "But I won't. You're a beautiful woman, Michaela Dunn, and way too attractive to a man who's been celibate for longer than he cares to remember...especially now that you've apparently ditched your perfume bottle."

"I haven't abandoned it." She turned back to the bacon frying on the stove. "Just laid it aside for when I return to Toronto."

"Good idea." He picked up the tray and headed out among the tables, a sinking feeling in his gut. "That stuff costs a lot."

Her announcement of her return to Toronto

shouldn't bother him. He'd known her residency at Promise Lodge was temporary. As he set the tables, he tried to comfort himself by conjuring up the scent of that despicable perfume. It didn't work.

****

An hour later, as he harnessed his team, the Premier and his entourage emerged from the Lodge.

"Ah, there's our musician." Shane Gray came down the steps toward him. "Great entertainment you provided last night, Travis."

"Thank you." Travis straightened and saw Michaela watching from the verandah. "Just helping out."

"And who are these fine lads and lasses?" The Premier turned to the dogs. "Absolutely beautiful. I've never seen huskies this particular color."

"Actually, they're malamutes, sir, the dray dogs of winter sledding. They can pull heavy loads over long distances. This particular strain is known as Moon Glow malamutes."

"Do you offer rides? Although I haven't the slightest idea how to drive a team like this, I'd enjoy a trip into the bush."

"It's not a feature of Promise Lodge at the present time, sir, but climb aboard. We'll be glad to take you for a run across the lake."

"Sir, I must remind you, you'll be presenting a security problem." One of his group stepped forward. RCMP, Travis guessed. "We can't guarantee we can keep up with a team of running dogs and…"

"Then don't. I excuse you from responsibility, in front of witnesses." He climbed into the sled. "Let's go, Travis. This is something I've wanted to do all my life."

"Very good, sir." Travis straightened the dogs in their harness, jogged to the back of the sled and yelled, "Hike, hike!"

The dogs bounded off. Shane Gray let out a

whoop.

****

After they'd returned and the Premier and his group had headed off along the trails, Travis went up onto the verandah to join Michaela. She'd been seeing them off with thermoses of coffee and soup.

"Seems like a nice guy," he commented, pulling off his mittens.

"Very nice. Too nice to be impressed with our Crown Attorney." Michaela squinted up at him in the blaze of sunlight.

"I agree. Any coffee left? I didn't have time for breakfast."

"If that's a hint, come inside. There are lots of leftovers. I didn't have time to eat either. We can keep each other company before I start the clean-up."

****

"You know, I've had a couple of ideas of what I'd do if I were the owner of this place. And you're the reason for them." Michaela replaced her coffee cup on the table after they'd polished off a breakfast of beans, biscuits, eggs, and ham.

"You've got my attention." Travis pushed away his empty plate and leaned back in his chair.

"Well, the guests really enjoyed your music last night. Maybe a little old-fashioned, down-home entertainment might add to the ambience. Second idea: today when the Premier took such pleasure in that ride in your sled...maybe a musher with a bunch of well trained dogs...it would definitely be in keeping with our philosophy of respecting the environment. No fumes from snowmobiles, no oily leaks."

"Are you offering me a job?" His mouth quirked up at one corner. "You want me to host some kind of Dude Dog Sled thing and provide music at night?"

"Well, you've just admitted you're no trapper

and you have lots of spare time, and..."

"Listen, Ms. Dunn." He stood and went to the counter to pour himself another cup of coffee. "You're only here temporarily. Your relatives will be back shortly to take over the reins. I don't think they'd appreciate your making major changes. Anyhow, to add dog sledding to a place like this would require a sizeable investment. Suitable dogs and sleds would have to be purchased, pens built in a portion of the barn to house them, outdoor runs constructed."

"Okay, okay, but just for now...will you continue to help out at night by providing music...and during the day with an occasional dog sled ride...just to see how it catches on?"

He turned back to her, rested his hips against the counter, and pursed his lips.

"Okay," he said finally. "I'll give it a go for a week or so. But after that, no promises."

"Fine. Perfect." She got to her feet and began to gather up dishes. "Since there's no need to sing or provide dog sled rides at the moment, how about bussing these tables with me? I want to get finished asap. I have to make a run to town for more supplies."

"How do you normally do that?" He grabbed a plastic container and began to clear tables.

"I drive Uncle Norm's snowmobile to the snowmobile garage, with a sled filled with insulated containers attached. He keeps a truck there in winter. From there, it's a five-minute drive to the market. You seem concerned. Don't you think your repairs will hold?"

"Yeah, I guess. You need a new machine, you realize. It wouldn't be as dependable as a dog team, but still a notch up from that rig you drive now."

"Maybe I'll buy one before Uncle Norm and Aunt Ida return." She paused thoughtfully. "A nice anniversary present for them."

"You must have been pretty successful in the big city to have that kind of cash." He clattered plates and utensils into his container without looking at her.

"Not a very subtle way to inquire about my financial status." She took her snowmobile pants from a hook by the door and stepped into them.

"Sorry. Bad manners. If you're not back in two hours, the guys and I will go after you, okay?"

"Okay, but I'm hoping I won't need you to rescue me again."

****

Michaela was pushing a cart piled with groceries around the Carleton supermarket when a woman's voice stopped her.

"Mikey?"

She turned to see Jenny Murdoch overtaking her.

"Jenny, hi. I suppose this is your second home, with two growing daughters and a husband to feed." She waited while the woman brought her cart up beside hers.

"Sort of. Is it true Travis MacDonald is no longer a person of interest in Ralph Frame's death?"

"Happily, yes. You don't appear overjoyed about it."

"I...I don't know the man. He's some sort of weird hermit, isn't he? Are you sure he's innocent? Andy says Travis MacDonald was stealing from Ralph's traps. He says they had a fight. He says Travis MacDonald threatened to kill Ralph..."

"Andy seems to be doing a lot of talking." Michaela's reply came out quick and sharp. "Jenny, I think your husband is trying to make Travis MacDonald look guilty."

"Oh, I know it's wrong to wish anyone trouble." She lowered her head and looked at her hands twisting on the cart handle. "But now the police are questioning Andy. They found out Andy owed Ralph a lot of money, and that they'd quarreled about it when Ralph refused to give Andy more time to pay up. Mikey," she looked up at her, desperation in her eyes. "They've taken Andy to the RCMP detachment for questioning, and I'm afraid!"

"You think he might be guilty?" Michaela asked softly.

"No, no, Andy would never do anything like that, but other innocent men have been wrongfully convicted. Mikey, will you defend him?"

"He probably doesn't need an attorney. At any rate, I couldn't take the case. I've already committed my services to Travis MacDonald. The best I can do for Andy is to help him find competent representation. I'm sorry."

"Yes, well, I'm sorry, too." Jenny's lips tightened, her face hardened. "I would have thought helping a high school friend would take precedence over defending some backwoods savage. I hate Ralph Frame. Even from the grave he's haunting us, causing our family distress. And still there's Karen Dollard. Why can't she leave my husband alone?"

"Jenny, what are you talking about?" Michaela was startled by the expression of pure hatred that transformed the woman's pale face. "Surely you don't think Karen and Andy...?"

"He was always up at Promise Lake with Ralph Frame. When they'd come back, Ralph would say things about their meeting up with Karen, how Andy still had the hots for eye-candy like her!"

"Surely you didn't take Ralph's remarks seriously!" *Ralph running true to form, a troublemaker at every opportunity.* "Karen hasn't the least interest in Andy, I assure you. Ralph was just trying to upset you. He was a master at innuendo."

"That's not the worst." Jenny moved close to Michaela and lowered her voice. "He said her

146

daughter is Andy's child."

"Jenny, really! You knew Ralph as well as I did. He was nasty to the core. He'd say or do anything to make others miserable."

"Maybe." Her eyes narrowed. "But you're Karen's best friend. You know the truth."

"Sorry, but I don't. Karen has never told anyone, to the best of my knowledge, and she plans to keep it that way."

"Fine, don't tell me. And don't defend Andy!" Jenny Murdoch grasped her shopping cart and shoved it ahead of Michaela's. "If all this leads to the breakup of our family, I hope you suffer for it!"

"Jenny…!" Michaela started after her, but when she realized nearby shoppers had heard Jenny's last, heated remarks and were staring, she wet her lips, forced a weak smile in their direction, and proceeded to the checkout.

She was loading groceries from the truck into the containers on the snowmobile sled at the garage when Karen pulled up beside her. She climbed out of the Department of Natural Resources vehicle she'd driven and greeted Michaela with a broad grin.

"Howdy, friend. Need a hand loading them thar supplies?"

"Sure." Michaela straightened and smiled at her friend. "It's clouding over. I want to get back to the Lodge before it snows. I left Travis in charge, and I'm not sure how long he'll be happy playing host."

"Travis is a great guy. Not to worry." The ranger began hoisting bags into the sled.

"Karen." Michaela paused, a canvas bag in her arms. "I know I said I'd never ask, but will you at least tell me who isn't Melissa's father?"

"Why?" She rounded on her so quickly Michaela backed off a step. "Has somebody been implying something?"

"Yes, as a matter of fact. Jenny Murdoch thinks

147

Andy is Melissa's dad."

"Yeah, right. Like I'd be making love with him after he dumped me!"

"It wouldn't be the first time a woman tried to win a man back."

"Mikey, I thought you were my friend. Now it turns out you're as cynical as everyone else about my daughter's parentage! Who's your next guess? Travis MacDonald? He arrived here in the right time frame. Why don't you check with him?"

She turned and strode back to her Jeep, her back ramrod straight.

"Karen, I didn't mean to pry! I'm sorry…"

The Jeep roared off.

"Damn!" Michaela grabbed the last bag of groceries and thrust it into place in the sled. *Just what I needed to do…alienate my best friend!*

Chapter Thirteen

Driving back to the Lodge, Michaela decided she wouldn't confront Travis with her suspicion that he was Melissa's father. Even though the question scorched her curiosity she couldn't risk ruining another relationship. Right now Travis MacDonald was proving a valuable addition to the hosting of Promise Lodge and providing entertainments that might make the inn even more popular.

She turned into the Lodge dooryard and swung around toward the rear kitchen entrance.

"You're back sooner than I expected." Travis came to the door, pulling on his parka. "Let me unload while you get started on the food. Our guests are due back for lunch within the hour."

"Okay, fine, thanks."

She went up the steps, through the pantry, and out into the restaurant .

"Oh, wow, this is wonderful!" She gazed out over a room where all the tables were set in readiness for the next meal. "Travis MacDonald, you're a keeper...at least as long as I'm managing Promise Lodge."

"You had me...right up to the qualifier." His voice from the pantry made her flinch.

Way to go, Michaela. Alienate another friend.

****

Fueled by Michaela's cooking and Travis's music and hosting skills, the evening was another success. Praising both the food and the hospitality, the Premier's party booked return visits before they headed off for bed.

149

"Best wilderness lodge I've ever stayed at!" one robust middle-aged man declared. "I own a couple of newspapers in the USA. When I get back home, I'll be assigning one of my writers to tell the story of my visit for our readers. Okay if I take a few pictures tomorrow?"

"No problem. Snap away." Michaela felt a smile stretching from cheek to cheek.

"Can I also book a ride in a dog sled? That would really flesh out my piece...if you'd take a few photos of me with the dogs."

"Travis?" Michaela turned to him.

"Sure, why not. The dogs like an early morning run. 8:00 a.m. okay?"

"Fine with me, if I can have breakfast first." The newspaper owner grinned at Michaela. "I wouldn't want to miss whatever this little lady has in store for us."

"I start serving at seven, so no problem. Tomorrow it will be pancakes with blueberry syrup, sausages, and homemade biscuits."

"Another great day." The man put his arm around his wife's shoulders and headed her toward the bedrooms. "Hettie, we're going to have to make this an annual event."

"That went well." Travis sank down onto a chair at a table. He and Michaela were finally alone. "Bookings are movin' right along, and now free advertising."

"Yes, without Ralph Frame getting me shut down on false charges, things are really picking up. No small thanks to you, Travis MacDonald."

Although she knew it was entirely the wrong thing to do, she raised on tiptoes and planted a kiss on his bearded cheek.

"Is that the best you can do?" Blue eyes twinkled wickedly down at her. "After all, I did set the tables."

She hesitated, then slowly slid her arms up and

about his neck. She felt his breath catch as he looked down into her eyes. He lowered his head to cover her mouth with his. Throwing caution into a snowbank, she responded with heartfelt passion.

"Miss Dunn?" The newspaper man's voice made her jump back as if struck by an electric shock. "Any chance of a hot choc-... Oh, sorry." He started to turn back down the corridor.

"No problem, Mr. Irwin." Michaela was quick to stop him. "Would you like one for your wife, as well?"

"That would be terrific...but I don't want to interrupt."

"Actually you arrived at just the right moment." Michaela headed behind the counter and took out a pot. "Mr. MacDonald and I were about to head off to bed."

The moment the words were out of her mouth, Michaela felt a hot blush spread over her face. "I mean, separately, of course. We're not...that is, we weren't about to..."

"No need to explain, my dear." The big man chuckled. "I understand. A couple of attractive young people running a Lodge away up here in the wilderness, sparks are bound to fly."

Stop digging yourself in deeper, Michaela Dunn. Just shut up and make the chocolate. Michaela turned on a burner and poured milk into the pot.

As she stirred chocolate into the hot milk, she heard Charles Irwin whisper to Travis in a not-too-subtle tone, "Lovely creature, MacDonald. Hope you're planning to make it right by her. Not many young women blush any more. She's an old-fashioned girl if ever I saw one."

"Thank you, sir. I'll try."

****

Cheeks flaming, Michaela handed the newspaper man a tray holding two mugs of steaming chocolate. "I hope you'll enjoy these, Mr. Irwin."

"I'm sure we will. Good night, Miss Dunn." He nudged Travis with an elbow. "Remember what I said, young fella. Do the right thing."

"Well, that was embarrassing." Michaela rinsed out the pot after the man had disappeared in the direction of the bedrooms.

"Why? Like the man said, we're a couple of young people alone in the wilderness…"

"Oh, be quiet. My face is still hot."

"Maybe Charles Irwin is right. You are an old-fashioned girl, and I should do the right thing by you…now that we've been caught in a compromising position. Would you consider marrying me, ma'am?"

"For heaven's sake! How old-fashioned would I have to be to think a man would propose based on a single kiss?"

"Maybe refreshingly old-fashioned." He turned toward the bedroom corridors. "And, if you'll recall, this was only one in a series of knock-your-socks-off kisses. Now I'm off to bed…alone. See you in the morning. Come on, Doc."

****

Alone with the dog in his room, Travis stripped to the waist and went to the window to look out at the star-studded sky. On impulse, he shoved it open and stood for a minute, letting the cold night air cool the heat Michaela had sent racing through his body. Trees cracked in the frost. Nearby an owl hooted. Farther back in the bush a coyote howled. From the barn his dogs answered. What a perfect night. Haunting and beautiful. Man, he loved this wilderness. And now he just might be starting to love the woman whose family owned a big chunk of it.

"No, damn it, no!" He slammed the window shut and headed into the bathroom. "I won't let it happen, Doc."

Doc stared after him as he shucked the

remainder of his clothes and turned on the water in the shower. The dog whined a long, low, wistful sound.

"That'll do from you, my friend." Travis jerked the curtain back and stepped into the spray. "Someone else has already been giving me advice I plan to ignore."

But he couldn't belay his thoughts of Michaela, of that kiss and the previous kisses, and how close and comfortable they were becoming. Friends with one hell of a physical attraction. A dangerous combination.

He and Jessica hadn't been friends. Not really. They'd worked for the same company, toward the same goals, at least for a while. They'd companioned each other to social events and visited each other's parents at Christmas and Easter. In short, they'd done all the mechanical things that had made them a couple in the eyes of the world, right down to sharing that overpriced glass-and-chrome apartment in an upscale highrise. But they'd never been friends.

He shifted in the bed and tried not to remember his return from that land acquisition trip to northern British Columbia, the night he'd come quietly into the apartment planning to surprise her. *Ah, damn, damn, damn!*

He turned and pummeled his pillow. Did a man ever really get over finding the woman he'd been about to marry in bed with another man? A man he'd regarded as his friend? *Hell, no. Hell, no, no, no.*

The topping had been her charging him with deliberately failing to acquire the land in Northern British Columbia vital to their company's expansion. Recalling the nasty triumph on her face when the CEO had asked for his resignation, he wondered he could ever have believed he loved her.

Doc's whine stopped him.

"You're right." He flopped over on his belly and drew a deep breath. "I have no right to destroy Lodge property just because I got suckered by one bitch of a woman and a two-faced bastard. Good night, boy. Sleep well. "

****

Travis began to unharness his weary team. The Premier, his wife, Charles Irwin, and the rest of their group had finally left after repeated sled rides across the lake. He was glad. It had been a busy morning. Now there was only a small group of new arrivals having breakfast in the dining room..

A snowmobile roaring into the Lodge yard made Travis pause and suppress a sigh. *Another unexpected guest? Well, face it. All paying customers are welcome.*

The rider skidded to a halt. He dismounted, pulling off his headgear. *Andy Murdoch. What was he doing here?*

"Stay," he ordered Doc as the newcomer approached. The malamute rumbled in his throat. "It's okay. He's alone."

"Where's Mikey?" Andy Murdoch's face bore a stubble, and his eyes were red-rimmed and bloodshot. *Drinking again. Losing his buddy hasn't changed a thing.*

"Good morning." Travis's words pointed out the other man's lack of manners. "Now what was it you wanted?"

"Don't play games with me, MacDonald. The police have hauled in my wife for questioning. I need Mikey to be present...make sure she doesn't say anything stupid!"

"Oh, I'm sure Ms. Dunn would never say anything stupid...especially to the Mounties."

"Real smart, aren't you, probably one of those guys who got straight A's in English composition in high school. Now, where's Mikey?"

"Serving breakfast." A malicious streak caught Travis. "If you'll watch the dogs, I'll take over."

He handed Doc's lead to the man and headed for the house. Behind his back he heard Doc mutter. A grin creased his face. *Make him sweat, Doc, make him sweat.*

"Andy Murdoch wants to see you in the yard." Travis pulled off his parka. "It sounds important. I'll take over here."

"Really? Obviously he's been released, so what can it be?" She paused in putting dishes into the washer.

"I'll let him tell you. Everyone about ready for another round of coffee?" Picking up the pot, he raised his voice on the last sentence.

"Sure am, Travis, honey." A full-breasted redhead waved her cup. "I've been ready for you most of my life."

The three other women sharing her table laughed and tapped empty mugs on the table. "Hey, sweet buns, over here!"

"Coming, ladies. More toast? Muffins?" He bent to fill the redhead's cup, then flinched as her nearest companion pinched his bottom.

Catching the scenario as she crossed the restaurant, Michaela stopped beside the table to slip an arm around Travis's waist.

"You can window shop to your heart's content, ladies"—she winked at them—"but this merchandise is all mine."

Letting her hand slide to the seat of his jeans, she gave him a squeeze that popped his eyes wide open. Then she sauntered outside.

****

Ten minutes later Michaela came back into the restaurant. The guests had finished their meal and left. They were alone. Her forehead furrowed, she took a chair at a table. Travis dropped the container

155

he'd been using to bus the tables and sat down opposite her.

"Well?"

"You have a mean streak, do you know, Travis MacDonald, making Andy hold your team when you could very well have tied them to the verandah." She looked over at him, eyes narrowed and twinkling.

"Yeah, guess I'm one nasty piece of work. I wanted Doc to get a bit of revenge for all the times Andy and Ralph threatened to shoot him. So what's the story? Are you going to head into Carleton to take care of Andy's wife?"

"I don't think things have progressed to the point where she needs an attorney present." Michaela toyed with a fork. "In fact, I think my arriving at this point would only serve to exacerbate her position. The reason they called her in for questioning is because she'd been heard uttering threats against Ralph."

"Seems a lot of people are seeking your advice." Travis stretched long legs out under the table.

"Seems a lot of our guests are pinching your bottom."

"Yeah, about that. What did you mean 'this merchandise is all mine'?"

"Sexual harassment is unacceptable in my establishment. Just keeping my staff safe."

"Your staff? Hey, I'm a free agent. I'm only helping out. Because if I was officially on staff, I'd have to protest the boss lady with the roving hand."

"Okay, okay. So you enjoy being groped. Next time I won't infringe on your perverted pleasure."

"Groped! It was a pinch on the butt. I think you were jealous." His eyes twinkled.

"Jealous? Get real. As if! Jealous of four randy female snowmobilers?" Michaela struggled to sound indignant but felt a hot flush starting to rise up her neck.

"Okay, fine. We'll just say you really were concerned for my safety and leave it there. Let's get back to discussing the murder. Maybe at some point you'll have to discover who's been naughty and who's innocent in order to know which way to turn."

"You mean solve the case?" She guffawed, glad to get the subject away from Travis and the four female guests. "I'm no detective. I'll leave all that to the police."

"And if they come up with the wrong solution? Seems to me Corporal Palmer and Constable Roy don't know any of the suspects as well as you do. How could they? You went to school with most of them."

"I wouldn't know where to start."

"Okay, so maybe I'll help. But right now I've got dogs to tend."

****

"No more guests for two days!" Michaela sank down on the couch in the lounge and looked out at the coffee cups, utensils, and dessert plates waiting to be bussed. "Never mind that now, Travis." She stopped him as he reached for the plastic pan. "Come and sit. We've earned a few minutes with our feet up."

"You're the boss." He set it aside and took a chair across from her. "Business is good, right?"

"Very good, in no small way thanks to you." She smiled at him and he felt the glow.

"Glad to help. You did save me from a murder charge, remember?"

"About that. Travis, were you serious when you said we should try to find the murderer, that that's the only way we'll clear the air?"

"I think we can do it." The idea of being involved in a partnership with Michaela, any partnership, never mind one that could be exciting and maybe even dangerous, made his blood sing. "You know, the idea that a murderer is loose in the area might start to affect business."

"Now, there's a thought. Okay, Sherlock, where do we start?"

"Well, first, I think we should make a list of possible suspects, then establish their motives and windows of opportunity."

"Sounds like some kind of board game."

"Maybe, but we have to start with known facts before we begin questioning people and ferreting around for more information. Have you got a laptop?"

"Of course."

"Charged up?"

"Of course."

"Okay, then we're in business. Get it, and we'll start our lists."

She headed down the bedroom corridor. Travis watched her go, admiring once again the way her bottom filled out those expensive jeans.

"Mikey, are you here?" The door opened. Karen Dollard poked her head inside.

"She's gone to get her laptop. Come in. Join us. We're about to embark on our own investigation of Ralph's murder."

"Why?" The ranger advanced across the room, helmet under her arm, and stood behind the couch.

"Because a lot of innocent people are being placed under suspicion. Michaela can't defend them all."

"So that means she has a client?"

"Not really, unless you count me, but she's been asked for help by others."

"And she's refused?"

"Karen, what are you getting at? You weren't going to ask for Michaela's legal advice, were you?"

"No...yes...sort of. Travis, you remember that day when we swapped secrets...after I discovered you were dismantling Ralph's traps and I agreed to turn a blind eye to the situation? You didn't tell anyone what I told you, the reason why I let you keep on doing a number on Ralph?"

"Swore I wouldn't, didn't I?" He stood. "Karen, what's happened? Is someone giving you grief because…?"

"Hi." Michaela came into the room, laptop under her arm, a smile breaking over her face as she recognized her friend. "Travis, fire this up." She set the computer on the coffee table. "Karen, you can help us. Take off your jacket and get comfortable."

"Mikey…"

"Oh, come on! With Ralph out of the way and Travis not really a trap raider, you must have a few spare minutes."

"Okay." Karen removed her jacket and sat down. Travis resumed his seat and turned the computer to "blank document."

"Let's see. There's myself." Travis quickly typed his own name. "Possible reason to want to see Ralph Frame dead: abhorrence of trapping, plus the fact that he and Andy Murdoch recently beat the tar out of me. Who's next?"

"Might as well be me." Michaela drew a deep breath. "Hated him for having the Lodge closed down, and…"

"And for something that happened during your high school days?" Travis held his fingers poised over the keys and looked up at her.

"Okay, okay. Karen knows, so you may as well, too. We have to be honest or we'll never get anywhere." Michaela went to stare out into a blustery day. "I had a thing for bad boys when I was in high school, and Ralph was one of the wildest. When he offered me a ride home on his snowmobile after a Christmas dance, I didn't think twice. It was only when he drove down a road into the woods and stopped at a deserted cabin—the old Wilson place—that I realized what he wanted."

When she'd finished the tale, she looked down at her clasped hands and heaved a sigh.

"She's soft-peddling it, Travis." Karen's tone reflected bitterness. "He attacked her and beat her before she managed to get away. She had a dislocated shoulder and a major black eye, not to mention multiple scrapes and bruises. Nevertheless, she stopped his bleeding with snow, bound his wound with her scarf, and then drove him to town for medical help."

"Sweet Jesus! Why wasn't he charged with attempted rape?" Travis felt his gut knot. The man had almost, but maybe not quite, deserved what he'd gotten.

"If my parents had found out what really happened, I'd have been grounded for months. I was a teenager. I couldn't bear the thought. I told them I fell on some ice, dancing on the school steps. They believed me. Back then I was always getting into scrapes, wasn't I, Karen?"

"You sure were, Mikey." The ranger smiled ruefully. "But I guess that scar you put on Ralph's face left him forever bitter."

"I'm glad I didn't hear this story while he was alive." A nerve in Travis's jaw twitched. "Otherwise I might really be guilty of murder." He paused. "But didn't you recognize the place, Michaela, when you were there lately?"

"No." She looked up at him, frowning. "I've never been back."

"Mikey, Travis's cabin is the old Wilson place." Karen Dollard sounded incredulous. "I thought you knew."

"Oh, God!" She closed her eyes, and Travis saw her gulp. "That's why...that's why..."

"What, Mikey?" Karen sat down beside her.

"What's wrong?"

"I had a flash the first time I stepped into it… There was blood and terror, and I didn't know why."

"Flash?" Travis didn't understand.

"Mikey has always had some kind of sixth sense about good and evil," the ranger explained when her friend remained silent.

"Psychic?" He looked from Karen to Michaela.

"Go on, scoff. Every man I know does." Michaela strode across the room to stare out the window, arms crossed on her chest.

"I'm not about to scoff. I can't prove one way or the other regarding the existence of psychic phenomena. Therefore I have no right to deny the possibility."

"Really?" Michaela turned to him, eyes widening.

"Really. Now let's get on with our crime-solving." He typed rapidly.

"What motive did you give me?" Michaela moved to stand behind him. "Oh, right! I hated him because he was a bully!"

"Well, he was. No need for details."

"Put me down next, Travis." Both Michaela and Travis turned to stare at Karen. "You know the reason. I'll have to tell Mikey if I want her to help me out of the mess I'm in."

"Mess? Karen, what's happened?" Michaela stared at her friend. "Surely they can't think you…"

"Surely they can, Mikey. You see, they're only a bit of DNA away from proving Melissa is Ralph's daughter."

"Karen, no!"

"Mikey, yes. Look, you almost had a major moment with Ralph. The fact is, I actually did. It wasn't by force, either."

"But why? When?" Travis watched Michaela's face transformed by shock. She'd had no idea.

"It was the week after Andy jilted me for Jenny. I wasn't...myself. I felt I was the laughingstock of Carleton. I had a few drinks at the hotel bar. By the time Ralph came in, I'd had too many to be rational. We ended up in a room an hour later...and every night for the rest of that week."

"Oh, Karen, you must have been in such pain to..."

"To take up with the likes of Ralph Frame? Yes, I must have been. At first he was funny and charming and affectionate. On the last night he got very drunk and told me he'd had a bet with Andy that he could bed me on the rebound. It had been fun but, now that he'd won, he was finished with me."

"Oh, God, Karen! No wonder you didn't want to tell anyone who Melissa's father is. But how did you manage to keep it a secret? This seems like the type of thing Ralph would love to howl from the rooftops."

"He had no desire to pay child support or get caught into taking any kind of custodial responsibility. But now the whole thing has come to light, and I was dragged in for questioning this morning. That's why I came to see you, Mikey...to see if you'd represent me if I get called in again."

"But no one knew about your relationship with Ralph. Why would the police think you had anything to do with his death?"

"Apparently he bragged to Andy Murdoch shortly before he died. Seems they got into some kind of stupid, drunken argument about their virility. Andy bragged he had two kids while Ralph had none. Ralph shot back that Ranger Karen Dollard had had no trouble getting knocked up from him."

"So Andy told the police, in an effort to save his own skin."

"No, not Andy. Jenny. Apparently Andy told her. Jenny has always been afraid Andy and I will get back together, so when they questioned her, she blurted out that if anyone had a reason to hate and kill Ralph Frame, it was me, the mother of his bastard."

"Damn it!" Travis rubbed his hands along the legs of his jeans. "Scared people can be dangerous. Michaela, can you think of any possible damage control?"

"Maybe it won't be needed. The police haven't charged any of us yet...except you, Travis. Maybe they'll find the actual killer, and that will be the end of it. Since Ralph is dead, Karen and Melissa won't have to worry about any further trouble. Anyhow, we're going in circles." Michaela pushed back her hair. "I'm exhausted. Let's take a break. I'll get apple dumplings and coffee. I feel the need for some serious comfort food."

****

"Hello." The man stepped into the Lodge, helmet tucked under his arm and looked around. "Is Michaela Dunn here?"

Karen had left a half hour earlier. Travis had been polishing tables. When he heard a snowmobile approaching, he'd continued, thinking it was only another guest looking for a meal.

"She's doing up the rooms." He straightened and faced the newcomer. Tall and well built, with professionally streaked brown hair, the man wore a black leather snowmobile suit so new Travis wondered if all the price tags had been removed. "And you would be...?"

"Randall Kirby." Travis felt his insides go hollow. *Ah, hell!*

"I'll see if I can find her. Have a seat."

Travis headed down the corridor, annoyance, anger, and apprehension swirling into a bilious mix in his belly. So this was the BF, the sort-of-engaged-to guy. Definitely not the skinny, bespectacled little man Travis had hoped he was. But then, could he honestly have believed Michaela would take up with that kind of man?

Yeah, if he was kind and good and loved kids and animals.

"You have a visitor." Travis paused at the door of the room where Michaela was spreading a snow-white sheet over the bed. "From TO."

"Who?" She glanced up at him, reminding him of a deer in headlights. Not the expression of a woman with any hope of it being her lover. The swirling slowed to a churn.

"Randall Kirby, your sort-of fiancé." Although he hadn't intended it, bitterness colored his words. *Watch it, buddy. Not cool to get nasty.*

"Randy? What is he doing here?" She dropped the sheet, brushed past Travis where he stood in the doorway, and strode down the hall.

Didn't stop to check herself out in the mirror. Good. But that nickname! Hope he doesn't live up to it.

He followed her, telling himself he wasn't jealous, that she was a free agent, that she could do as she wished, that it was nothing to him.

"Randy." He got to the end of the corridor just in time to see Michaela pause a few feet from the newcomer. "What are you doing here?" She put her hands on her hips.

Good again. No rushing into his arms. No hugs, no kisses. Great, in fact.

"Michaela." Randall Kirby had removed his jacket to reveal a green cashmere sweater. In three long strides he crossed the room to gather her into his arms.

She remained with her hands on her hips. Randall Kirby slowly released her and stepped back to look down at her, his expression contorting into a puzzled frown. Travis stifled his satisfaction and stood back, hoping he looked as disinterested as he didn't feel.

"What's wrong, babe? Surely you didn't believe that crazy gossip about Melinda Bowes. Is that the real reason you left TO in such a rush?" A smug smile crept across his handsome features. "You were jealous, I knew it! I never thought you so altruistic as to give up your career to come down here into the boonies to help out an old aunt and uncle."

"Think again, Randy. That's exactly what I did do, am doing. And," she walked over to stand beside Travis. "Travis is helping me." She linked her arm into his and leaned her head against his shoulder.

Randall Kirby stared. Then he broke out laughing.

"Come on, Michaela! Are you telling me you're involved with this Grizzly Adams lookalike? God, he's little more than a caveman. You always did have a taste for the wild side, babe, but this is going way too far."

"Okay, Randy, that's enough. Travis recently saved my life and has been a good friend ever since. Tell me what you're doing here. Then I'll be grateful if you'd be on your way." Suddenly her annoyed tone changed so abruptly Travis glanced down at her. "It's not Mom or Dad? Has something happened to them?"

"Nothing more than a small piece in the Globe about a murder near a northern New Brunswick snowmobile lodge owned by the brother and sister-in-law of the famous Toronto criminal defense team of Michael Dunn and his lady wife. Nothing beyond the fact that the murder victim was trying to pressure Norman and Ida Dunn into selling out to him. Nothing beyond that article mentioning that Mike Dunn's daughter is currently running aforesaid Lodge after suddenly leaving the family practice. Although all this may seem trivial, you know your parents. Damage control, damage control, damage control. That's why I'm here."

"And you plan to do what?" Michaela's lips set into a hard line.

Good for me. The thought darted across Travis's mind.

"I'll have to ferret around, see if there's any way I can distance your name from this fiasco. I've already booked a room at the hotel in Carleton, but I'll need one here, as well. I'll be doing a lot of travelling back and forth."

"No, you won't." Michaela walked across the room and opened the door. "You'll be on the next flight back to Toronto. You can tell my mother and father that I'm just fine and perfectly capable of doing any necessary damage control all on my own."

Randall Kirby stared at her. Then a sardonic grin crossed his handsome features.

"Okay, fine. I'll go. But only as far as Carleton. I have a feeling you're going to need help, Michaela. When you do, I'm betting this mountain man won't be of much use."

Snatching up his jacket and helmet, he strode toward the door.

"His charms are really well hidden." Randall Kirby shot one more arrow of sarcasm before exiting the Lodge. "I assume he's hot in bed?"

"Get out!" Michaela grabbed a plate from the counter. Randall Kirby ducked before it crashed into the wall above his head.

"Still the same old Michaela!" Laughing, he slammed the door shut. "Can't wait until you come back to me. The make-up sex will be great."

As the sound of his snowmobile gunning out of the yard reached them, Michaela strode behind the counter. She stood gripping the edge of the dishwasher, her back to Travis, her shoulders rigid.

"So do you think we need Mr. Studio Tan and

166

Salon-Streaked Hair?" Travis hadn't meant to blurt out sarcastic remarks. but the guy had provoked him to the core. He'd done well not to take a swing at him.

"Travis, I'm sorry." She turned slowly to face him. "He had no right to take verbal swipes at you. No right or reason."

"Don't worry about it." He grinned. "I've been insulted a lot better than that. I'm flattered he thinks I have to be super good in bed to make up for my mangy looks."

Green eyes met blue for a moment. A grin slowly spread over her face to match his.

"You're a good man, Travis MacDonald. I don't care where you came from or what you did before you arrived at the Promise. I like you."

"Just like?" He crossed his arms on his chest and planted his feet firmly apart.

"I'm not in a position to offer more." *Do I see regret in those emerald eyes?* "After we get this all sorted out and Uncle Norm and Aunt Ida return, I'll be heading back to Toronto. I promised my father."

"And you were going to tell me this when?"

"Travis, it's not like you and I are an item. Let's just take one day at a time."

"Why do I get the distinct feeling you don't want to go back, that somewhere along the line you've made a deal with a devil named Randall Kirby?"

"Try Michael Dunn." She drew a deep breath. "But right now I'm going into Carleton to talk to Jenny and Andy Murdoch. Someone has to advise them of the damage they're doing, throwing wild innuendoes around."

"Sounds as if they're running scared. Do you think one of them might be guilty? You know them both a lot better than I do."

"I think they're each afraid the other may be guilty, and that's making them desperate. After all, they have two little girls. I'm hoping neither killed Ralph Frame, but they each had reason to hate and fear him."

"And if you discover one of them did?"

"I'll cross that bridge when I come to it. Hopefully I'll never get to the river."

****

"Jenny?" Michaela smiled as the woman opened the door of the elegant multi-story house on the outskirts of Carleton. "Do you have a few minutes to talk to me?"

"I...I'm just about to go to Mom's to pick up the girls, Mikey." Jenny Murdoch pushed her hair back from her forehead and held onto the door handle with the other.

"This will only take a minute. Please, Jenny. It's important."

"Well, okay. Come into the den."

Michaela pulled off her snow-crusted boots. She'd walked the short distance from where she'd left her snowmobile at the garage. It hadn't seemed worth starting up her uncle's old truck. She placed her boots on a mat by the door and followed Jenny into a room where a black leather couch and two matching chairs semi-circled before a wide white-brick fireplace. A polished oak floor reflected the flames crackling on the hearth. On the walls were various trophies: deer heads, fish, and even a set of moose antlers. Michaela winced.

"Sit down." Jenny indicated a place on the couch as she sat on one of the chairs. "What is it, Mikey?" Her voice rose hopefully. "Have you decided to be our attorney?"

"No, I haven't. Is Andy here? I'd like to speak to him, as well."

"He just stepped out." Her tone became belligerent. "So why have you come?"

"I'm concerned about the innuendoes you and

Andy have been spreading about a number of us who knew Ralph Frame and had reason to dislike him. They're hurting innocent people."

"But we've only said what's true. Travis MacDonald had every reason to hate Ralph. And Karen Dollard is the mother of his child, a child he refused to acknowledge. As for you, Mikey, you had a few motives of your own to want Ralph dead."

"But you have no definitive proof. Travis was arrested largely on Andy's claims about his having trouble with Ralph over traps and a fight where Travis was injured."

"You're not mentioning the fact that Travis MacDonald was having an affair with Amanda Best." Jenny glanced smugly over at Michaela. "You may think you're the only woman he's had since he came to the Promise, but you're not. Amanda told Ralph and Ralph told Andy that she and Mountain Man have been an item almost from the day he arrived."

"Travis denies it. I believe him."

"I wouldn't, if I were you." Jenny shrugged and stood. "Now if that's all you want…"

"Jenny, if you know who killed Ralph Frame, if you're certain of it, you have an obligation to come forward, even if…"

"Even if it's my husband?" Her voice rose shrilly. "Well, it wasn't Andy. And it wasn't me. So you can just get out of my house, Ms. Dunn. You're no longer welcome here."

"I'm sorry." Michaela got up and went into the foyer. She was pulling on her boots when the door opened. Andy Murdoch stepped inside, accompanied by Constable Roy and Corporal Palmer.

"There she is." Andy Murdoch pointed at Michaela. "There's the woman who killed my buddy Ralph."

Chapter Fourteen

"Let's go over this again, Miss Dunn." Corporal Palmer clasped his hands behind his back and looked down at Michaela seated in a hard, wooden chair in front of his desk in the interrogation room of the RCMP detachment. "You threatened Ralph Frame much more recently than a dozen years ago. Two witnesses who heard you threaten him the day before he died have come forward."

"Ralph's lady friends from his chalet," she breathed. "I'm guessing Andy Murdoch brought them to your attention."

"Not relevant." Corporal Palmer drew a deep breath. "The salient point is they're ready to testify that you threatened to kill Mr. Frame only hours before he died."

"I spoke out of anger. I had no intention..."

A knock at the door of the interview room interrupted. The detachment secretary stuck her head inside.

"Miss Dunn's attorney has arrived," she said. "He's demanding to be present during the interview."

"Of course." Corporal Palmer heaved a sigh. "Show him in."

Michaela caught her breath as Randall Kirby, impeccably dressed in a business suit, briefcase in hand, stepped into the room.

"Randall Kirby, Ms. Dunn's attorney." He addressed the two Mounties crisply, offering his hand. "I'll be advising the lady."

****

170

"What are you doing here?" Michaela stopped short on the steps of the RCMP detachment. Travis MacDonald leaned against the railing at the bottom.

"I wanted to know how things turned out." He straightened and cast that incredible blue-eyed gaze over her.

"He thought you might need professional help after the convenience store owner saw you in the back of the patrol car." Randall Kirby put a possessive arm about Michaela's shoulders. "He sent the news to MacDonald."

"Seemed the right thing to do." Travis shrugged. The detached coldness in the words sent a chill washing over her. *Not very caring. Definitely not very caring.*

"What about the Lodge?" She struggled to dispel the icy feeling that embraced her. "Did you leave the door unlocked, with the sign for visitors to…"

"I left it in good hands. Ranger Dollard is holding the fort."

"Karen? But how could she spare the time? How…"

"Without Ralph and me to chase after, her job has become a lot less time consuming. You said so yourself. She happened along just as I got the news from Sam. She said she could handle the Lodge while I went to town. Everything okay with you?"

"Thanks to her brilliant attorney, Ms. Dunn is in the clear." Randall Kirby hefted his briefcase and winked at her. "We'll discuss my bill later. Right now, how about dinner at the hotel? I'm sure this Ranger person and MacDonald can handle your backwoods bed and breakfast for a while longer."

"No problem." Travis turned away before Michaela could speak. "Go for it. I hear they serve a great beef tenderloin. Ranger Dollard and I will whip up a little something back at the Lodge." He gave the last sentence a deliberate sexual spin and winked at Randall Kirby. "See you later, boss lady."

"Travis, wait!" She started after him, but Randall caught her by a sleeve.

"Come on, Michaela. Let him go. Damn, he's little more than a Neanderthal. Grow up and start looking at men who shave and bathe."

"Just what do you mean by that?"

"I overheard a bit of what those officers were saying about your past relationship with Ralph Frame. Apparently he was a misfit, too. This penchant for wild men does little to enhance your image as a member of one of Toronto's most prestigious law firms."

"So you're saying I should set my sights on someone like you?"

"You did once. It can happen again. You'll be coming back to Toronto soon. Your father told me about your deal. I know how adamant you are about promises...of all types."

He tried to take her into his arms, but she pushed away.

"We'll have to wait and see, Randall. At the moment the ambience is all wrong to start me seriously thinking about highrises, three-piece suits, and claustrophobic courtrooms. Let me finish up what I have to do here. When I get back to Toronto, we'll see what develops. Deal?"

She held out her hand.

He hesitated, then took it in his leather-gloved one.

"I don't have time for dinner at the hotel." She glanced after Travis retreating down the street. "I have to get back to the Lodge."

"Actually, it's not a good idea for me, either. I have a ton of e-mails to answer. It's better if I order a sandwich from room service."

He trotted down the steps and strode off toward the hotel. He hadn't bothered to ask if she had a way back to the Promise.

With a sigh, she hunched her shoulders against the rising wind, wrapped her arms around her body, and turned toward the garage. She was cold and tired and hungry. She hoped her old snowmobile would start. It had sputtered and coughed all the way into Carleton.

"Need a lift, lady?" An SUV had materialized out of the blowing snow. Doc stuck his head out the open window next to Travis and barked a greeting before his master continued, "We're on our way to collect the rest of the team and the sled. We'll give you a ride back to the Lodge. You can leave your snowmobile at the garage. Duffy McLean says it's badly in need of a tune-up. We'll come back for it tomorrow."

"Thanks." The idea of heading home beneath a warm rug, safe in Travis's care, brought a cozy feeling flooding over her. She scuttled around to the passenger door and climbed in. He'd cranked up the heat. The warmth felt like heaven. She pulled off her gloves and rubbed cold hands together.

"Hungry?" He glanced over at her.

"Ravenous. Must be something about a police interrogation that spurs the appetite." She slanted him a sideways glance and grinned.

"I think it's inspired by the relief that comes when it's over."

"You've had the experience?"

"Don't you remember? You bailed me out."

"I meant previous to that."

"Always trying to dig into my mysterious past." He swung the truck around a corner and into the McDonald's drive-thru. "Nice try. How about a McHappy meal or whatever it's called?"

"Sounds good, only I think that's a kid's lunch. I'm in the mood for a biggie everything."

"Okay. I'll see if they can fire up the grill."

173

Doc, sitting between them, barked sharply.

"Okay, okay. You can have a cheeseburger. Just remember not to tell the rest of the team."

****

"You're pretty darn amazing, Travis MacDonald, do you know?" Michaela polished off her fries, rolled her hamburger wrapper into a ball, and shoved the garbage into a paper bag.

"How so?" He set aside his soft drink.

"Like some kind of super hero, you always turn up when I need you...or at least when you think I need you."

"Are you telling me you didn't need Kirby's help back there at RCMP headquarters?"

"I could have managed."

"What about that old adage that only a fool acts as her own attorney—or lawyer—or however it goes?"

"Yes, well, like most clichés, it's riddled with exceptions." She gathered up the garbage, pushed Doc's exploring nose aside, and opened the door to scamper through swirling snow to the nearest garbage can.

"Whew! Quite a blow coming up. We should be heading home." She scrambled back into the SUV.

"Okay." He turned the key in the ignition, glancing sideways at her. "When are you heading back to Toronto?"

"Two weeks. Uncle Norm and Aunt Ida will be back from Florida. They won't need me here any longer."

"You'll be glad to go?" He put the truck in gear and started across the snow-crusted lot to the road.

"You knew I was only filling in."

"Sure." He turned the vehicle down a road empty of traffic in the encroaching storm. "I thought you might want to see this thing out, discover who actually did murder Ralph Frame."

"I will." She leaned back in the seat and closed her eyes with a sigh as Doc lay down and rested his head in her lap. "We should be able to solve the case in fourteen days. Right now, I'm tired. I'm going to catch forty winks."

She eased an eye open just enough to see grim lines tighten about his lips. *He doesn't want me to go.* The idea sent a pain like heartburn through her chest. *And I don't want to, either.*

****

The storm had intensified by the time Travis stowed the truck inside the garage. Michaela helped harness the team, her efforts awkward and often needing correction, but when she saw the pleased expression her attempts brought to Travis's face she continued to struggle with dancing, eager dogs and tangling harness.

I could get to love life with this man. Then*: Stop it, Michaela Dunn. He's a hermit who doesn't want a lawyer in his life. What do you know about him, anyway? He could be a serial killer hiding from justice in the backwoods. Just because we've become friends, come to care about each other's welfare, doesn't mean...*

"Climb aboard!" His voice brought her out of her thoughts. "The storm's getting worse."

Obediently she got into the sled and pulled the robe up to her chin.

"Hike, hike!"

The sled lurched at Travis's command. They sped off into a world of howling, trackless white.

Although she could see only a few feet ahead, Michaela didn't worry. She trusted the man to get her safely back to the Promise. She'd have been lost without him, both figuratively and literally, on more occasions than she cared to count in the past couple of weeks. *He* hadn't left her cold, tired, and hungry on the steps of the courthouse. *He* hadn't been uncaring of her need to get back to the Lodge before the storm isolated it.

She snuggled deep beneath the insulated blanket with a sigh. It felt good to be cared for, cared about. If only he cared for her as a woman and not simply as another human being.

"Hike, hike!" The sled lurched, then stopped. Travis floundered past her toward Doc and his team. "Hike, hike!" Again the sled jerked but didn't move forward.

"Travis, what is it?" Michaela scrambled out of the sled and sank to her thighs in powdery, swirling snow.

"Snow's too deep and soft," he shouted above the roaring gale. "The dogs can't pull a load." He turned to her, beard and eyebrows iced with snow. She remembered the day he'd found her in that blizzard. A chill of apprehension washed over her.

"So I'll walk with you." She tightened the drawstrings on her hood. "Come on, it can't be far." She grinned up at him with a face that felt as if it were frozen and cracking. "Hike, hike, MacDonald."

His mouth quirked in one corner. He caught at Doc's harness and pulled the dog forward. "Hike, hike!" he yelled as she floundered into his footprints.

****

"We made it!" Travis halted the exhausted team in late evening darkness at the foot of the Lodge steps. "Go on inside and get warm. Lights are on and smoke is coming from the chimney. Ranger Dollard is apparently still on duty."

"No, first I'll help you settle the team in the barn." Although she longed for the comforts of a fire and dry, warm clothes, Michaela was determined to finish this expedition shouldering equal responsibility.

"Okay. That tone tells me it would be a waste of breath to argue. Especially when I don't have a whole lot left to spare."

At the barn he led the weary dogs inside, pulled off his mittens, and began to release harnesses. Michaela saw his fingers were stiff from cold. She set about helping him. Hers weren't much better, but she managed to free three of the dogs and get them settled in straw-filled stalls.

"Now we feed them?" She headed for the food Travis had stored in the tack room.

"No, not right away. It's not good to feed exhausted animals. I'll come back later. Right now, they need rest." He indicated the big dogs stretched out in the bedding. "Come on, Doc. You can come up to the Lodge."

He paused at the barn door and looked down at her.

"You're a pretty darned remarkable woman, Michaela Dunn." He reached out and ran a finger down her cold face. "Even if you are big city and used to smell like it."

Her breath caught in her throat as he looked down at her with those amazing blue eyes. Was he going to kiss her? *Please, please, don't turn away, Travis. Not now!*

But he did, opening the door for her to precede him outside into the savagery of the storm.

Damn, damn, damn!
****

Their brash entrance, snow-caked and ghost white, startled Karen Dollard, who'd been reading in front of the fire.

"Good lord!" she gasped, jumping to her feet. "I was hoping and praying you'd decided to overnight in Carleton. I never thought anyone could make it through a storm like this."

"I had an excellent guide." Michaela began to remove her frozen outerwear. "And seven wonderful dogs. But we could both go for a hot toddy."

"Afraid I don't know how to make such a thing." Karen shook snow from Michaela's outdoor garments and took them to hang by the fire to dry.

"Ah, but I do." Michaela rubbed her hands together and grinned wickedly. "You two get comfortable. I'll find the makings in Uncle Norm's private stock."

She scuttled off down the bedroom corridor while Travis finished hanging up his snow-crusted clothes by the hearth.

She got the brandy bottle from her uncle's apartment, then went into her own room for a quick shower. Dressed in a comfortable sweatsuit and moccasins, she returned to the main living room and started her preparations in the kitchen area.

"One absolutely amazing hot toddy coming up," she called out to the pair sitting in front of the fire.

"Nothing too strong for me." Travis stretched long legs out toward the fire. "I still have the dogs to feed and water."

"I can do that." Karen stood and headed for the door. "It's been boring, sitting around here all afternoon. I need to move around."

"You know how much to give them? Don't overfeed, or they'll…"

"Travis, take it easy. Remember, you showed me the day I brought Melissa to your cabin?"

"Right." He settled back with a sigh. "Thanks, Karen. I owe you another one."

"Forget who owes who, Travis. It's gotten way too complicated. Mikey, save one of those toddies for me. I'll be staying the night. I'm not about to venture out in this weather."

"What about Melissa? With her grandmother?"

"Safely and happily with Grammie. I drove over to your place this afternoon, Travis, and called her to tell her not to worry if I didn't get back. I knew a storm was brewing. Now behave yourselves, you two.

I'll be right back." She pulled the door open on the black, blustery night and vanished into the storm.

"Here." Michaela approached Travis with two steaming mugs. "Get this down you, my lad, and you'll live to fight another day."

He sniffed it suspiciously. "I don't know if I should. The last time I drank one of your potions, I crossed the lake and got myself accused of murder."

"Well, you're not going anywhere farther than a room down the corridor tonight, so what's to worry about? The only thing that can happen is that you'll have a great sleep and wake up feeling ready to take on the world. Or"—she sat down opposite him—"are you afraid of getting tipsy alone with two beautiful women? Are you afraid we'll take advantage of you?"

"That would be a dream come true for most guys." He took a sip, winced, and frowned over at her.

"But you're not most guys?"

"No."

"Explain."

"I'm the monogamous type."

"You mean one at a time? Or forever?"

"Both."

"Wow. Not many of you left."

"I guess not."

"Who was she?"

"What?"

"Who was the woman you decided was the forever one? It's obvious it didn't work out, or you wouldn't be up here living like a hermit. I'm guessing she was a city girl, maybe a lawyer with a preference for expensive perfume?"

He took a gulp from the tankard, choked, and stood.

"I'll finish this in my room. Come on, Doc."

"Afraid it might loosen your tongue, MacDonald? Afraid you might actually tell me what turned you off women?"

"Possibly. No point in taking chances. See you in the morning."

She watched as he disappeared down the bedroom corridor. *Why did I start cross-examining him? Michaela Dunn, you should know by now when to ease up on an interrogation.*

By the time Karen returned from taking care of the dogs, Michaela had finished her drink.

"Where's Travis?" Karen doffed her outerwear.

"I scared him off to bed with questions about his past." Michaela felt mellow and talkative. "Here's your drink. Come and sit with me, Ranger Dollard. Tell me all you know about the mysterious hermit of Promise Lake."

"Michaela Dunn, are you falling for him?" She looked squarely into her friend's eyes. "Don't try to lie. I know you too well to be fooled."

"Okay, maybe, possibly, I don't know." She leaned back on the couch and closed her eyes. "Oh, God, Karen, you know my track record with men...always the wrong one. Until I met Randall, that is. He seemed perfect. Law-abiding, respectable, eager to climb the legal ladder to success..."

"But?"

"Yes, of course, there is a 'but' coming. He's emotionally cold and professionally calculating. We never laugh together, never do anything crazy, never have any fun. And I've definitely never partnered with him in the way I do with..."

"Travis." Karen finished the sentence and grinned. "I'm not even going to inquire about physically. Even with that hair and beard, Travis MacDonald can put that artificially browned, beauty-parlor-streaked Kirby to shame on his worst day. I met him in town shortly after he arrived. He was asking directions to the Lodge."

"You're saying Travis is naturally sexy,

naturally earthy, naturally virile."

"Yeah. Mikey, he's all you've ever looked for in a man...good looks and an untamed spirit, not to mention a mysterious past. But best of all, he's a truly good man who cares about this place and you. You could do a whole lot worse."

"I could, couldn't I?" She stood a little unsteadily. "The only trouble is, he's not interested. Wow, I'd better head off to bed. I'm so bushed that one drink hit me like gangbusters. See you in the morning, Ranger Dollard. And thanks for everything...including your well intentioned but inapplicable advice on the man in bed down the corridor."

Chapter Fifteen

"Guests due for lunch." Travis greeted her with the announcement when he entered the Lodge. She hadn't heard him get up and go out.

" 'Good morning' is a more traditional greeting." She turned to fill a cup from the percolator on the counter.

"Sorry. Guess I'm getting into this innkeeper thing too intensely. Good morning. I've been checking on the dogs."

"No, I'm sorry." She turned back to face him. "I'm just grumpy. This murder case is getting to me. Thanks for making the coffee, by the way."

"No problem." He shucked his outerwear and came to pour himself a cup. "Can't say I enjoy being a suspect either. So where did we leave off in our last discussion?"

"We were convinced that you, Karen, and I are innocent. Not quite so about Andy and Jenny Murdoch, although frankly I don't think either of them has the inner fortitude to do it."

"Then who does that leave?" He sat down at the nearest table.

"What about your lover, Amanda Frame?" She skewered him with a look.

"Lover? What are you on about, woman? I've already told you she's blowing smoke. I'm the hermit of Promise Lake, remember? Taking lovers isn't in the job description."

"Maybe not, but what has it been, over four years since you came up here? Doesn't seem likely you've remained celibate all that time."

"Doesn't it? Let me tell you, it's perfectly possible when a man has been betrayed and belittled by a woman so severely that even…" He stopped and turned to look out the window.

"That even her choice of perfume turns his stomach?" She had a flash of understanding.

"Yeah, even that."

"And when we first met…"

"You were drenched in it."

"Hardly drenched. How could I have known?"

"You couldn't. So that's one mystery solved. Let's move on to the much more important one at hand."

"But…" She burned to continue the questioning, to find out more about this woman who had done something so despicable, so terrible she'd driven a man who'd cared for her—Michaela wouldn't think loved—deep into hiding in the wilderness.

"Come on, Michaela." He swung back to face her, stubborn determination scowling his face. "Moving on."

"Okay, okay." She threw up her free hand, took a sip of coffee, and turned back to the stove. "Let's deduce while I make us a couple of omelets. You know"—she held up the cup—"this is good. You're learning."

"I'm glad. Now let's get to work. Let's start by putting Amanda Best on our list. For some reason she's trying to make me look guilty by claiming an affair we never had, although why that would inspire me to kill her brother I don't know."

"How do you explain that oh-so-sexy nightie she brought out of your room?"

Michaela cracked eggs into a bowl.

"Think, woman! She brought it with her. Lots of room in snowsuit pockets, and from what you've described, it wouldn't take up all that much space."

"I suppose." Michaela began whipping the eggs with more than necessary vehemence.

"You know, looking at this objectively, I'm probably the most logical suspect." He replenished his coffee and sat down before continuing. "I was in the vicinity at the time. You witnessed my crossing the lake that night. Ralph and I were enemies. He and his friend had beat the tar out of me just days before. Andy Murdoch heard me threaten to kill him over the trap lines. So there you have it, motive and opportunity, the two prime ingredients to prove murder."

"But forensic evidence has already proven it wasn't your gun that killed Ralph."

"The gun they *found*. What's to say I didn't have another one, a hand gun, secreted somewhere? If Colin Best hadn't been afraid of your father and out to ingratiate himself with the Premier, he might have opened up that line of inquiry."

"I'm sure Corporal Palmer thought of that possibility but chose not to pursue the investigation for two very good reasons. First, I don't believe he was ever convinced of your guilt. Second, finding a hand gun hidden away in the Promise Wilderness by a man who knows the area like his own backyard would be like finding a single particular snowflake in a blizzard."

"Makes sense. Moving on, who else could possibly want Ralph dead? Others who may have owed him money because of those poker games? Some other woman he molested? Or maybe it was someone he cheated at business. He did run the only recreation vehicle business in Carleton."

"I'm sure the Mounties have already checked out those avenues." Michaela placed a skillet on the stove. "No, I feel it's someone we know."

"Feel?" He narrowed his eyes as he looked over at her. "What are you saying, that your sixth sense is telling you who's naughty or nice?"

"No...yes...I don't know." She paused and faced

him squarely. "Okay, you may as well know. It's partly why I'm here. My father banished me because I told him I felt a certain client of his was guilty of a particularly heinous crime. I told him he shouldn't defend him, even though I had no tangible proof of the man's guilt."

"Oh, oh. I can see where that kind of logic could get you into deep trouble with a hard-nosed defense attorney like Michael Dunn."

"You know my father?" Astonishment made the sentence come out in a gasp.

"By reputation. Doesn't most of Canada?"

"Why do I get the feeling you had to do a back flip to land on your feet after that one? You lived in Toronto, didn't you? Good lord, Travis, don't tell me you once had need of my father's services."

"Look, we're straying from our discussion. You were saying you have this sixth sense that tells you..."

"No, I did not. I should never have confided in you." She poured the beaten eggs into the skillet. "I don't have spider instincts that start tingling in the presence of a criminal."

"Spider instincts?"

"Oh, don't act so sophisticated! Don't tell me you haven't seen the movie *Spider-Man* or read a single comic!"

"Oh, yeah, right. Spidy sense. That guy."

She caught the chuckle in his voice and turned on him, prepared to be angry. Their eyes met. Suddenly she was chuckling, too.

He stood and rounded the counter to take the bowl from her hands and place it on the counter. Gathering her into his arms, he drew her close and lowered his head until he was kissing her neck.

"Feeling anything now?" His voice was deep and sensuous. "Can you tell if I'm in the good or the evil category?"

She gasped as he nipped at her ear.

"Tingling yet?" He adjusted himself against her and raised his head to look down into her eyes.

"Yes, oh, yes." She pulled him down into a kiss that turned the tingle to an all-out shock wave.

The sound of approaching snowmobiles pulled them apart.

"Damn. Breakfast guests." Michaela patted her hair and hoped her lips didn't look freshly, decidedly, kissed.

"To be continued," he grinned, stepping back. "Definitely to be continued."

****

Guests filled the following day and night. After they'd gone, Michaela came outside to where Travis, waving the last guest goodbye, had stopped beside his dogs. Exhausted from taking people for sunrise rides, the malamutes had flopped down on the snow, tongues lolling out of their mouths. The wilderness glistened in the sunlight of a beautiful winter day.

"I'm going to Carleton." Dressed in snowmobile clothing, she carried her helmet under her arm. "I'll ferret around and see what I can learn about anyone who had a grudge against Ralph Frame. Think you can hold down the fort?"

"Definitely. But I thought maybe you and I might spend a little quality time together now that the Lodge has emptied. Take up where we left off, that kind of thing."

"About that. Travis, I've been thinking."

"Damn, here it comes. It's never good when a woman uses that sentence."

"You're right. It isn't. You may as well know I'm not into quickie affairs. That's all there ever could be for us. I'm headed back to Toronto in less than two weeks; you're determined to stay here. Having a casual fling might be okay for you, but it won't work for me. I'm into the HEA stuff at this phase of my life."

"HEA?" He gave her a quizzical look.

"Happily ever after." She brushed past him, putting on her helmet. "See you later."

She mounted her snowmobile and revved the motor with more than necessary vehemence. It did nothing to relieve the sick feeling in her heart.

****

"Mikey." Andy Murdoch slid onto the bench opposite her in the booth she was occupying at McDonald's Restaurant. "I hear you've been asking around town about Ralph, about anyone who held a grudge against him."

"I have." She bit into her hamburger, chewed for a moment. "And that concerns you why?"

"Because you're stirring up a lot of dirt that would be better left alone. Ralph's got a sister, you know."

"A sister who's busy telling anyone who will listen that she and Travis MacDonald had a torrid affair. I'd hardly call her grieving."

"Yeah, well, Mandy can be a bit heartless."

"What about you? You don't appear incapacitated with sorrow. He was your best friend, wasn't he?"

"I guess." Andy drew invisible pictures on the tabletop with his thumb. "But I wasn't blind to the bastard he could be." He looked up at her, eyes suddenly bright. "He bragged to me about how you came on to him...Michaela Dunn, daughter of one of the town's leading families."

"I made a very big mistake accepting a snowmobile ride from Ralph when I was in high school." Michaela faced him squarely. "That in no way gave him an excuse to attack me."

"Yeah, well, Ralphie told it another way, Mikey. He said you did most of the attacking, and then when things started getting serious you lost your nerve and hit him. He never did forgive you for putting that scar down his face."

"I'm sorry about that, but he gave me no choice. Ralph must really have been scrounging for something that would save his flagging reputation with the ladies, to come up with a whopper like that."

Although outrage was threatening to clog her throat, Michaela kept her cool and calmly crumpled the wrapper from her hamburger into a ball. "May I treat you to lunch, Andy? Or are you headed home to a romantic moment with your wife, now that Ralph's chalet can no longer offer any of its charms?"

Remembering the two women in body-hugging clothes she'd seen at the chalet, the witnesses to her death threat, she looked over at him, narrowing her eyes.

"You always did have a really nasty way with words, Mikey." He shot to his feet, his face red and contorted. "Just watch where you stick your nose around this town. Remember, no one knows anything about Travis MacDonald...not where he came from or why. He's probably a fugitive, hiding behind all that hair. He's the guy who murdered Ralph."

"You're floundering, trying to pin the murder on someone else. The more you do, the more I'm getting skeptical of your own innocence." Michaela stood and faced him squarely.

"You're so crazy about Travis MacDonald, you wouldn't believe he killed Ralph if you'd caught him standing over him with a smoking gun. Just don't go trying to build a case against either my wife or me, Miss TO Lawyer. It won't work. You don't live here anymore. The locals will support their own."

"It'll be a sad day when justice is meted out by geographic residency. I have to be going. I have more people to see, more questions to ask."

"You and Travis had better watch your backs!" he yelled after her as she headed for the door. Customers turned to stare at him. "You'll be sorry if you keep throwing suspicion on a lot of innocent people."

Stupid, stupid man. Michaela strode out of the restaurant and headed for her uncle's Jeep. *To issue threats in front of a roomful of witnesses. He must be desperate.*

"Mikey!" Amanda Best's voice hailed her as she was fitting the key into the driver's side lock.

Damn!

"I assume you're heading up to the Lodge?" The woman dressed in an elegant, calf-length fur coat caught up to her breathlessly, a small shopping bag clutched in black leather gloves. She smelled of something heavy and sensuous.

"Yes, I am, Mandy. What is it you want?"

"Here." She thrust the container into Michaela's hand. "A little something for Travis, to cheer him during this dreary investigation."

Michaela looked down at the glittering black faux-leather bag with the logo of the town's only sex shop on its side.

"A little reminder of happier days and a preview of things to come." She winked at Michaela. She gave her long, salon-blonded hair a shampoo-commercial toss and sauntered away.

Damn the woman! She'd been a tramp and a bitch in high school. Apparently nothing had changed. She opened the Jeep's door and flung the bag into the passenger seat.

By the time she pulled into the garage to collect her snowmobile she'd calmed down. A slow smile slid over her lips. It might be fun to see what was in the bag. And still more fun to watch Travis's reaction to it.

Chapter Sixteen

"I have a gift for you." Michaela sauntered into the Lodge twirling the bag in her fingers.

"You bought me something?" He straightened from where he'd been replenishing the fire on the lounge hearth. The eagerness and pleasure in his tone daunted her. She was being mean.

"No, but Amanda Frame did." She held it out to him.

He stared.

"Well, take it. It won't bite...at least I don't think it will."

His face a quizzical mix of annoyance and chagrin, he crossed the room and took it from her.

"Well, aren't you going to open it?" Michaela cocked her head to one side and gave him a sly glance.

" Maybe later."

"Oh, come on, Travis. If there really is nothing between you and her, the contents might be good for a laugh. But if you're lying..."

"Okay, okay." He opened the top, riffled through the black tissue paper inside, and let out an expletive Michaela had never heard him use.

Muttering more outrage, he strode to the blazing fire on the hearth and thrust bag and contents into it.

"Travis, no! Not before you let me see..."

Michaela rushed forward too late to save the flaming parcel.

"Darn! Now I'll never know what turns you on!" She feigned disappointment.

"Well, that stuff wouldn't, so you missed out on nothing." Long strides took him back into the restaurant, where he began to dress in his outerwear.

"Where are you going? Come on, Travis. There's no need to get huffy. I was just teasing."

"Yeah, well, I think I need some time to myself. I'm heading back to my cabin."

"When will you be back?" She followed him to the door, feeling concern puckering her face. The idea of him leaving sent a hollow feeling wafting over her.

"I'll be around if you need me." He slapped on his false fur hat.

"Travis, don't go..." She caught him by his sleeve.

"And if I said that to you, 'Don't go back to Toronto, Michaela Dunn,' what would you say?"

Her hand released him and fell to her side. She dropped her gaze to the boards beneath her feet.

"I thought so." He went out, slamming the door after him.

****

Michaela made a ham sandwich and a cup of tea. That was all the supper she felt she could stomach after Travis's bitter leave-taking. She knew there was no solution to their relationship, yet it hurt, hurt, hurt. Leaving Randall Kirby in Toronto had been nothing like this. In fact, it had come as a relief after his constant pressuring her to marry him. He hadn't loved her. He simply wanted to be a permanent part of the most successful team of criminal defense attorneys in the country.

She'd been on the verge of agreeing. After all, wasn't it about time she abandoned her dreams of a hero rushing in on a white horse, a man of mystery as well as of honor, a man who could make her senses tingle with a single kiss?

Then along came Travis MacDonald. Even if his team of malamutes was white only when snow-crusted, he did drive an ivory-colored SUV—and he had the power to propel her senses right off the radar with a kiss. His mysterious past intrigued her more than she cared to admit. His treatment of people and animals branded him a man of honor and integrity. What more could she want?

Out of that miserable promise, that's what. But if she hadn't made it, Travis would most likely still be under arrest for murder, maybe even on his way to trial, his name forever smeared no matter what the outcome. He'd saved her life, she'd saved his. They were even. If only she hadn't fallen in love with him!

She choked on her sandwich. *What was that?* Had she just admitted she loved a man she'd known only a couple of weeks? A man who'd originally deceived her, lied to her about his way of life—a man who'd made it clear he'd never settle for a Toronto attorney.

The sound of an approaching snowmobile broke into her thoughts. It drew to a stop at the Lodge steps. Footsteps thudded up onto the verandah. Randall Kirby stepped into the room, snowmobile helmet under his arm.

"Michaela, I had to see you. I have to leave for Toronto first thing tomorrow." He pulled off his mittens and jacket. "I want to settle things between us before I leave."

He took a small box from his pants' pocket, snapped it open, and removed a ring. He crossed the room and caught her left hand in his. "I want to be waiting for my future bride in two weeks' time at Pearson International."

"No!" She jerked back when he tried to slide the diamond band onto her third finger.

"Come on, Michaela. Be sensible. You know it's

what we both were planning, what your parents expect." Annoyance flooded across his handsome features. "We've got a big future, you and I. For God's sake…!"

His voice rose as she whirled away from him and strode behind the counter.

"I can't." She swung back to face him. "I'm sorry."

"But before you left Toronto…"

"Things were different then."

"Ah, I see." His eyes narrowed, his face contorting into a sneer. "Different before you met Nature Boy, before you got into some hot, primitive affair with him, is that it? Well, let me tell you, Ms. Dunn, you're not fitted for life in the backwoods. As for that hairy ape you've taken up, he hardly looks like something ready to mate for life. I'd be willing to bet he has all the loyalty of one of his sled dogs chasing anything in heat."

"Get out! Right now!" Michaela rounded the counter and advanced toward him, rage filling every inch of her body. "Travis MacDonald is a decent man, a man who didn't leave me cold and tired and hungry on the steps of a courthouse simply because I refused his invitation to dinner. Travis has stuck by me through all the problems I've had since I came here. And for your information, although you don't deserve it, I'm not having an affair with him. We're just good friends who can rely on each other."

"Okay, okay!" He raised his hands in a defensive gesture. "But I can't go now, tonight. Listen to that wind. Drifting snow will have obscured the trail. I'm no woodsman. I'd be lost in five minutes."

Michaela drew a deep breath and listened. It definitely was blowing hard enough to cover the trail back to Carleton.

"Very well." She turned away. "You can have Room Two, on the left. I'll leave sandwiches and coffee outside your door before I go to bed. Just get yourself down there and don't show your face until morning. Otherwise, I may feel obliged to chuck you out, gale or no gale."

****

Michaela was preparing breakfast when she heard dogs yelping. Her heart did a flip. *Damn! What was that? I'm no teenager with her first crush...*

When the door opened and Travis MacDonald entered, it happened again. Remembering her thoughts about being in love with him, she instantly felt shy in his presence.

Oh damn, I'm blushing!

"Good morning." He pulled off his fur hat. "Can you spare a cup of coffee for a man who doesn't deserve it?"

"What do you mean, 'who doesn't deserve it'?" Michaela filled a cup to avoid facing him. *Color fade, color fade.* The heat in her cheeks evidenced her command wasn't being obeyed.

"After the way I stomped out of here last night." He opened his jacket and walked to the counter. "I don't know what gave me the idea you might by some strange twist of fate decide you wanted to stay here. I had no right to get annoyed when you stated the obvious. You have a life in Toronto, a future with your parents' law firm. You no doubt worked hard to become an attorney. It wouldn't make sense for you to throw that away to live in the backwoods."

"No, it wouldn't." She handed him the cup. Their fingers touched on its warm surface. Green eyes began to drown in blue.

"Travis." His name came as a whisper from her lips.

"Good morning all." Randall Kirby emerged from the bedroom corridor, naked except for a white towel about his hips, his hair damp. "Michaela, is there a

194

blow dryer in this rustic retreat?"

Taking the cup with him, Travis jerked back from her, eyes narrowing, lips drawn back in a hard, thin line that reminded her of one of Doc's snarls.

"Kirby." He acknowledged the other man's presence. Pausing, he looked him up and down critically. "Spent the night, did you?"

"Yes, as a matter of fact." He sauntered over to Michaela and put an arm possessively about her shoulders. She jerked away and went back behind the counter. Gripping the edge of the dishwasher until her knuckles whitened she lowered her head and kept her back to the two men.

"I'll be on my way." Travis MacDonald replaced his cup on the counter, zipped up his jacket and slapped on his hat.

"Yes, you should leave. And not come back. Last night I asked Michaela to marry me."

"Congratulations." He strode to the door and yanked it open.

"Travis!" His name was a cry as she whirled toward him.

"Good luck, Ms. Dunn," he threw back over his shoulder. The blaze of morning sunshine he let in blinded her. She saw only his silhouette for a moment before he slammed the door. His dogs yelped eagerly as he pounded down the steps.

"Damn you, Randall Kirby!" Michaela rounded the counter and struck him hard on the bare chest with the flat of both hands. "Damn you, damn you, damn you!"

"What's the big deal? You're honor bound to come back to TO in two weeks. There's no future for you with that 'before' section of a male grooming ad. Let him go find some hillbilly who suits his lifestyle."

He gave her a slap on the buttocks before he sauntered back into the bedroom corridor. Michaela had to battle to keep her clenched fists at her sides.

****

An hour later Michaela guided Randall Kirby back to Carleton. As they drew up to the storage garage on the outskirts of town, Amanda Best, dressed in fancy snowmobile gear, stood ready to mount a machine. Seeing Michaela, she abandoned her stance and headed over to her, waving.

"Mikey!" She greeted her with a hug and double kiss that didn't touch either of Michaela's cold cheeks. "I'm heading up to visit Travis. Maybe we could ride partway together."

Although she would have liked to deny it, Michaela knew she had to return immediately. She had guests due for lunch, with no Travis acting as backup.

"Okay, fine. I'll gas up and we'll be off."

"Aren't you going to introduce me?" Amanda preened and shook her long, golden locks as she looked over at Randall Kirby removing his helmet and balaclava.

"Amanda Best, Randall Kirby." Michaela was abrupt.

"Mrs. Best, allow me to offer my condolences on your recent loss." He was immediately the smooth, socially correct being he always appeared to be in public. He took her hand and held it.

"Thank you, Mr. Kirby. However, I must say my brother's passing left me very little pain. He wasn't a nice man...was he, Mikey? We can both testify to that fact." She glanced over at Michaela, eyes narrowing.

"Mrs. Best, perhaps you might do me a favor." Randall smiled the cold, calculating smile Michaela knew all too well. "I'll be leaving for Toronto later today and won't have time to make an engagement announcement. Perhaps you could spread the word that Ms. Dunn and I are to be married. That information might serve to keep unwelcome attention from any of the local swains to a minimum."

"Really! How exciting! Mikey, congratulations! I hope you'll be inviting some of your old friends up to Toronto to the wedding. I adore Toronto, Mr. Kirby."

"Randall, please…" Michaela tried to interject a protest.

"Of course you'll be invited, Mrs. Best." He ignored Michaela's words, putting his arm around his intended's shoulders to plant a kiss on her temple. "I'll tell my secretary to make a note of it the minute I return to my office." He gave her a quick squeeze. "Love you, darling, but I have to run if I'm to get to the city in time to catch the noon flight. See you in two weeks. A pleasure meeting you, Mrs. Best."

He strode off into the blinding sunlight. Michaela heaved a sigh. No use protesting further. She'd deal with Randall and his unacceptable marriage plans when she got back to her office.

"He's adorable!" Amanda Best gushed turning to Michaela after Randall had vanished around a corner of the garage. "I'd never have suspected you might be having it off with Travis if I'd seen what you have waiting at home. Mikey, you sly minx!"

"Yes, well, one never knows, does one. Now I have to gas up and get back on the trail. Is your machine ready?"

****

"Mikey, he's gone!" Amanda burst into the Lodge as Michaela was bussing the last of the lunch dishes.

"What are you talking about? Who's gone?" Michaela was glad the last of her guests had hit the trails. The woman's outburst would have attracted unwelcome interest.

"Travis, of course! I went up to his cabin to find it closed up. All his personal stuff is gone."

"What about the dogs?" He'd never leave

197

without his dogs. Amanda had to be wrong.

"Dogs, too, of course. Do you seriously think he'd leave those mutts to fend for themselves? Damn it, Mikey, of course he's gone...for good!"

"Calm down, Amanda." Michaela willed herself to speak as she advised. "He may simply have gone away for a few days. He couldn't very well leave his team unattended."

"With everything he owns, right down to his underwear?" She tossed her blonde hair, eyes glowering. "He's gone forever, and it's all Ralph's fault!"

"How can you possibly blame your brother? He's deceased. Be rational, Amanda."

"Deceased, and Travis is the number one suspect for putting him in that condition. Don't you see, Mikey? Travis killed Ralph, and now he's afraid the police are getting too close to the truth, so he's decided to disappear. God, how I hate that idiot I married. Ralph was responsible for that, too, you know. If my dear, sweet husband"—her words dripped with sarcasm—"hadn't needed money to finance his political aspirations, I never would have married the self-centred egotist!"

"Colin needed money?"

"You remember our family, Mikey. Poor as church mice, our father a bum, our mother cleaning houses to keep us fed. Ralph was always ambitious, I'll give him that. As soon as we graduated from high school, he began to make money...gambling—cheating, I guess. I never asked. He managed to start a recreational vehicle business with the proceeds. It grew into the biggest in northern New Brunswick. Then some of his shady schemes started to catch up with him.

"Colin was already Crown Prosecutor. When he started investigating some of Ralph's business ventures, my darling brother sent me out to seduce him and get him off the case. I didn't think it would work, but by then Colin had political ambitions that required campaign financing. Ralph was in a position to provide it. But Ralph felt he couldn't propose a mutually beneficial arrangement without some further means of cementing Colin's forever turning a blind eye to his doings. The way to do that, as he saw it, was to get me married to the Crown Attorney. Colin wouldn't risk scandal by proposing any warrants against his brother-in-law, not if he hoped to be the area's next political representative. He had visions of becoming a cabinet minister, then Premier."

"So you managed to marry him." Michaela stared at her. "How?"

"Feminine wiles, Mikey, feminine wiles. Colin always was a bookish type, never had many girlfriends. I swept him off his feet." She flung her hair over her shoulder, a sly, smug expression crossing her face. "I've done all right by it. I have a big house, a sports car, and a position in the community I never thought I'd have. People have to look to me, invite me to parties I wasn't considered good enough to do maid service at, previously. Being the wife of the Crown Attorney has its perks...even if my husband is the world's worst lover."

"That must be disappointing." Michaela couldn't keep the sarcasm out of her own tone.

"For a while it was. Then along came Travis MacDonald, with those absolutely amazing blue eyes, killer body, and mysterious past. He made Colin look like the ultimate nerd. Well, you know what I mean, Mikey."

"What will you do now?" Michaela hid her disgust at the woman's confession. "With Ralph gone, you don't have to stay married to Colin. On the other hand, Travis MacDonald is no longer available."

"Men are like ships. There'll be another one passing before too long. In the meantime, I think Andy Murdoch might be willing to comfort his friend's sister."

"He's a married man with children!"

"He's as unfulfilled in his marriage as I am in mine. He married for money just like Colin did. He might be interested in a little fun with a woman who has a whole lot more flash and dash than Jenny Mouse."

"You're despicable!" Michaela's anger burst free. "You haven't a kind or caring bone in your body. Your brother is dead, your supposed lover has disappeared, and yet all you're concerned about is finding a new man to seduce."

"Come on, Mikey. Don't act the prude. Ralph told me all about you and the major moves you made on him when you were in high school. Hardly the actions of an innocent little girl!"

"Get out, just get out!" Michaela advanced toward her. Suddenly she understood the term murderous rage.

"Okay, okay!" Holding up her hands to protect her face, Amanda Frame backed toward the door. "Geez, Mikey! You must really have it bad for that Neanderthal! He's all yours...if you ever find him."

Seconds later the roar of a snowmobile engine marked her departure.

Mikey sank down at a table and put her face in her hands. Travis gone! Randall Kirby and Amanda Best had driven him away. *Damn them, damn them, damn them!*

She rubbed her temples and tried to organize her thoughts. *Be reasonable, Michaela. They weren't solely responsible. You were the one who told him he had no future with you. You were the one who promised to return to Toronto. You were the reason Randall Kirby showed up. You're getting what you deserve, what you set yourself up for.*

She swallowed hard over the lump in her throat. *Okay, get on with it. He's gone and he won't be back. You have a Lodge to run. Don't let Uncle Norm and Aunt Ida down.*

****

Two hours later, she placed bread dough in a bowl to rise, covered it carefully with a damp cloth, then a dry one, and washed her hands. Barbecued chicken and ribs were on the menu for dinner that evening. She removed thick packages of each from the freezer and set them to thaw. Coleslaw and baked potatoes, fresh rolls, and a pineapple upside-down cake would complete the meal.

She poured herself a cup of coffee and headed for the lounge. The sound of approaching snowmobiles ended her plans for a break. With a sigh she placed her mug on the counter.

Business is brisk, mustn't complain.

She opened to door to see three snowmobiles pulling up. Two of them bore the insignia of the RCMP. *What now?* She forced a smile across her face. *Start out on the right foot.*

Her lips straightened into a hard line as the man riding the unmarked snowmobile dismounted and doffed his headgear. Colin Best. This had to be serious to have brought the Crown Prosecutor all the way up here in sub-zero temperatures.

"Ms. Dunn." His breath formed a frosty cloud as he headed toward her. "We're looking for Travis MacDonald. We'll be obliged for any information you can give us regarding his whereabouts." He stopped at the foot of the steps and squinted up at her.

It didn't take Amanda long to spread the word of Travis's disappearance. She probably used her cell from his cabin the moment she discovered he was missing. Not exactly the act of a heartbroken lover.

"He might be at his cabin." Michaela decided to

play dumb.

"My wife was out for a run on her snowmobile earlier. She stopped at MacDonald's cabin to see if he could spare some gas. Her machine was running a bit low. She called me on her cell to tell me he was gone, with all of his personal belongings, even those brutes of dogs. He's apparently fled the area or gone into hiding." He fumbled inside his leather jacket and pulled out a sheet of paper.

"This is a second warrant for his arrest for the murder of Ralph Frame. I'm sure even your friend Judge Anderson will have no choice but to notarize it when I present him with the facts. If we didn't have sufficient proof to hold him on the first occasion, we do now. Only a guilty man would decide to disappear in the heart of a murder investigation in which he's a person of much interest."

"That's your case?" Michaela, in spite of the thrill of fear rippling through her body, managed to put on her best defense attorney expression and smile tauntingly. "Well, Mr. Best, I'm glad I won't be in your shoes in any courtroom where they choose to try Travis MacDonald."

"You know there's a whole lot more!" he snapped.

Michaela saw small beads of sweat on his forehead in spite of the temperatures.

"Such as?" She wanted to keep him talking, to keep him and the Mounties off Travis's trail for as long as she could. If he was running, she'd buy him as much time as possible.

"You know very well he and my brother-in-law were fighting over trap lines, that Ralph and he had a physical altercation over them. Furthermore, you'll be testifying. You'll be telling the truth, the whole truth, and nothing but the truth about witnessing Travis MacDonald and Ralph Frame threatening each other over those trap lines, about your finding

MacDonald severely beaten by Mr. Frame, about how both men had rival romantic interest in you. MacDonald's sudden disappearance is just the icing on the cake of his guilt!"

"Just because Mr. MacDonald has seen fit to move away from the Promise area doesn't prove he's guilty." Michaela looked down at him, hoping the contempt she felt for his reasoning was written in her expression.

"*Ran* away, you mean. He realized he's become our prime suspect."

"You're blowing smoke, counselor." Michaela deliberately failed to call him "Crown Prosecutor." He wasn't worthy of the title.

"Fine, have it your way." Colin Best managed to regain his professional demeanor. "I'm taking this to mean you won't assist us in our search."

"Not won't. Can't. I have no idea where Travis MacDonald is."

"Aiding and abetting a murderer is a serious offense, Ms. Dunn. I'm sure your parents wouldn't welcome their only offspring being so charged."

"My parents are experts at refuting false accusations." She smiled tauntingly. "They'd just see this as another challenge...a very small challenge, given the resources behind a firm like Dunn and Dunn. Be forewarned, Mr. Best. They're noted for making mincemeat out of people preferring false charges, and they're experts at exacting severe reparations."

"Yes, well, we'll see." He replaced his headgear and returned to his snowmobile. His bravado appeared to have drained at her last remarks. *Good.* She'd been running out of bluff, praying what she had would work. "Let's go, gentlemen. Maybe we can pick up a trail at MacDonald's cabin. Or at least a few clues as to where he's gone."

"Shouldn't we search this place first, sir?"

Constable Roy waved a hand to indicate the Lodge and its grounds.

"We don't have a warrant, Constable." Corporal Palmer brought his young colleague up short. "We need to move fast. We want to make a thorough search of MacDonald's place before the light fades. If it snows tonight, chances of finding tracks will be gone."

"I'd like to wish you luck." Michaela crossed her arms on her chest. "But since you're after the wrong person, I can't."

"Argh!" Colin Best started his machine, revved the motor, and gunned out of the Lodge yard.

"Good day, Miss Dunn." Corporal Palmer touched the front of his helmet.

"Good day, gentlemen." Michaela never ceased to be amazed at the politeness of members of the RCMP under trying circumstances. She'd dealt with many Mounties over the years. Without exception, such had been the case.

Michaela watched them out of sight, then went slowly back inside the Lodge. Why had Travis MacDonald chosen to leave so suddenly? Was it because she'd made it clear there was no future for them? He wasn't a stupid man. Surely he must have realized how his disappearance would appear to the authorities. What could he have been thinking?

She leaned her back against the old plank door and heaved a deep sigh. He'd left without so much as a goodbye. Didn't he care? Didn't he think she'd wonder, worry? What should she do? Ignore his leaving and go on with her business as if she'd never met him? That would be the wise thing to do. She shouldn't connect herself with a suspected murderer, but they'd become close. She'd even been crazy enough to think they were headed into a serious relationship.

She needed advice—advice based on logic and

good old-fashioned common sense. Grabbing her cell, she made a decision. Ten minutes later she was headed across the lake and up the mountain to where she could make a call.

"Janet? It's Michaela. Is my mother in?"

"You're in luck, honey. She just got back from Vancouver. Let me tell you, she wasn't at all pleased to hear what transpired between you and your father in her absence. She was going to try to contact you as soon as she got settled. I'll put you through to her office. Good luck."

"Thanks, Janet."

****

"Laura Dunn here. How can I help?" Her mother's well-modulated voice soothed her the minute she heard it. Nothing ruffled Laura Dunn, attorney at law.

"Mom. How are you? How did the case go in BC?" She aimed for casual conversation as an opener to a conversation she feared might not be an easy one.

"Michaela, what on earth has been going on between you and your father?" The news-anchor voice changed into the sharp tones of a concerned parent. "I come back to discover you've had some kind of ridiculous argument with your father and gone off to New Brunswick..."

"It was the Lawson case, Mom." Michaela launched into the explanation. "The man was guilty. I refused to be second chair. Dad wouldn't accept my decision. He suspended me. I decided it was an excellent opportunity to give Uncle Norm and Aunt Ida a much-needed vacation."

"Michaela, I understand you sometimes believe you get these flashes. Your grandmother claimed to have them, too. But you can't go applying them in a murder case. Feelings are all well and good, but..."

"Mom, can we discuss this later? Right now I

205

need some motherly advice."

There was a pause. "Michaela, what kind of trouble are you in now? Your father told me you asked his help to get some man exonerated from a murder charge. I hope you didn't do this on feelings alone. Have you found out he's guilty?" Her voice was rising.

"No, no, Mom, nothing like that. It's just that...this man. I've never met anyone like him. He's really something, Mom. I know you'd like him. He's strong and brave and kind and..."

"And you've fallen for him?"

"Big time, Mom. I've never felt anything like this before."

"Well, then, darling, if you're sure about him, if your heart tells you he's the one..."

"I do...think he's the one, that is. The problem is I'm not sure he's all that committed to me. You see, he's disappeared without so much as goodbye."

"Then go after him." Her mother's advice startled her. "You'll never feel satisfied until you know for certain one way or the other the state of your relationship. Michaela, my darling, I've been in love with your father for over thirty years. It's a wonderful way to live. I would be a very poor mother if I didn't wish the same happiness for you."

"But Dad..."

"Leave your father to me. I've just gotten home after several weeks' absence. I think he's in a perfect state of mind to listen to anything I might propose."

"You're one devious lady, Laura Dunn." Michaela felt a grin starting to spread across her face.

"How else do you think I've managed to be both wife and partner to a man as brilliant and volatile as Michael Dunn all these years? There's always a woman behind the throne, darling, and don't you forget it. Now go out and find that man who can send you flying off the face of this earth with a single kiss."

"How did you know...?"

"Not all that difficult. Well known symptoms of a woman in love."

"Okay, fine. Will do. Thanks, Mom. Love you."

"Love you, too, baby. Good luck."

Go after him. Michaela shoved the cell back into her pocket and climbed aboard the snowmobile. As she drove down the mountain, she marveled at her mother's advice, then began planning how she would carry it out without the police getting wise.

Traveling in a white SUV packed with seven malamutes, Travis would, at least initially, be easy to spot. He'd be aware of the fact. He'd find a place where he could temporarily deposit the dogs in safety. But where, where?

His dogs were a unique breed. Moon Glow malamutes. He'd said he got them from the breeder who developed the strain. Maybe they had a web site. She had to get access to the Internet. She had to go to Carleton.

She had guests arriving for supper. She'd have to wait until tomorrow morning and hope Travis's trail hadn't gone cold.

****

At 10:00 o'clock the following morning, Michaela sat in the small cyber café in the Carleton Hotel, typed in "Moon Glow malamutes, New Brunswick" and held her breath. Although it seemed minutes, within seconds she had a hit.

With a backdrop of a team of beautiful golden-red malamutes, the words "Moon Glow Kennels, Jane and Jake Hudson, proprietors" flashed in front of her. Their address told her they lived only an hour's drive away. With no guests scheduled until late afternoon, she'd have time to visit the kennel.

"Thanks." She threw a twenty to the desk clerk

as she dashed through the lobby.

"But, Miss, it's only five!" he yelled after her.

"Tip." She rushed out the front door into a bitterly cold grey morning.

An hour later she found a roadside gate adorned with a large likeness of what looked like Doc's head and the words "Moon Glow Kennels" emblazoned in golden brown above it.

She drove through a tunnel of lofty white pine until she emerged into the dooryard of a neat log bungalow. Equally tidy outbuildings, with dog runs attached, flanked it.

A cacophony of barking began as she stopped and got out of her uncle's truck. In the runs she saw a number of beautiful dogs similar to Travis's team. Similar—no! Her breath caught in her throat. The dogs in that first run *were* Travis's team. A white SUV parked in the trees beyond the kennels sent ripples of pleasure coursing through her. Travis was here!

Half running, she skittered across the slippery yard. Doc, howling at full volume, leaped almost to the top of the eight-foot chain link.

"Doc!" she cried, clutching the fence in both hands. "Doc, it's so good to see you!"

Through the chain link she rubbed his nose while his team mates gathered around him, dancing and yelping.

"Can I help you, miss?" A man had come up behind her. Tall and broad-shouldered, he had a weathered face, twinkling blue eyes, and a friendly smile.

"Yes, you can." She turned to face him. "I hope I'm not trespassing, but your gate was open."

"Visitors are always welcome. But it appears you're more than a visitor. Doc here seems to know you."

"He does. I'm Michaela Dunn, a friend of Travis

MacDonald's."

"Aha!" The big man nodded knowingly. "I'm Jake Hudson. Travis said you'd probably show up. Come over to the house. Jane has coffee on."

"Is Travis here?"

"No, he's been and gone."

Michaela's hopes plummeted.

"I'll be back," she managed to reassure Doc before she followed Jake up to the snug bungalow.

"Jane, Michaela's here," Jake Hudson called as they entered the sparkling kitchen.

A slender woman with streaks of grey beginning to show in her dark hair entered the room. Her complexion darkened by the elements, she was an attractive woman in jeans and a forest green turtleneck, clothing suited to her vigorous manner.

"Welcome, Michaela." Smiling, she caught the younger woman's hand in hers. "We were wondering when you'd arrive. Sit down. I've made fresh coffee. There's scones from earlier this morning. You must be cold and hungry after your drive."

Puzzled, Michaela sat down at the polished maplewood table as a cup of steaming, aromatic coffee was placed in front of her. What had Travis been thinking? He'd told the Hudsons to expect her. Did they know where he'd gone, why he'd chosen to disappear?

"Have a scone." Jake Hudson had divested himself of his outerwear and joined her at the table. He slid the plate of golden biscuits toward her. "Jane is quite a cook, along with being the best musher I've ever met. That's why I married her." His blue eyes twinkled.

"Enough!" Jane Hudson brought two more cups of coffee to the table, placed one in front of her husband, and sat down opposite Michaela with the second. "You'll be taking Doc back with you, I suppose. Travis thought you might. Actually it would be best if you did. Doc's not really a kennel dog."

"Travis thought I might..." She was completely puzzled.

"He was confident you'd track him this far." Jake Hudson's face became serious. "Although he wanted to take Doc, he knew having the dog with him would be as good as waving a red flag in the face of anyone wanting to find him. He told us to give him to you when you arrived."

"Then you know he was running away?" She approached the subject carefully, not sure how much he'd told the couple.

"Not running away, disappearing...again." Jake Hudson leaned back on his chair, his broad chest puffing out against his plaid shirt. "That's his way."

"I see. I take it you helped him disappear five years ago."

"Travis came to us burned to the core." Jane Hudson met Michaela's gaze steadily. "We didn't ask for details. We knew he had to get away from whatever it was that had injured him. He wanted to buy a team, to hermit himself away in the woods up at the Promise. We know the area. We knew it was a good place for our dogs. We also knew he'd take proper care of them. He's that kind of man."

"So you sold him his team."

"And we didn't make a mistake." Jake Hudson reached for a scone and began to butter it. "Those dogs are in wonderful condition. I couldn't have taken better care of them myself."

"Travis loves those dogs." Michaela took a sip of her coffee. It was excellent.

"Agreed. Now I'll get Doc out for you. He'll need a bit of a frolic around the yard before you put him in your vehicle for a long drive. He's been penned up since Travis left."

"Left to go where?" Michaela could restrain

herself no longer.

"No idea." Jake Hudson stood and reached for his jacket. "We didn't ask. He was hurting again, we could tell, and needed to get away. That was enough for us."

"But I saw his SUV parked beside the kennels. He couldn't have left on foot."

"No, he didn't. He left it for us to use. We only have one vehicle and it will come in handy, a state-of-the-art truck like that. All he wanted in return was for one of us to drive him to the city. Janie did, let him out at the bus terminal, then drove back. That's the last we saw of him. Sorry." Jake Hudson's blue gaze reflected the sincerity of the last word. "We gathered you were pretty special to him, even though he said very little. I'll let Doc out for a run."

When he'd gone, Jane Hudson reached a hand across the table to cover Michaela's.

"Travis is a fine man, Michaela. We know all about the trouble at Promise Lake and, believe me, there's no way Travis MacDonald could have been involved in that man's death."

"Do you know anything about his past?" Michaela looked over at the woman, hope making her words shaky. "Where he came from? Why he came here?"

"Nothing." Jane Hudson shook her head as she withdrew her hand. She wrapped her fingers around her coffee cup and leaned back in her chair. "He must have had money, because he came with that fancy SUV and paid cash for the team and sled, which are more expensive than you might imagine. He had less hair and beard back then. He was just beginning to let both grow, but that made him look disreputable." She gave a little laugh.

"At first glance, we were inclined to deny his request to buy our dogs, but after he'd stayed with us for a week to learn mushing...he already had a good knowledge of canines, we discovered....we knew he could be trusted. Our dogs are our babies, Michaela. We'd never let them go to anyone less than a stellar caregiver."

"I'm sure you wouldn't." She stood. "Thank you so much, Mrs. Hudson. I have to be going before the trail gets cold."

"You sound as if you've become a genuine wilderness woman." Jane Hudson got to her feet and smiled. "No wonder Travis felt confident leaving Doc in your care. Anything else?" Her eyes twinkled.

"Yes." Michaela felt she could trust these kind people who'd been unquestioningly supportive of Travis. "I'm in love with him." Relief flooded through her. It felt wonderful finally to admit it to other human beings.

"Good. That's exactly what Travis needs. The love of a good woman. I think..." She paused and looked deep into her coffee cup.

"Please. Go on."

"I think Travis was hurt, deeply hurt, in a relationship with a woman. I think..." She stopped again.

"Mrs. Hudson, please!"

"I think she deceived and hurt him in more ways than one. I think she tore away his ability to trust, and therefore, maybe..."

"His ability to love another woman?" It wasn't hard to finish that sentence.

"Yes." Jane Hudson looked up at her. "But, mind you, I said tore away. There's nothing to say it can't be mended. From the way he spoke about you, Michaela, I think you're the one to do the repairs."

"What exactly did he say about me?" Michaela couldn't resist asking, even though she felt like a teenager inquiring about her first crush.

"He said he was leaving Doc for you. He said he knew you'd take proper care of him and that he'd look out for you. He said you needed looking out for, but that he couldn't stay around to do it. He also said you'd be leaving shortly and that would make you safe. He said..."

"Yes?" Eagerness highlighted the word.

"He said he wished things had been different, that it could have worked out."

"Anything else?"

"No." Jane Hudson shook her head sadly. "He looked so forlorn and out of place standing outside the bus station, I felt like crying. With his long hair and backpack, in his gray parka, he was an absolute anachronism among the other travelers."

"Then it shouldn't be hard to trace him." Michaela headed for the door, her spirits revving. "Someone is bound to remember him. Someone will recall him purchasing a ticket, where he was planning to go."

"Good luck!" Jane Hudson called after her. "Bring him back to pick up the rest of his dogs when you find him. They miss him."

****

"No one answering that description bought a ticket here two days ago, miss." The elderly ticket agent peered at Michaela over his granny glasses. "I'd remember."

"But a friend said she dropped him off here. Are you quite sure?"

"Sure as anything. Sorry."

"Hey, wait a minute!" A custodian who'd been sweeping the floor came to join them. "I saw that guy standing outside a couple of days back. A lady driving a white SUV dropped him off."

"What did he do? Where did he go?" Michaela was firing questions more rapidly than she'd ever shot them at a witness on the stand.

"Well, as I recall," the man scratched his scraggly beard. "He stood there for a couple of minutes, and then he picked up his backpack and headed off down the street."

"In which direction?"

"Toward the mall. It's about a five-minute walk."

"Thanks." She shoved a twenty into his hand and headed off at a run.

Inside the mall door, she paused. Where would he go first? A barber's. A shave and a haircut would go a long way to assuring no one would recognize him. She saw a hair salon a few doors up.

"Did a man come in here with long dark hair and a full beard?" she questioned the girl behind the front desk.

"A little over six feet, great body, killer blue eyes?" The blonde fanned her face with her fingers. "Hot stuff. Hard to forget him. He looked even better after Eric gave him a hair styling and a shave."

"Do you know where he went from here?" Michaela pulled out another twenty.

"Wish I knew." She grinned. "I'd have been hot on his trail if I hadn't had to work the rest of the day. He said something about getting new clothes."

"Thanks." Michaela headed back into the mall walkway and looked around. Several stores up, men's clothing hung on racks out front. Expensive men's clothing. She entered and gave the sales clerk a description of Travis as best she could imagine him sans hair and beard.

"Sorry, no one answering that description or anything like it came in here. Wish he had. Business has been terrible."

She stood for a few moments in the middle of the walkway thinking. Ahead, a giant Wal-Mart sign indicated the department store as one of the mall's anchors.

Of course! Travis wouldn't go into an elegant men's store where business was slow and he would be remembered. No, he'd go for a mass sales place.

Almost running, she headed for Wal-Mart.

She had to buy a variety of items to pass through each checkout to question the various cashiers. Finally, at checkout number thirteen, she found a woman who remembered the tall, good-looking man with killer blue eyes.

"Bought a fake leather jacket, jeans, and a grey turtleneck." She smiled as Michaela paid for a bottle-green scarf she didn't want. "I saw him go into the washroom over there," she indicated the direction. "When he came out he was wearing the entire outfit. I don't usually watch customers once they've passed through my cash, but he was something else, you know what I mean?"

"I surely do. Thanks." Michaela gathered up her package.

"Is he your boyfriend?" The young woman looked at her. "If he is, you're real lucky."

"I guess maybe he is...or was." Michaela waved goodbye and headed out to the SUV, where Doc waited.

"What now, boy?" She ruffled the dog's fur. "It's getting late, and I have guests coming. I can't check the railway station, the bus depot, and the airport today. We'll have to go back and take up the trail tomorrow or the next day. Hopefully it won't have gone cold by then."

Chapter Seventeen

She was cleaning up breakfast the following morning when the sound of approaching snowmobiles drew her attention. Doc whined and got up from his spot by the lounge fire.

"I agree." She put her hands on her hips and sighed. "I'm glad business is good, but it's exhausting. I miss your buddy."

She avoided saying Travis's name. She'd discovered it sent the dog into a flurry of searching.

The machines came to a stop. Less than a minute later, Colin Best and the two RCMP officers stepped into the Lodge. Doc emitted a low growl.

"Hush!" Michaela admonished him in a whisper. She got a grip on his collar and braced herself. "Gentlemen, what can I do for you today?"

"To begin, you can explain how you come to have Travis MacDonald's dog when you said you had no idea where he is." Colin Best's expression was smug as he deposited his helmet on a nearby table and indicated the malamute.

Doc muttered something Michaela interpreted as the canine equivalent of a four-letter word. She tightened her hold on the big dog.

"I found him wandering along the edge of the road." Michaela had her story practiced and ready. She'd been anticipating something like this, only not so quickly. "How did you find out?"

"You were seen letting him out of your uncle's truck at the garage in Carleton," Corporal Palmer said. "He's an easily identifiable animal, what with that distinctive color."

"Yes, he is. That's how I came to notice him. He appeared lost, so I picked him up. I plan to keep him. If I need a license, I'll purchase one." She smiled and rubbed the malamute's head as he pushed against her leg.

"The animal's legally a stray." Colin Best looked down at the dog. "Constable, take him."

"That may not be the best idea, sir," Corporal Palmer said as Doc again rumbled in his throat. "Carleton's animal shelter is small and overcrowded. Furthermore, I know from experience that he can be a difficult case. If Miss Dunn is willing to pay for a license and take responsibility for the animal, I'm sure the good folks at the SPCA will be grateful."

"Thank you, Corporal." Michaela went behind the counter and took a checkbook from a drawer. "What does a dog license cost?"

"Very well, you win this round." Colin Best turned and headed for the door. "We're leaving. But be advised, we'll be watching you, Michaela Dunn. If you try to contact Travis MacDonald in any way, we'll be right there to intercept both of you. Aiding a murder suspect is a serious offense, as I'm sure you're aware."

When they'd gone, Michaela sat down on a stool at the counter. Whining, Doc licked her hand, his eyes wide.

"You're right. With a potentially dangerous man like Colin Best hot on his trail, Travis has to be warned. It's up to us to do it—and make certain we're not followed."

****

At midnight, dressed for the night's bitter cold and with Doc at her heels, Michaela headed toward the back of the Lodge, where her snowmobile waited. She was glad she had no guests to detain her. A raw wind howled down out of the northeast. Pines and spruce surrounding the inn bent and moaned. She mounted the machine, started the motor, and drove out of the yard and into the trail leading to Carleton.

Doc bounded easily along beside her, silent as a ghost of his wolf ancestors. She couldn't have had a better companion, unless it was his master. She felt in tune with the black velvet of the star-studded night, the wilderness, and even the wild, restless wind, with the great wolf-dog a natural companion. She belonged here. This was where she'd be happy...with Travis MacDonald.

****

He appeared suddenly, materializing as he had the night she'd been lost in the blizzard. Swerving to avoid him, she swung her machine broadside across the trail. The motor sputtered and died, and she sat facing the luminous ghost of winters past, the Promise's phantom protector.

He stared at her. Her heart pounded at her ribs. Whining softly, Doc fidgeted close beside her.

As if pronouncing a benediction, the spectre's features softened. His head nodded assent before he slowly evaporated into the wind and darkness.

Doc threw back his head and howled, his cry blending into the gale in primeval harmony. Mesmerized, Michaela sat astride her snowmobile, her hands clutching the handlebars.

"You saw him, too, didn't you, Doc?" Her hand shook as she reached out to lay it on the dog's snow-crusted neck. "He was here, wasn't he? He came to tell us we're doing the right thing trying to find Travis, that I've made the right decision, deciding to stay here with him."

The malamute leaped away from her and cavorted sideways down the trail toward Carleton. He paused, looked back at her, and barked.

"Okay, okay, I'm coming...if this old machine will start and I can get my shakes under control. I know this guy is a good ghost, but he still scares the beejeebers out of me."

She fumbled with the key. The motor roared to life. With a quaking sigh, she headed toward the town.

Relief flooded through her when she saw the dark outline of the snowmobile garage looming ahead. She'd deliberately left her uncle's truck parked at the back. No one would notice it missing until morning, she hoped.

She left the snowmobile behind the building and loaded Doc into the vehicle's passenger seat. With the truck's headlights turned off, she eased out onto the slippery road and headed toward the city. Once on the highway, after glancing in all directions and reassured she wasn't being followed, she snapped on the lights and breathed a sigh of relief.

"Should be clear sailing from here on, Doc." She patted the dog. He whined and licked her hand.

She'd decided to start her search at the airport. It would be open all night. The train station might not.

Repeating Travis's description at each, she traveled from airline desk to airline desk, explaining that she was a private investigator trying to find him to inform him of an inheritance. Lying wasn't something she sanctioned, but in this case she could think of no other ploy. In each instance she flashed her legal society membership card, breathing an inward sigh of relief when no one paused to examine it closely.

After an hour of unsuccessful inquiries, she bought a cup of coffee and sat down to think. She'd felt confident he'd be heading for Toronto, that it was where he'd come from five years ago, but she'd checked all the airlines offering flights to the city and no one remembered him. Of course, nearly two days had elapsed since he'd disappeared. Other agents could have been on duty when he purchased a ticket.

"Excuse me, miss." A tall woman with bright orange dyed hair approached her. "You were looking for a man wearing a black leather jacket, a gray turtleneck, and jeans? A really good-looking man?"

"Yes." Michaela jumped to her feet. "Did you see him?"

"I was on duty two days ago when a man of that description bought a ticket to Halifax. Some people have all the luck, don't they? Killer good looks and now an inheritance? Wow!"

"Yes, wow." Astonished at Travis's unexpected destination, Michaela was at a loss for words. "The flight he took would have gotten him to Nova Scotia when?"

"Late in the afternoon on Tuesday. Maybe you can trace him through the car rental service at Stanfield International. That is, if he rented a vehicle and didn't take the shuttle into Halifax or had someone waiting for him."

"Thanks." Michaela felt suddenly weary, suddenly reluctant to pursue Travis MacDonald any further. Then she had an inspiration. "Under what name did he purchase his ticket? I want to be sure I'm chasing the right man."

"Thomas Donnelly." The redhead looked at Michaela, suspicion beginning to contort her features. "Are you sure you're trying to find him to tell him about an inheritance? Are you…"

"Yes, yes. Thanks." Michaela turned and headed out of the airport. "I'll inform Mr. Donnelly of your cooperation. I'm sure he'll want to offer you some kind of reward."

"Maria James," she called after Michaela, suspicion vanishing. "My name is Maria James."

****

"What a shameless liar I am!" Michaela told Doc as she turned the truck back out onto the highway.

It was beginning to snow, big whirling flakes smashing silently into the windshield, mesmerizingly dangerous to drivers. The roads, slick with the fine stuff on top of ice, made her long to be back in the dogsled, with Doc and Travis keeping her safe. "Now all I have to do is lie more information out of the car rental people in Halifax when we come to a pay phone...at a decent hour, that is. Do you realize it's only five a.m.? Let's find an all-night diner and have breakfast. If they won't allow you in, I'll get you a take-out."

****

"No one by that name has rented a vehicle from us in the past four days." The male voice on the phone turned Michaela's hopes to mush. "Perhaps the person you're looking for took the shuttle into Halifax."

"I've already contacted all the drivers who might have been on duty when he arrived." Michaela tried to keep the wheeze of defeat out of her voice. "He's not remembered there, either."

"Then the only alternative is that he was picked up by someone."

"Yes, I suppose it is. Thank you for your time."

"Not a problem. I hope you find Mr. Donnelly. He'll be pleased to discover he's the recipient of an inheritance."

"Yes, I'm sure he will."

Michaela punched off her cell and leaned back against the truck seat.

"Did *she* pick him up, Doc? Is *she* maybe in Halifax on business, and he went to be with her?"

Doc nuzzled her and whined.

"You're right. She hurt him too much. But then where did he go? Why Halifax? I was sure he'd lived in Toronto before coming to Promise Lake."

She sat for a few minutes, staring out into the grey, cold morning. The snow had stopped, but the temperature had dropped like a stone to far below freezing. She longed to be back in the Lodge, fires crackling on the hearths, she and Travis serving well-satisfied guests.

A thought struck her. She turned on the motor and revved it into action.

"We're going to the library, Doc. I need a Halifax phone book."

An hour later she felt vindicated on her third call to one of the many Donnellys listed.

"Sure, he's my nephew, Angus's boy," a friendly male voice informed her. "Angus has a dairy farm up the valley."

"Up the valley?" Michaela, unfamiliar with Nova Scotia parlance, was confused.

"The Annapolis Valley." The voice suddenly tinged with exasperation. "You aren't from Nova Scotia, are you?"

"New Brunswick. Would you have a phone number for the farm?"

"Sure." He gave her a 902 number, which she memorized in the absence of a notepad. "Say hello to Tom for me when you get in touch. Tell him it's high time he came to visit his Uncle Callum. Haven't seen him in a dog's age."

"Mr. Donnelly, can you tell me if he once worked in Toronto?"

"Sure did. He was one of those big, high-power business people you read about in the financial pages of the newspaper. He got turned off by something that happened up there and took to living in the backwoods. Never would tell anyone exactly where that was. He always kept in touch with his folks, though. He didn't want them to worry about him. He's a fine young man."

"Yes, I believe he is. Thank you, Mr. Donnelly. I appreciate your help."

After she'd rung off, she started to tap in the

number Callum Donnelly had given her. Doc's paw on her hand stopped her.

"What?" She paused to look at the malamute at her side. "Are you telling me not to take this any further? Or are you just hungry?"

Either way, the dog's action gave her pause. Contacting Travis or Thomas or whatever his name was might not be wise at this point. She could be leaving a trail that would lead Colin Best and the Mounties right to his door. No, she'd leave things as they stood and get back to her investigations. After she'd solved the murder and exonerated Travis...that would be the time to make a call to Nova Scotia.

"Thanks, Doc." She started the truck and eased it out onto the road. "Whatever the reason for that paw on the hand, it gave me time to decide the best course of action. I think you've just earned yourself one very choice steak when we get back to the Promise. But, hey!" She braked to a skidding halt and had to maneuver quickly to keep the vehicle from landing in the ditch. "That doesn't stop me from checking up on Thomas Donnelly's past in Toronto. I know just the person to do the sleuthing up there." She punched a number into her cell and waited.

"Hi, Janet. Michaela here again. I'd be grateful if you'd do a little detective work for me."

****

Michaela divided her time over the next hour and a half between a coffee shop and taking Doc for walks. When her cell finally rang, she snatched it from her pocket.

"Janet? What did you find out?"

"Thomas Donnelly was the chief land acquisitions officer for Havens Drilling up until five years ago." Michaela recognized that efficient Janet was reading from notes she'd made. "At that point

223

he appears to have had a falling out with company executives and left."

"Havens Drilling? Oil exploration, isn't it?"

"Yes, one of the biggest and most successful in Canada, I gather from quick research. Their chief endeavors are in Alberta and northern British Columbia. However..."

"However what?"

"From further inquiries into the business community here, I've been given to understand Havens Drilling people have a reputation for ruthlessness. Lately they've been cited for ignoring the requests of ranchers to respect their land and running roughshod over their grazing areas and crops. They've also been in trouble for a lack of concern for the environment."

"Could the falling out Thomas Donnelly had with the company have had anything to do with this?"

"Not only could, did. Apparently when he was sent to northern BC to clear the way across ranchland to drilling sites, he became totally disillusioned with the mess Havens Drilling was making of perfectly good agricultural land...land that had in many cases been in families for three or more generations. He went back to Toronto to try to talk the CEO and the rest of the company executives out of going into the area. When they refused, a bitter argument ensued."

"So he isn't a fugitive." Michaela heaved a sigh. "Only a man who stuck to his principles, who wouldn't allow a natural area to be destroyed."

"Well..."

"Come on, Janet. What is it? There has to be more. I know that tone."

"They tried to make a case against him that he'd leaked information to a competing company. Then..."

"Oh, for heaven's sake, Janet, get on with it!"

"He had a fiancée at the time. Jessica Wells. She was one of Havens' senior attorneys. Gossip has it he found her in bed with the company CEO in the apartment he and this Jessica person had been sharing since their engagement. Right after that, Thomas Donnelly vanished. The company used his disappearance to add fuel to the charge that he'd been providing information to a competing company. He's never been seen or heard from since."

The line went silent.

"Michaela, are you there? Michaela...?"

"Yes, yes, I'm here, Janet. Thanks so much. This makes a whole lot of things clear."

"Do you want me to tell your parents we've spoken? Do you want me to tell them exactly when you'll be coming back?"

"Not necessary. And regarding the last bit...that's on hold pending further consideration."

Chapter Eighteen

Thomas Donnelly, alias Travis MacDonald, leaned against the door of the milking theatre and watched his older brother inspecting the Holstein in the milking stall while one of the farm hands looked on. Robert Donnelly was a farmer born and bred. Thomas had had no qualms about leaving the family farm in his capable hands. Robert had made a success of a business in which many failed.

"Hey, brother." Robert turned toward him. "Come on in. Haven't become afraid of cows, have you?"

"Helen says coffee's on." Thomas grinned as he joined him. "Fine-looking animal. Same as are all the others I've seen since I arrived. You've done a great job, Bobby."

"Yeah, well, I didn't have much choice." He was grinning too. "What with my little brother running off to university and then to TO."

"You know you love this farm. You know all you ever really wanted to do was marry Helen, have a few kids, and turn Donnelly's Dairy into the best in the province. Looks like you're closing in on that goal." He waved a hand to indicate the big snow-white milking theatre and the line of obedient Holsteins patiently waiting their turn to have their udders relieved.

"I am pretty happy with it all." Robert slapped an arm about his brother's broad shoulders and headed him toward the door. "Keep 'em moving, Taylor," he called back to the man working the machines. "Jamie will be along to relieve you in fifteen minutes."

"No problem, boss." The man returned, whistling, to his work.

"Contented employees. A sure sign of a successful business." Thomas grinned.

"You'd know, Mr. Master of Business Administration." They stepped outside into the thin film of snow that covered the barnyard.

"Come on now. You always said you wanted to go to agricultural college, not university."

"Your way of life never was mine and never will be. Toronto and a high-pressure job in land acquisitions...definitely not for me. As for a woman like Jessica..." He cast a sideways glance at his brother as they walked and winked at him. "Way too sophisticated for a country boy like me."

"And me, too, apparently."

"Ah, Tommy, forget it. I shouldn't have mentioned her. She's old news. What I'd like to hear about is what you've been up to these past five years. You kept in touch, but that was about it. Come on. Tell me."

They went up the steps into the farmhouse kitchen. Warm air and the scent of fresh baking hit Thomas the moment the door opened. The century-old house held nothing but good memories.

"Come in, Tom." Helen took a pan from the oven of the electric stove squeezed in beside the big wood-burning range that heated the room in winter. "Fresh scones and coffee."

"Feels like I never left." He pulled off his leather jacket and sat down at the old wooden table in the centre of the room.

"Too bad Mom and Dad aren't here." Robert stepped out of his coveralls and hung them on a peg by the kitchen door. "But they really needed a vacation. These days, with the farm showing a nice profit, it was the perfect time."

"Now tell us, Tom." Helen poured coffee into the three mugs waiting on the table.

"What brought you here now? We haven't had a chance to talk without the kids around. With them in school for the day, you can give us the real story."

Thomas Donnelly drew a deep breath. He looked from his pretty, blonde sister-in-law to his handsome, dark-haired brother. "I hope you're both up to this...and willing to keep a secret."

****

"Man, that's quite a story." Robert Donnelly pushed back in his chair and rubbed his neck. "We never once thought of looking for you at Great-Uncle George's cabin. It should have been a logical place. After all, you did spend time there with him every Christmas vacation. I remember you boarding the train, as soon as the festivities were finished here at the farm, and heading for the Promise. You loved the place, especially in winter. I guess we just assumed you'd become too big-city to hide out in a place like the Promise Wilderness."

"We also didn't think you could be at the Promise because we figured that old place would have fallen down years ago," Helen interjected. "And, like Robert just said, we thought you'd choose a lot more posh location."

"Posh?" Thomas Donnelly guffawed. "I've had enough posh to do me a lifetime. Anyhow, log cabins are durable. All I had to do was evict the mice and raccoons, clean it, and bring in some decent furniture and appliances. Luckily, with the trails frozen hard and no snow that October I moved in, five years ago, I was able to drive a 4x4 rental truck right up to the door."

"I can't say I approve of your running away when you're still a person of interest in a murder investigation." His brother's blue eyes met his squarely. "Furthermore, you left that girl Michaela in one hell of a mess. Not like you, brother, to desert a lady in distress."

"No, it isn't. But in this case, I thought it was the only solution. My disappearance would temporarily divert suspicion from her. Furthermore, she's one smart lady. Without the difficulty of trying to protect me, she'll be free to pursue an investigation of the case. I've no doubt she'll find the solution. As I've told you, she's a defense attorney. Her mother and father are probably the most famous team of criminal defense lawyers in Canada. If all else fails, she'll have the resources of their firm behind her."

"Why do I get the feeling there's a whole lot more?" Helen stood and went to refill their cups. "Why do I get the feeling that this Michaela is a great deal more than a friend, someone you happened to discover in a blizzard? Thomas, are you in love with her?"

"You never change, Helen." Thomas Donnelly quirked a corner of his mouth. "Cut right to the chase. Okay, yes, maybe I have feelings for her. But after Jessica, I'm not about to get burned again. Michaela Dunn is another Toronto attorney, for God's sake. When I first met her, she was drenched in fancy perfume. You must remember that scent from your visit to my apartment? The place reeked of the stuff. Furthermore, she's going back to the city as soon as her uncle and aunt return from vacation. She has a sort-of fiancé waiting for her there. I never want to see Toronto again. Future for Michaela Dunn and Thomas Donnelly? Effectively cancelled."

"Thomas, I've never known you to give up easily." Helen Donnelly faced him across the table. "Go back to Promise Lake. Tell her you love her. Convince her to stay there with you. From what you've told us, she loves the place, is a real outdoors type of woman. You could make a good life together.

You owe it to both of you to give it your best effort."

"Sorry, Helen." Thomas got to his feet. "She's not about to end up with a farm boy turned wilderness recluse. Come on, brother. I'll give you a hand. I haven't forgotten how to milk a cow."

****

Thomas Donnelly sat on the bench against the barn wall and watched the handsome black-and-white Holsteins enjoying their dinner. There was something soothing about being in the warm barn, out of reach of the raw wind that raced across the acres of pastureland and cultivation beyond its doors, with animals contentedly munching their carefully prepared diet. He'd spent a lot of time there as a child and young man, especially when he'd had serious thinking to do.

His thoughts took him back to Promise Lake and Michaela. Green eyes sparkling out at him from beneath a parka wreathed with snow... Soft cheeks glowing pink in the cold as she smiled up at him... Man, he missed her!

He wondered if his leaving had diverted suspicion from her. He wondered if she'd discovered who murdered Ralph Frame. She was clever, and familiar with how murder investigations were conducted. He had no doubt she'd figure it out. But when?

Did it matter when? All that mattered was that in a week she'd be on her way back to Toronto.

He wished he could solve the murder. Now. Instantly. That would give him time to go back to her, try to work out their dilemma, maybe convince her to stay with him for a while.

Who had killed Ralph Frame? Who had a motive strong enough to warrant killing another human being? Andy and Jenny Murdoch? Not likely. In spite of their frequent attempts to shift guilt to others, he, like Michaela, doubted either had the internal fortitude to kill the man. Karen Dollard, the mother of Ralph's child? Although she was a strong, determined woman, he couldn't imagine her suddenly deciding to kill the man after she'd contained her animosity for years. Furthermore, she loved her daughter. She wasn't about to risk the child's losing her mother to a murder charge.

What about Amanda Best? She'd gone out of her way to make Travis MacDonald a major suspect. Why? Had she finally gotten fed up with her brother's jaded lifestyle casting shadows over her and her Crown Attorney husband?

His mind wouldn't leave the woman. Somewhere in her behavior was a clue, a major clue. Who could she be protecting by implicating Travis? Who...

Damn it! He jolted straight on his feet. Why hadn't he remembered it earlier? A conversation overheard between Colin Best and the Premier ricocheted across his mind. A conversation that involved Ralph Frame. A conversation that had brought a black scowl down over the Crown Prosecutor's features. A murderous scowl.

****

Michaela curled up in front of the fire, a cup of hot chocolate in her hands. It had been a long day, tracing down Travis MacDonald, a.k.a. Thomas Donnelly. Although she'd been successful, she felt bone tired.

"Time for bed, Doc," she told the dog dozing at her feet. He raised his head, cocked it to one side, and listened.

She heard it, too. At least one approaching snowmobile.

"Not now!" She placed her cup on an end table and stood, stretching weary muscles. "Let's hope just this once they pass us by."

The motor stopped at the steps and booted footsteps tramped up onto the verandah. The door opened to admit Colin Best.

Doc snarled.

"It's late, Mr. Best." He was wild-eyed, his skin a sickly gray. An icy prickle suddenly tingled over her. "Is there something I can do for you?"

"We need to talk."

Doc muttered.

"But first, lock that creature up somewhere. I don't enjoy him glowering at me."

"Sorry. He stays. Taking Doc by the collar, she looked up into the man's bloodshot eyes. She'd seen enough desperate people in her days as an attorney to recognize one now.

An overwhelming sensation of recognition shot through her. Its intensity made a wave of paralysis start deep in her stomach. *What's happening to me?* She fought the dizziness suddenly buzzing in her head and managed to stay on her feet.

Travis MacDonald's countenance crossed into her mind, grinning about her "Spidy sense." *Oh, God, no, it couldn't be...* The same miserable sensation she'd experienced when she looked at her father's client and known him guilty of murdering his wife and daughter.

Keep cool. Don't make him suspicious. You can't prove anything. You could be mistaken. You could just be coming down with a virus.

"What's wrong with you?" Colin Best advanced toward her, eyes hard and cold, his skin suddenly appearing stretched like plastic wrap over his cheekbones. "Why are you staring at me? You don't think that I... You couldn't possibly think *I* murdered Ralph!"

His face contorted into a vicious leer. "That *is* what you think, isn't it? Good God, you must be crazy! But then you'd have to be, getting yourself involved with the likes of Travis MacDonald."

"Yes, I'd have to be." Michaela's mouth had gone

so dry she could barely speak. Her head swam. *Don't let me pass out, please don't let me pass out. I could be wrong.*

"I'm tired of you ferreting around, questioning people, trying to find out who killed my dear brother-in-law." He whipped a gun from inside his leather jacket. "I think it's time for Travis MacDonald to return and get rid of you once and for all."

Snarling, Doc wrenched free. He lunged, an explosion rocked the Lodge, and the malamute fell to the floor, blood spurting from his chest.

"Doc!" Michaela screamed.

A blow to the side of her head silenced her. Unconscious, she fell beside the body of the dog.

Chapter Nineteen

Thomas Donnelly knew he was breaking the speed limit. He only hoped the cops didn't get on his tail or that he didn't skid off the snow-packed road. He had to get to Promise Lodge and Michaela as fast as possible. He had to be there, just in case that crazy sixth sense she'd told him about suddenly kicked in and she did something rash, like confronting Colin Best.

He turned off the heater. Sweat coursed down his body in spite of the bitter northeast wind that was all but pulling his brother's Silverado off the road. Did it have to be winter in the Maritimes? Did this Cobequid Pass through the centre of Nova Scotia have to be "snow-packed and slippery," as the highway conditions information office had described?

Just let her be safe. Please let her be safe. Never an especially religious man, Thomas Donnelly caught himself praying. *She can go back to Toronto, she can even marry that phony, Randall Kirby. Just let her be safe.*

Entering New Brunswick, he rolled stiff shoulders as he headed the truck across the wide plains that were the Tantramar Marshes. In summer, fat cattle grazed on this wide expanse of grassland. Tonight it was a barren, windswept desert of shifting white.

He gripped the wheel until his knuckles whitened as he peered into the swirling snow. Another two hours and he'd be in Carleton. Another two and a half hours and he'd be back with Michaela.

****

"Sam, I need to rent your snowmobile." Thomas burst into the convenience store. "And an outfit of snowmobile clothing." He'd left the farm in the jeans, jacket, and sweater he'd bought at Wal-Mart.

"Sure." The convenience store owner reached under the counter and pulled out a set of keys. "It's parked behind the garage, all gassed up and ready to go. What's wrong?"

"I think Michaela may be in danger." He pulled his wallet from his jacket pocket. "How much?"

"For a guy who always pays up for his klepto dog, it's on the house. Especially if Mikey's in danger." He pointed to a suit of leather outerwear and helmet hanging on a back wall. "Take those."

"Thanks, Sam." Thomas snatched up the outfit. "I appreciate this more than you know." He grabbed the keys from the man's hand and headed for the door. There he stopped and turned back.

"Not everyone would lend property to a man with an unknown past and who's now suspected of murder."

"Hell, Travis, I've been running this store for thirty years. Don't you think I've learned how to tell who I can trust and who I can't? Now go on, get out of here. Norm will never forgive me if something happens to his niece when I could have helped prevent it. Bundle up. It's settling in to be the coldest night this winter."

"Right." Thomas turned and dodged out into the blowing snow.

He paused at the garage to dial Michaela's cell, on the slim chance she might be somewhere within range. Maybe she was okay. Maybe he'd overreacted. He listened as it rang repeatedly. So she was somewhere within reach, just not answering. Where? And why?

If she was somewhere in the Promise

Wilderness, she had to be either up the mountain across the lake or at his cabin. The first idea didn't make sense, not on a night like this, full of screaming winds, sub-zero temperatures, and snow beginning to thicken to blizzard intensity.

Maybe she'd come to the same conclusion he had. Maybe she'd gone to his cabin to call the police.

Another thought stopped him. He punched in 911 and waited.

"Police and emergency services," the efficient voice informed him.

"I'm Michaela Dunn's uncle, Norman Dunn. I can't rouse her on her cell phone, and I'm worried. She hasn't been reported injured or missing, has she?"

"No, sir. No one by that name has been reported in trouble."

"Okay, fine, thanks."

"Sir? How long has it been since you've been in touch with her? You realize you can't file a missing person's report until the individual hasn't been located for forty-eight hours."

"Yes, yes, I realize."

He rang off, adjusted his helmet, mounted his friend's snowmobile, and revved off into the bitterly cold night.

He didn't take the trail that led first to Promise and on to his cabin. Instead he used a shortcut through the woods. He emerged on the dogsled trail running between his cabin and the shed where he housed his truck. With a rough road at his disposal, he made better time.

He pushed the machine to its limit, hoping it was air cooled and that the bitter night was doing its work on the engine. If it broke down, he'd have to run a good distance in temperatures cold enough to freeze the lungs of anyone who dared to exert themselves under such conditions.

****

He saw the flames as he rounded the final bend that would take him to his cabin.

"Sweet Jesus!" He gunned into the dooryard, met by orange tongues of flame shooting out a side window. "Michaela!"

He swirled to a halt and bounded up the steps. The door, never locked, seemed wedged shut. Kicking out, he sent it hurtling backward into a room filled with smoke. Flames licked out of the bedroom. On the floor of the main room Michaela lay, gagged, hands and feet bound, green eyes round and desperate.

Choking, he pulled his balaclava over his mouth and nose and dived toward her. Gathering her into his arms, he staggered out into the snow. Behind him, his cabin exploded into a fireball. At the edge of the trees, he fell to his knees and eased her down beside him. The sweet, heavy odor of gas gushed over him on a wave of wind. Arson and attempted murder.

He returned his attention to Michaela. Blood from a head wound matted her hair above her left ear. She flinched when he yanked the duct tape from her mouth. As he struggled to remove her bonds with fingers that felt like icicles, she vomited.

Concussion. I have to get her somewhere warm. Fast.

"Travis," she sputtered. "Is it really you? You came back?"

"Yeah, what else could I do?" He forced a small grin and flung aside the ropes. "You make it hard to leave, lady. Now I have to get you onto the snowmobile and back to Promise Lodge. It's the closest place where we can take shelter from this storm. Think you can hold on behind me, or should I hold you in front of me?"

She swallowed hard and tried to smile. "In front

of you? As if! What do you think this is, a romance novel, and you've got a white horse?"

"Okay, okay. Behind. Come on." He started to get her to her feet, but she caught him by an arm. "Colin Best, he…"

"I know. Later. Right now we have to get ourselves out of this storm, or he'll be adding two more bodies to his list." He pulled a survival blanket from the snowmobile's emergency kit and wrapped it around her.

"Travis." Looking up at him, green eyes filling with tears, she caught at his sleeve. "He shot Doc."

****

The blizzard must have blanketed out the sound of their snowmobile. At least that's what Travis surmised as he brought the machine to a stop in the trees at the edge of the Lodge's dooryard. Lights blazed from the windows.

"Wait here." He dismounted.

"No!" she protested. The word was a shudder. He had to get her inside and warm, asap.

"I'm only going as far as the Lodge." He pulled off his helmet but left his balaclava in place. "I won't be long. Stay here."

"But what if Colin Best is inside, what if…" She hugged her shaking body.

"He'll be surprised to see *me*, don't you think?" He made his tone sound devil-may-care.

"Travis, he's got a gun!"

"Quiet. Sit. Stay." He bent forward and kissed her beneath the hood he'd fashioned around her face from the survival blanket.

"That was highly unsatisfactory." Through the storm and darkness, he caught the twinkle in her words. *Recovering nicely.*

"Just wait until I get back, lady." He touched her cheek with a gloved hand, then turned and headed toward the Lodge, hunching against the

238

wind and snow.

He'd managed to stanch the flow of blood from the bash above her ear.

She'd be okay.

But not Doc.

Colin Best will pay. Yes, Colin Best would definitely pay.

He slunk up onto the Lodge verandah and crouched under a window beside the door. With his pulse pounding at his eardrums, he took a chance and raised himself to peer inside.

Colin Best, his face gray-green, sat at a table, a liquor bottle clutched in his hand.

A wide blood stain on the floor caught Thomas's attention. It smeared its way over the boards and behind the counter.

Doc.

The man had dragged his dead dog across the room and probably thrown him out the service entrance into the snow. First Michaela's attempted murder, now this.

Rage-induced adrenalin belched through every inch of his body. He stood, strode to the door, and kicked it in.

"Shoring up your courage, Mr. Best?" Travis pulled off his balaclava. Colin Best's face blanched.

"MacDonald! What are you doing here?"

"Rescuing Michaela Dunn from the fire you set to cover up her murder. Bad plan, Best. Never use the same MO twice. The police love that kind of thing."

"They're convinced you're guilty." Colin Best's hand crept inside his jacket. "They're…"

Travis tackled the man as he pulled out the gun. It discharged with a reverberating roar.

****

"Travis!" Michaela burst into the Lodge. "What happened? Are you all right?"

"Yeah, except for a banged-up knee and maybe a skinned elbow." Travis finished tying Colin Best's hands with the man's belt as he straddled the Crown Prosecutor's back on the floor.

"Travis..." She turned and stumbled down the corridor to the bedrooms.

"Michaela?" He trussed the man's feet with his own belt, then followed her. Outside the closed bathroom door of Room One he stopped.

"Michaela?"

"I'm...okay. Just a little nauseated. Must have been the bump on the head." He heard her retch, and cursed. *Damn Colin Best to hell.*

"Travis? Have you found Doc?" The dog's name was a hiccup. "He was trying to defend me."

"You take it easy." His voiced sounded alien as the words bumped over the lump in his throat. "I'll find him."

He returned to the restaurant where he'd left the trussed-up Colin Best.

"Where is my dog?" he demanded.

"Dead." The sneered response all but drove Travis to attack the man again. "I threw his carcass out the service entrance. He's probably stiff as a board by now."

"You're trying my patience, Best. Don't push me any further, or I might just take my boots to that pretty face of yours."

"Try it, and I'll have you for attempted murder. I've already got you for assault."

"And we've got you for murder. Unless I'm badly mistaken, the bullet they retrieved from Ralph Frame's chalet will match those in your gun. So shut up!"

Travis turned and followed the trail of blood out the service entrance and into the blizzard.

"Doc." Travis dropped to his knees beside the big dog's snow-crusted body. "Sweet Jesus! Doc!"

He ran a hand over the animal's body. *What was that? God, could it be...yes, it was! A heartbeat. Faint, but definitely a heartbeat!*

"Doc!" He gathered the malamute into his arms. Stumbling under the hundred-pound body, he struggled back into the Lodge.

Chapter Twenty

"That's the last of them." Thomas Donnelly closed the Lodge door and came to join Michaela where she sat ensconced on the couch in the lounge, a blanket pulled up to her waist. "Can't say I'm sorry. I'm bushed. Not often guests opt to head back at night, but they have a plane to catch early tomorrow morning."

On the rug in front of the fire, Doc lay snoring, seemingly unconcerned about the heavy swath of bandages around his chest and shoulders.

"Trav...Thomas, you're going to have to allow me to start back to work," she said as he sprawled in a chair opposite her.

"You've got a bunch of stitches above your ear, not to mention a concussion. I hardly think you're in any shape to be serving guests."

"It's been five days since Colin Best was carted away by Corporal Palmer and his sidekick. Both Doc and I are mending fast."

"Yeah, well, let's just say I've made the arbitrary decision you both need more rest." He pulled himself upright, his face hardening. "Man, I wish I'd given that bastard a few choice punches when I had the chance!"

"You did the right thing." Michaela looked over at him, her expression gentle.

Damn, she's beautiful even with a section of her hair shaved away, even with her face still pale from trauma. How in hell will I ever learn to live without her?

"I barely recognized you after you rescued me

from your burning cabin," she continued, a slight smile playing over her lips. "Without the hair and beard..."

"Disappointed, were you?" He grinned.

"You're one handsome man, Thomas Donnelly." She slanted him a sideways glance that sent his hormones racing. "With or without the hairy trimmings. A woman could do a lot worse. However, I must admit..."

"Yeah?"

"I do prefer the wilderness-man look."

"Still got a taste for that kind of guy? Well, hair and beard grow back. Is that what you'd like?"

"Yes. But not guys with fake IDs. What about that driver's license and birth certificate in your wallet? You're not from Yellowknife."

"You snooped my underwear drawer?" He feigned horrified surprise. "Is nothing sacred anymore?"

"Stop avoiding the question."

"Okay, okay. I had them made before I left Toronto. Not hard to come by up there, for the right price. I wanted to disappear, remember. Luckily the RCMP investigation into my involvement in Ralph's death didn't last long enough for them to check it out when I was arrested, but I'm betting they knew it was false shortly after I did my disappearing act. I think it might have taken them a while to trace it all back to me, since I have no criminal record and my fingerprints as Thomas Donnelly aren't on file anywhere, that I know of."

The noise of approaching snowmobiles broke into his thoughts. More guests. He dragged himself to his feet as the door opened. A tall, barrel-chested man stepped into the Lodge, pulling off his headgear. Behind him, a petite, grey-haired woman did the same.

"Uncle Norm! Aunt Ida!" Michaela threw aside

her cover and got to her feet. Too quickly. Thomas caught her as she staggered.

"Are you all right, child?" Ida Dunn hurried to join them, her suntanned face creased with concern.

"Of course I am." She stepped away from Thomas's support to hug the older woman. "A little bump on the head, that's all. Nothing serious."

"That's not the story we heard in Carleton." Norman Dunn joined them, his height and broad shoulders eclipsing his small wife. "According to Sam, at the convenience store, you probably wouldn't be alive if it weren't for Travis here." He extended his right hand while he slapped the younger man on the shoulder with the other. "We'll be hard pressed to fittingly thank you, my boy."

"No need for thanks, Norm." Thomas quirked a grin. "Once you hear the entire story, you'll discover I was just returning a favor."

****

"That went well." Michaela returned to the lounge where Thomas sat nursing a glass of wine from the bottle her aunt and uncle had opened to celebrate their return. "They're settled into their quarters as if they'd never left. Would you believe, Aunt Ida's already planning dishes to replenish the freezer?"

"I have been hitting her supply hard." He stood. "I guess this is where I should vanish back into the wilderness like any decent ghost, but unfortunately I have no place to go."

"That definitely isn't the thing to do." She paused close in front of him, green eyes sparkling. "Not after the commitment I've just made to Uncle Norm and Aunt Ida."

"Commitment?"

"I've agreed to take over the Lodge so they can retire and build the cabin of their dreams on the site of your former home...that is, if you'll allow them."

"You're staying...here?" He felt something—his heart, he assumed—lurch in his chest.

"If you'll agree to be my business partner in running the place and protecting the Promise Wilderness."

He saw a flicker of doubt in those amazing emerald eyes. "Or do you want to go back to being a hermit? Or maybe to Toronto? Or to your family farm?" The words galloped out.

"What about your parents? Your promise to your father? Randall Kirby?" He almost choked over the name.

"I called Mom and Dad yesterday when you took me into town for a checkup. I told them I wouldn't be coming back."

"And they said?"

"At first Dad ranted and raved, said he'd give Randall Kirby my partnership in the firm."

"And you said?"

"I said go ahead. Told him he could adopt Randall Kirby, for all I cared."

"Really?"

"Really. Then Mom, the voice of reason, chimed in. She reminded Dad that in the beginning their relationship hadn't exactly been blessed by his family. She reminded him of a young law student who'd promised his family he wouldn't get serious about a woman or marry until he'd graduated and established his career."

"And I take it he broke that promise."

"Definitely. And just look where it's gotten him."

"So you're advocating the breaking of promises?"

"Only those the keeping of which will result in unhappiness and be counterproductive."

"You're sounding more and more like a lawyer."

"Sorry. I know how you feel about lawyers, especially of the female type."

"Not any more. At least not all female lawyers.

But getting back to the bottom line with your father... He agreed to let you stay?"

"Let's just say he accepted defeat, something he's not all that familiar with. But what about you? You haven't answered my question about our forming a partnership...or your leaving."

"Come here." He was chuckling as he drew her into his arms. "I'm not going anywhere. This is where I want to be...with you, Michaela Dunn. And not just as a business partner."

He lowered his head to kiss her. With a contented sigh she settled against him.

"You know," he said, against her hair that still smelled vaguely of disinfectant and he couldn't have cared less, "It's strange how I happened to find you in that blizzard. That wasn't my usual route. Something made me turn down that old logging road. It was almost as if some strange force willed me in that direction."

"Maybe a genuine ghost of winters past?" Michaela looked up at him, green eyes twinkling. "I saw him that day, you know...the phantom First Nations caretaker of the Promise. He was there, just before you arrived."

"Okay, okay, so you're the gifted one, the one who can see ghosts and sense good and evil a mile away." He swung her up into his arms and started down the bedroom corridor. "But right now I'm hoping I'm going to be right in sensing what we both want to happen next. Your place or mine?" He paused between their rooms.

"Yours." She snuggled against him. "Just in case the slightest hint of that dastardly perfume is lingering in mine. I don't want anything to turn you off tonight."

"Argh!" He chuckled as he struggled to open the door without putting her down.

Back in the lounge, Doc threw back his head and

howled, his cry as natural and feral as the surrounding wilderness.

Across the lake, a tall straight figure in snow-white buckskins nodded slowly, the planes of his strong features sliding into a contented smile. He turned and slowly vanished into the night.

A word about the author...

The award-winning author of twenty published books, Gail MacMillan is a graduate of Queen's University.

Two of her nonfiction books, *Biography of a Beagle* and *Ceilidh's Quest*, have garnered Maxwell Medals. Her short stories and articles have appeared in magazines in Canada, the USA, and Europe.

She lives in New Brunswick, Canada with her husband and three dogs.

You can visit Gail at her website:
www.gailmacmillan.ca

Thank you for purchasing
this publication of The Wild Rose Press, Inc.
For other wonderful stories of romance,
please visit our on-line bookstore at
www.thewildrosepress.com.

For questions or more information
contact us at
info@thewildrosepress.com.

The Wild Rose Press, Inc.
www.thewildrosepress.com

To visit with authors of
The Wild Rose Press, Inc.
join our yahoo loop at
http://groups.yahoo.com/group/thewildrosepress/

www.ingramcontent.com/pod-product-compliance
Lightning Source LLC
Chambersburg PA
CBHW060416180626
46817CB00007B/2598